The Breedling & the City in the Garden

BY

Kimberlee Ann Bastian

ISBN 13: 978-1-945769-04-7
eISBN 13: 978-1-945769-03-0

Library of Congress Catalog Number: 2016941466
Printed in the United States of America
First Printing: 2016

20   19   18   17   16   5   4   3   2   1

Cover and interior design by Steven Meyer-Rassow

Wise Ink Creative Publishing
807 Broadway St. NE, Suite 46
Minneapolis, MN 55413
www.wiseink.com

To the Bastian Loons:

Mum, Duke, Andros, & Budz

"In any moment of decision,
the best thing you can do is the right thing,
the next best thing is the wrong thing,
and the worst thing you can do is nothing."

~Theodore Roosevelt

Element I: Chicago, 1934

The Musings of the Tales Teller

The Tales Teller burst through the front door uninvited, her transparent skin turning red to mirror her frustrated mood. It was her intent to use her volatile emotion and give the Apothecary a piece of her mind, having grown tired of the waiting, uncertain of his plans. She expected to find him at his kitchen counter fussing over his herbs, no doubt to brew some elixir that would calm her temper, but she would not be restrained. Not until she had gotten out every last thought.

She searched every room but the Apothecary was nowhere to be found, and shortly she was back in the kitchen, greeted by the sound of bubbling water and the aromatic smell of lavender and lemon balm, scents she had not previously noticed. Secretly, the two calming herbs tried to work their magic on her, but she continued to pace, awaiting the Apothecary's return. She tried to piece together the fragments of his plan, but he had not shared all the details with her and rightly so, for his mistrust in her was not ill-placed. After all, she was still subject to the commanding will of the Fates, the ancient trinity who lorded over the creatures of Euxinus, a realm predating the creation of Eden and mortals.

The shade of her skin lightened as she lingered in the kitchen, her temper waning, her mind focusing more on the hope of liberation.

For far too long, the cruel neutrality of the Fates had stifled the will of their subjects, suffocated the realm with desolation, and governed the destinies of the four Creators, who in their infancy were once known as the Elements. In her library, she had studied the scrolls chronicling the origin story, committing to memory every sin the Fates had committed, before pledging an existence to perpetual neutrality.

Euxinus was once a vast, boundless black sea, wrapped in the bosom of darkness. From its depths there arose a mountain of earth, and at its peak, there burned a vibrant flame that danced in an untamed wind. On this mountain slope, the Fates made their home and, in Euxian lore, their fellowship with the Elements became known as the Rule of Seven. Yet the strength of this unity could not prevent the births of betrayal, jealousy, and greed.

Without provocation, the Fates stole the powers of the Elements and refashioned Euxinus to fit their vision. For the Elements, it was the end of their physical forms and in order to survive they ascended. Fearful of this transformation, the Fates banished the Elements to three corners of the universe, subjecting the Spirit of Flame to the intolerable desert of Hell and the Spirit of Wind to the lofty snow-capped clouds of Heaven. For the Spirits of Earth and Sea, the Fates created the sublime realm of Eden, using what remained of the four Elements. It was a halfhearted attempt to make amends, but the gift soured when neither Earth nor Sea took ownership of the realm, leaving Eden vulnerable to the manipulation of a vengeful Flame and a broken-hearted Wind.

The Tales Teller pulled the whistling kettle from the hot stove and filled a beaker with the blistering water. In it, she steeped lemon balm and mint with pulverized, dehydrated pomegranate the Apothecary had smuggled from Eden upon his previous secretive visit. She inhaled the fragrant steam and placed the beaker to her lips.

"I see you have begun without me, Madam Teller," spoke a deep, disembodied voice.

Startled, the Tales Teller dropped her beaker, the glass shattering at her feet. Her feline eyes narrowed and her skin flushed beet red. She found the Apothecary standing near the front door, his bronzed face hinted at a smile. She placed her hands on the counter, crushing the herbs beneath her palms.

"Master Apothecary, where have you been?" inquired the Tales Teller. Her usual melodious voice was hidden by the curt tone of her temper. "I have been beside myself, as have the others of the council. Why have you not assisted the Breedling Bartholomew in his escape? Why the delay? Are two hundred Eden years not long enough?"

"You certainly have a way with your greetings," said the Apothecary, his voice pleasant.

"My Eldest," said the Tales Teller. "Are you ill? This is no time for jests."

"I do not jest, Madam Teller," said the Apothecary, joining her at the kitchen counter, the wrinkles of his seasoned skin accenting the sternness in his voice.

The Tales Teller recoiled, removing her hands from the counter, releasing the scents of thyme and rosemary. Her skin softened to a pleasing plum, depicting her embarrassment.

"Beg your pardon, my Eldest, I…"

The Apothecary silenced her with the raise of his hand. "Your honesty has always been welcomed, Madam Teller, but as we have discussed on many occasions, Bartholomew must escape of his own volition."

"But why?" asked the Tales Teller, despite having been told this answer. "Why is it so important he do this alone? Would it not be easier just to tell him what needs to be done?"

"It would," agreed the Apothecary, "but assistance would only hinder him, not help him. As you and the other council members know, Bartholomew has been in prison all this time because he defied the Fates. He, a mere Breedling, the youngest of all the Euxian creatures, the ones who are meant to be the most obedient to the Fates. It is for this very reason that Bartholomew has to will himself to make the choice."

The Tales Teller's cat-like ears drooped and her skin altered to a somber shade of blue. She felt foolish and disheartened. She had expected to gain some answers or insight into the Apothecary's plan, but all she had managed to extract from him was the same rhetoric he had told her a hundred times over. She could not explain why it was still hard for her to accept the Apothecary's insistence on placing all his faith in a Breedling, whose primary purpose for being was to be a soulcatcher for the Fates. And yet, had she not witnessed Bartholomew's defiance for herself, she would never have believed the unwilled creature had the power to disobey. She recalled the youthful, emerald-eyed Breedling standing in the atrium of the Fates' palace, soaked to the bone, his clothes covered in mud. He had returned from Eden in custody and had been given the chance to report his findings. Bartholomew, Breedling of the First Grade, had found what had been missing: one of the Lost Creators. Bartholomew, however, had given no such report. Instead, he had remained silent and because of it, the Breedling was imprisoned for his defiance.

"And what of the mortal, Damek?" she asked finally, referring to one of the Apothecary's seven breadcrumbs to assist Bartholomew upon his escape.

"What of him?" asked the Apothecary, his almond eyes appraising the Tales Teller.

"You said you had blessed Damek with the necessary enchantment Bartholomew will need in order to bind himself to the mortal realm of Eden and reaffirm his charge once he has broken ties with the Fates."

"I did," said the Apothecary.

"Then I ask you again, my Eldest, why the delay? Damek will be an old man on his death bed, if Master Breedling does not act quickly and fulfill your expectations. And if Damek dies, what then? I cannot wait any longer and neither can the council. Bartholomew must find the Eden Wanderer, Stingy Jack, and bring him here soon, for I can no longer postpone the trial of the Shepherdess."

"Not to worry, Madam Teller, I have sent the Chameleon ahead to the City in the Garden to oversee Bartholomew's transition."

"Is that wise to send the Fates' spy? Are you certain the Chameleon is loyal enough not to betray you?" asked the Tales Teller.

"As much as I am certain about your loyalty, Madam Teller," said the Apothecary, without an ounce of hesitation. "Rest assured," he continued, "that events are in motion for Damek to find Bartholomew. And all I ask is that you play your part when the time comes. For now, you are dismissed."

The Tales Teller removed herself from the Apothecary's workstation, switching spots with him around the counter. As he passed, she smelled the rotten scent of sulfur, which for Euxinus was not uncommon. What gave her pause, however, was a distinct perfume of smoke. Her skin flushed a nervous shade of yellow, fear gripping her fragile state of hope. She wanted to confront him about it, but her feet continued forward, leading her out the front door. She heard the slam behind her and knew her opportunity was gone. She swallowed hard, pushing all doubt from her mind. Everything was contingent upon the Apothecary's plan, and without being privy to its full extent, she had no choice but to trust his words: *events are in motion.*

The Orphans of Chicago

Charlie Reese stood next to the vacant industrial railroad tracks, keeping an eye on his nine-year-old cousin, Jimmy. He watched the youngster intently, nervous that the child might hurt himself, while at the same time indulging the boy as he pretended to be a circus acrobat.

"Look at you, Jimmy," said Charlie with pride. "You're a natural."

Jimmy's stubby arms stretched out like the wings of a soaring bird, his underdeveloped muscles achy from holding their position for so long. He centered his balance and steadily walked along the imaginary tightrope.

"Behold, the stupendous Jimmy, as he masters the rail beam—a most formidable foe to freighthoppers, hobos, transients, and runaways," said Charlie, showcasing the young performer. "Watch as he executes his infamous about-face, a twirling stunt that combines the elegance of a ballerina and the cadence of a soldier."

Jimmy began to wobble, his giggles throwing off his equilibrium.

"Shhh, hush now folks," said Charlie as though they were really under the big top and he were the ring master. "We don't want to break the youngster's concentration. Now, drum roll, maestro." Charlie patted his hands on his thighs.

Jimmy paused as his cousin's claps grew faster and when the padded beats ceased, he spun around on cue in a pirouette. His foot landed on the dull metal to secure his stance before flawlessly dismounting. He threw his hands in the air and began to wave at his adoring audience, which realistically only consisted of Charlie, but Jimmy took the sounds of the city around him and transformed it into deafening applause. He bowed multiple times, and by the eighth, he paused mid-bend and reached for the ground. His pale fingers closed around a wadded ball and he stood upright, Charlie's fanfare no longer of interest. He unwrapped the paper to reveal the familiar image of a one silver dollar.

"Charlie," Jimmy squealed. "Look what I found." He extended the dirty piece of money to his older cousin, but to his surprise, Charlie refused to take it.

"That's yours, Jimmy," said Charlie. "Yours to do with what you will."

"I want to give it to you," said Jimmy, "as a birthday present."

"Jimmy, you already gave me a present," said Charlie, pulling the Big Top Orange Soda bottle cap from his pocket. It had been Jimmy's gift to him two days prior to celebrate his seventeenth birthday. The two of them had gone up to Navy Pier to spend the day watching the water vessels coming and going off Lake Michigan. The day had been enjoyable, one of only a few since his previous birthday, before the two of them lost everything–Charlie his parents and four siblings; Jimmy his father.

Charlie tried not to think about the horrific scene, especially not in front of Jimmy, but flashes of the burning farmhouse seized his mind. He was paralyzed by the image, and without warning, his eyes welled. He held back his tears, but it was already too late. Jimmy's watery hazel eyes stared back at him, the young boy's expression emanating the same heartache he felt. Charlie knew it was no place for a good cry, not with onlookers so close, the city street only a few feet away. He thought about what to do, his mind so lost in finding a way out that he did not notice Jimmy standing next to him until his cousin was holding his hand.

"I think I know what I want to do with my money," said Jimmy, and led his cousin away.

Charlie remained silent for the duration of the walk, allowing Jimmy to ramble on about topics he enjoyed. His mind temporarily unsettled with memories of the family they lost.

The grandfather clock struck half past one when he awoke to the smell of burning wood. He was in the living room, having fallen asleep there after spending extra time in the barn tending to his horse. The fire by then had gutted the kitchen and managed to beat a path toward the stairs, cutting Charlie off from reaching the front door as well as the second floor where his family lay sleeping. There was no escape save for the side window. Charlie lifted the pane before jumping out. He landed in his mother's favorite rose bush, ignoring the thorns scratching him as he scrambled into the yard and began throwing rocks at his Uncle Gert's window. It took a few good throws, but he managed to rouse the heavy sleeper. Uncle Gert instructed him to wait while he collected Jimmy then disappeared back into the smoking house. The wait was unbearable and as his uncle's absence became prolonged, Charlie feared him dead. He screamed into the night air, his voice a whisper compared to the growl of the fiery beast consuming every inch of his family's home. He cried for his mother, his father, and then his siblings, but none of them came to the window. He called for his uncle again, but only Jimmy emerged, his face stark white. Charlie yelled at his cousin to jump, just as a small explosion shattered the glass by the front porch and Jimmy flew out of the window.

"Why, thank you for your generous gift, Jimmy," said the priest, as Jimmy handed him the dollar.

"Charlie said I could do what I wanted with it," said Jimmy.

"Well, it's thoughtful of you," said the priest, acknowledging the youngster's selflessness, a trait his older cousin nurtured well.

Jimmy scuffed his foot across the grass in a bashful, "oh shucks" gesture, his hands stuffed in the pockets of his trousers.

The priest smiled, his long face pulling tight. He lifted his gaze to look at Charlie, who was leaning against the side of the church, his attention on his feet, lost in thought. He studied the poor condition of his faded charcoal pants and his long sleeve shirt. His broad shoulders rounded forward, his burly arms crossed over his chest showing his strength. He seemed to have the appearance of a full-grown man, but in many ways it was an illusion, for though the priest knew how grown up Charlie appeared, the young man had yet to forsake his youthful wonder.

"How is he today?" asked the priest, looking back at Jimmy.

Jimmy glanced over his shoulder. "He's all right," he said, "but you know Charlie."

"Indeed," said the priest, concerned about his young friend.

The bell on the front door of the rectory chimed, and a little girl dressed in a poorly sewn potato sack dress exited onto the porch, her dainty feet swiftly carrying her down the steps.

"Hi, Jimmy," she said politely, first addressing the visitor, just like her mama taught her.

"Hi," replied Jimmy, his eyes drawn to the mason jar of marbles she was holding.

"Father Van Lewen, may I play marbles on the sidewalk?" asked the little girl.

"Phyllis, I don't know how many times I have to tell you, you don't have to ask my permission," said the priest. "If your mother said it was fine with her, I see no harm. Why don't you show Jimmy your favorites while I have a talk with his cousin?"

"Sure," said the little girl. "Come on, Jimmy." She led the way out of the fenced yard, then ran down the block, forcing Jimmy to sprint after her.

Father Van Lewen laughed at the child and posed a question to Charlie that would make him think of the future instead of dwelling on the past.

"Are you prepared for the meeting tomorrow?" he asked, referring to the gang dispute Charlie had been asked to mediate, which was a nicer way of saying he was forced.

"As ready as I can be, I suppose," said Charlie. "It's not as though they gave me a say in the matter."

"Still, you did agree to act as their peacekeeper," said Father Van Lewen.

"I did," said Charlie. "But," he added with a shrug, "it doesn't mean I'm thrilled about the situation."

"Of course," agreed the priest. "Frankenstein and the Bogeyman managed to get to you the only way they can." He paused and looked at Jimmy up the block, aware Charlie's predicament went beyond the thought of a beating if he had refused. Father Van Lewen sighed. "It's as you say Charlie, sometimes one must do the things one doesn't want to do in order to survive."

"I know," said Charlie. "The thought of helping either of them really gets my goat, but there's nothing for it. I just don't need any trouble from the Poles or the Lithuanians, and I especially don't need either of them coming after Jimmy."

"Are you still planning on bringing Jimmy here in the morning?" asked Father Van Lewen, referencing a previous conversation on the matter.

Charlie did not answer right away, his attention distracted by the little girl, Phyllis, as she screeched out a victory. "No," he finally said. "I would—God knows it would be safer for him here, but he's their insurance to keep me in line. If he's not present, it will raise suspicion and there's no telling how they'll react. Besides, I'd rather him be with me than worry the whole time about him, or you. I just don't know if the Bogeyman is not below sending his minions to call on the home of a priest. I can't put you or those you're caring for in that sort of position. It wouldn't be right."

Father Van Lewen reflected on Charlie's outlook, formulating the right words of wisdom to impart. He was not about to make an argument against Charlie's chivalry. Instead, he wanted to be able to arm him with some sliver of reassurance. That no matter what happened tomorrow, it would all work itself out.

"Just remember Charlie, you are doing the neighborhoods a great service by preventing a gang war. This Depression has taken so much already—the last thing the Poles or the Lithuanians want is blood in the streets. If you think of it in those terms, it will make those two giants you stand between not seem so titanic."

"Sounds like something my mother would say," said Charlie, his thoughts reaching out for the image of her caring expression.

Father Van Lewen chuckled. "Wise woman, your mother," he said. "I so wish I could have met her."

"As do I," said Charlie, smiling at the notion of Father Van Lewen and Adele Reese chatting at great length. What a conversation that would have been. "I think she would have liked you," he added. "Although, I don't think she would have ever referred to the Bogeyman as a giant."

"No, I suppose not," said Father Van Lewen with a chuckle.

Charlie and the priest shared another good laugh before retreating to the porch, where they debated for several hours about baseball. All the while, Charlie kept a watchful eye on Jimmy as he and Phyllis played their game. At one point, Phyllis' mother came onto the porch offering glasses of freshly squeezed lemonade. It was definitely light on the lemon, but their thirsty mouths did not complain.

"Well, I suppose," said Charlie finally, derailing the debate of which team was better, the White Sox or the Cubs, "I think it's time me and Jimmy hightail it to the boarding house. Miss Schwarman gives out ten lashings for anyone caught out past curfew."

"Of course," said Father Van Lewen. "Don't need to get you in any sort of trouble." He rose from his chair and showed Charlie across the lawn. "You'll be sure to stop by and let me know how everything shakes out between Frankenstein and the Bogeyman."

"Will do," said Charlie. "Come on Jimmy," he called, "time to go."

Jimmy tried to ask for more time—Phyllis was beating him ten to five—but Charlie was insistent that they leave. He made a fuss, and the girl giggled playfully at his tantrum, but before he left she gave him one of her marbles.

"It's one of my favorites," she said, not entirely willing to let it go, although figuring it was the least she could do. After all, the dollar he had given Father Van Lewen would go to feeding her and several others seeking refuge from destitution. "It's called a sul-phide," she added. "My grandfather used to work in a plant back in Germany that made them. Most sulphides have animals encased in the center, but this one has a flower. Mama told me it's a hibiscus."

"Thank you," said Jimmy, inspecting the orange-colored flower inside.

"Jimmy, it's time to go," called Charlie.

Jimmy got to his feet and thanked the little girl again for the gift, placing it safely in his pocket. He met Charlie on the corner and waved back to Father Van Lewen as they crossed the street, the work whistles announcing the end of the day. The two cousins made their way through the streets of Chicago, back to the orphanage they would never call home.

History Repeats

Charlie tore himself from sleep, his night terror having made its twentieth performance in a row. The sheets on his bed stuck to his bare skin as he pressed his left ear into his pillow, his gaze focusing on the kerosene lamp sitting on top of the cobweb-infested bookshelf, its fuel nearly spent. He sighed, knowing dawn was near, even though the dormitory of the orphanage had no windows to reveal the lightening of the sky. He looked at the servant's door, its frame butting against the shelf, and thought about greeting the sun as it rose over the depressed city of Chicago. It would only take the picking of the lock, followed by a quick ascent to the second floor, then through the secret crawlspace above the kitchen ceiling, and a climb onto the roof. Charlie meowed a weak yawn, too tired to put forth the effort of an early morning rendezvous. Instead, he looked about the sleepy room, surveying the other beds. He counted the bundles beneath the sheets, each one a slumbering boy. He said each of their names softly aloud like counting sheep, reminding himself of their stories in an attempt to lessen the despair of his own. He reached the tenth bed, whose occupant was a boy named Orrin. Out of all the boys in the orphanage, Charlie had taken a shine to the youngster. Orrin had the type of personality that was irresistibly infectious, and when he was around all the troubles of the world were nowhere to be found. Often times Charlie found himself staring at a version of himself at that age.

He counted himself as eleven then moved onto the twelfth bed, which was currently empty, awaiting its new arrival. Finally, he rolled his head on his pillow to look at the thirteenth bed next to him, which was where Jimmy slept, but instead of finding his cousin, the bed was empty.

"Jimmy," he moaned, as he ran a hand through his sweaty hair, hoping this time he would be able to retrieve his cousin before being caught by Miss Schwarman, the warden of the boarding house. Last time, she had punished Jimmy by locking him in the cupboard under the stairs, denying him food and water for four days. Charlie had made a few attempts to slip his cousin the crusts of his bread after every meal, but without fail the old crone had caught him in the act, and for his troubles she swatted his hands with her twitch until they bled. Charlie had gone to Father Van Lewen for help, and though the priest and the warden had had a civil conversation, Miss Schwarman would not kowtow to the priest. On the fifth day, however, Miss Schwarman let Jimmy out as though it had been her idea. By then it was already too late and Jimmy had fallen catatonic from the abuse. It took Charlie days, with Father Van Lewen's assistance to bring his cousin around, and despite their best efforts, Jimmy's frame remained in a perpetual sickly state.

Charlie tossed his covers aside and rolled to the edge of his bed. He threw on a stained shirt, which instantly stuck to his skin, debating whether to check the second floor or outside first. It was not often he found his cousin outside, but every time he had, Orrin was always with him. Since Orrin was in his bed, it was safe to assume Jimmy had gone upstairs to the second-floor dormitory where he kept a box of treasures underneath a loose floorboard.

"Better check anyway," said Charlie and tip-toed towards Orrin's bed. In the center, he saw the small rise of the sheets, but when he lifted the covers, all he found were two pillows. "Dammit Orrin."

Charlie went back to his bed and put on his shoes. Then, without waking any of the others, he gradually made his way to the main door of the room. He reached for the knob, not expecting it to be unlocked, but much to his surprise it was slightly ajar. Charlie stepped into the hallway and crept towards the front door, stopping a few feet short. He peered around the banister at the closed study doors across the foyer and saw light breaking across the wooden floor, the sound of booted footsteps moving about behind them.

"Damn," swore Charlie under his breath, as the sliding door closest to him began to open. He retraced his steps and returned to the dormitory, securing the door behind him just as girly giggles entered the hall. He pressed his ear against the thin wood, listening intently for the path of footsteps, realizing they had halted on the other side of where he was standing. Unable to make a dash for his bed, Charlie pressed his lean body against the wall, using the opening door as camouflage.

"Shhh," said the slur of a female voice as a bright yellow glow filled the room and cast two distinct shadows on the white walls. "You don't want to be waking up the little ones," she whispered, her unsteady steps coming into the room.

Charlie shifted his weight to peer around the door, his eyes finding the silhouette of Hanna, the assistant caretaker of the orphanage. She was a ginger-headed young woman, who was only four years older than him, and unlike Miss Schwarman, possessed a kind heart. She swayed like a dancer, but with less grace. The skirt of her slender day dress obeyed the movement of her body as she floated down the aisle between the rows of beds.

In a soft voice, she said the names of each boy as the flame from her lantern wavered.

Charlie held his breath when she made her way to his bed, because unlike Orrin, he had forgotten to decoy his covers and feared she would notice the absence of its occupant.

"All is well," she said in a whisper.

Charlie rolled his eyes in disgust, but took stock in his good fortune that her drunken state had impeded her judgment. *Better she miscount than discover Jimmy and I are missing again.*

"What about the second-floor dormitory?"

Charlie's stomach flipped at the familiarity of the man's voice. He had heard it once before, a silky tone, a prime trademark of any charlatan, but he could not place where he had heard it. He watched Hanna move back to the door, her shadow meeting the taller one.

"The room is empty," she said. "Has been for a few days now. The City cut our funding so we had to ship the boys up to Minnesota."

"And what of the servant's hall, doesn't it connect this dormitory to the back bedroom?" asked the charlatan. "What about the spiral staircase in that hall, isn't it a secret passage to the second-floor dormitory?"

Charlie watched Hanna's face as it followed the point of the man's outstretched finger. He too panned his eyes to the far corner of the room next to the bookshelf and wondered why the man was so curious about the orphanage's hidden passageway. Charlie looked back at Hanna and inched a little further around his hiding place to get a better look at whom she was with, but the charlatan held back behind the door and he dared not risk exposure.

"I don't see how," said Hanna, lifting a hand to her forehead.

"The servant's door is always locked, so no one has access to the hallway." She began to lean backwards.

"I think you need to lie down, sweetie pie," said the charlatan, as he embraced a fainting Hanna.

"Oh, yes," said Hanna and disappeared from Charlie's line of sight.

Charlie listened to their footsteps as the door closed. He stood still until the skeleton key finished securing the lock. He waited another moment or two, half-expecting one of the boys to wake up after the less-than-subtle ruckus, but none of them did, and the room remained quiet. Charlie relaxed his shoulders and placed his hands on his knees.

"That was close," he said aloud, and reevaluated his plan to find Jimmy. He would be taking a risk heading out the front door, what with Hanna and the charlatan wandering about, which made him wonder why Miss Schwarman had not come out of her room and given the two an earful—and that was when it dawned on him. He had heard this charlatan once before, in Miss Schwarman's study. He had not intended to eavesdrop, but he had overheard them talking about insurance, particularly for fire. Charlie's stomach cramped and he quickly pulled a piece of wire from his pocket. He placed it in the keyhole and jiggled the knob, trying not to make any noise. He pressed his ear on the oak door, listening for the click, but instead he heard the charlatan's footsteps barrel down the hallway toward the kitchen. He paused a moment before resuming and just as the pick was about to spring the latch, a foul odor penetrated the air. Charlie could not hold in a sneeze as the scent of sulfur tickled his nose.

Kerosene?

Warmth from the doorknob began building around his palm and steadily it increased in intensity reclaiming his attention.

"Ah," he huffed, and released the burning metal.

Charlie rubbed his fingers against his palm to stem the tingling sensation and even sucked on his skin to cool it. The smell of burning wood began to permeate the air as puffs of gray smoke seeped through the cracks of the door. Terror seized Charlie's chest and he knew what it meant, the image of his nightmare returning.

"Everyone up!" he shouted, scrambling to his feet, beginning to rip the covers off each bed.

All of the boys groaned and a few snuggled back into their mattresses, ignoring Charlie. One of the boys in particular buried his head underneath his pillow to muffle the commotion.

"I said, up!" said Charlie, grabbing the boy's foot before pulling him off his bed.

"Come on, Charlie," said the pillow boy in a groggy protest, rubbing his sore bum.

"Yeah, what gives?" said another boy, stretching his arms over his static mop of red hair.

"We need to leave," said Charlie, his fingers picking the lock on the servant's door.

The pillow boy glanced in puzzlement at the redhead boy, both of them at a loss—at least until a six-year-old boy pointed out the smoke coming in from the hallway. After that everyone was awake, the boys all frantically talking at once.

"Quiet!" shouted Charlie, his voice commanding.

The nine boys fell immediately silent, waiting for Charlie to tell them what to do, but it had not been Charlie's intention to gain their attention. He needed silence to listen for the lock. He twisted his wrist and with a light push the spring released.

"All right," he said, grabbing the kerosene lamp. "Stay close and follow me."

Single file, Charlie led the boys down the dark servant's hall to the back bedroom. He passed off the lamp to the pillow boy in order to free his hands, and tested the temperature of the knob before picking the lock. There was some debate as to why they would risk breaking into Hanna's room and not use the secret crawlspace upstairs.

"Because this is faster," said Charlie, working on the keyhole. "And besides, there is no way of knowing how much of the building is already on fire."

There were a few nervous whimpers, especially from the six-year-old boy who clung to the arm of a boy twice his age. The lock clicked and Charlie cautiously pulled the handle toward him. A soft growl rumbled through the room and he paused for a moment before exposing himself and the others to the unknown.

Hanna's room was untouched by flames, but thick smoke lingered around the ceiling. Charlie instructed the boys to crawl on the floor. He stood briefly to unlatch the window facing the neighboring brick house. He would have used the one facing the backyard, but the hitch was hard to turn. Charlie lifted the pane and immediately the growl returned, only this time it was much louder.

"Charlie, look," said the boy wrapped in a blanket.

Charlie turned his attention across the bedroom.

"Is the door supposed to do that?" asked the blanket boy, his question intended for Charlie, although it was answered by another.

"I don't think so," said a boy with a baseball cap. "I ain't ever seen a door bow like that."

"It's because of the pressure buildup," said Charlie, continuing to press his luck by lifting the window. He managed to secure enough space to fit the tallest and chubbiest boy through. There was no argument from the others when he had the tallest go first, followed by his little shadow. After that Charlie got everyone else out, one by one, trying to ignore the swelling wood, his thoughts again on the explosion on the front porch of the farmhouse. He squeezed out the chubby boy, a plump German who smelled of onions, and readied to jump himself.

"Charlie, what about Jimmy?" asked the blanket boy.

"What about him?" asked Charlie, his fingers gripping the window's frame.

"He's still inside," said the German boy.

"Are you sure?" asked Charlie, panic crushing his sense of flight.

"Ja," said the German boy.

"What about Orrin?" asked Charlie, remembering he had found the boy's bed empty.

"I saw him sneak out," said the redhead.

"By himself?" said Charlie.

The boys looked at each other, neither of them answering. Charlie yelled at them to speak, but instead of their reply, the fire in the hall pounded on the door.

"Run!" shouted Charlie and threw himself into the dark hallway, kicking the door shut behind him.

He tried to cover his ears in anticipation of the blast, but he did not have the time. His ears rang, his mind disoriented. Smoke pumped through the cracks in the doors on both sides of the pitch-dark hallway. Charlie shook his head and grunted as he unevenly got to his feet. He held his hands out in front of him, feeling his way to the spiral staircase. If Jimmy was still inside, the second-floor dormitory was on his way out. For now, his only means of escape was the roof.

Charlie reached the landing of the staircase and picked the lock blindly. It took a little more finesse, but he managed to spring the lock. He opened the door, relieved only wisps of smoke loomed overhead, and began to search the room.

"Jimmy," said Charlie, spotting his cousin huddled underneath one of the naked beds.

"No, no, no!" cried Jimmy, his body coiled around his treasure box. His right hand clenched the marble.

Charlie crouched in order to engage his cousin in a calm voice, but his sense of urgency threatened to take over. "Jimmy, please," he said, reaching under the exposed springs, but Jimmy retracted his bony appendages like a hermit crab. "Jimmy, everything is fine. It's just me. Please, we have to go."

Jimmy bound his body tighter into a protective shell, crushing the cardboard box against his chest. The burst from downstairs had triggered vivid memories of the house fire and terror dulled his flight instincts, paralyzing him. His droopy eyes blinked uncontrollably to keep the sting of the smoke at bay.

Charlie tried again to coax his cousin out from under the bed, but his commands were not working and they did not have time for him to play out this game. "Very well, Jimmy, you stay right here then. I'm gonna go out into the hall," he said, hoping the strength of the fire had not yet reached the second floor.

Charlie stood and made his way to the brightening hallway. He placed the sleeve of his shirt over his mouth before leaving the room and was instantly surrounded by swirls of thick smoke. He had taken no more than four steps toward the stairs when he heard the scampering of Jimmy's feet. Charlie was glad for his own cleverness, knowing his cousin would not be able to tarry alone amidst chaos. He turned around to meet Jimmy's eyes. Charlie took a step toward Jimmy, but the bubbling crackle of wallpaper distracted him. He glanced over his shoulder, and from the corner of his eye, he saw the all-too-familiar hues of yellow and orange.

"Tinkers be damned," swore Charlie, as the flames ascended the old wooden stairs.

"Charlie," said Jimmy, his free hand tugging the fabric of his long underwear.

Charlie looked back at his cousin. The boy's hazel eyes were similar in size to those of a barn owl, and full of fear. Without warning, Jimmy pivoted on his toes and ran back into the empty dormitory, trinkets from his treasure box spilling out onto the floor.

Charlie pulled his sleeve away from his mouth. "Jimmy, wait!" he shouted and ran after him. He gripped both sides of the doorframe and paused briefly to survey the room. He heard Jimmy crying in the far corner and went carefully across the floor as if sneaking up on an injured animal, but the time for coddling was over. He had no time to play hide and seek, not with the blaze smoldering beneath them. They needed to evacuate or face perishing the same way as the rest of their family.

Charlie stumbled on one of Jimmy's treasures, his ankle twisting the wrong way. He caught his footing early enough to avoid a sprain, tweaking the ligaments. He looked at the object as it rolled out from under his shoe and saw the marble. He picked it up and placed it in his pocket, then found Jimmy curled in the corner. He knelt down, ready to use his stern voice, but the weary sight of his cousin softened his anxiety.

"It'll be all right, Jimmy," said Charlie reassuringly and tried again to reach for him, but stopped short as his peripheral vision caught sight of gray smoke seeping in from underneath the servant's door.

"Char-lie," said Jimmy, leaving his treasure box and crawling underneath the bed to the other side.

"Jimmy." Charlie got to his feet and rounded the foot of the bed. "Jimmy, this is no time for games. We…" He paused, his firm tone catching in the back of his throat at the sight of a young boy lying on the floor between the two beds.

"Charlie, I think he's hurt," said Jimmy, leaning over the stranger on his hands and knees.

Charlie stood dumbfounded. Where had the kid come from? He retraced his steps, knowing full well he had gotten all the boys out. Charlie thought of the empty twelfth bed and wondered if he had arrived in the night unbeknownst to everyone. He knelt down to assess the boy. The kid looked half-starved and his round face was a sickly shade of green. It was hard to tell if anything else was wrong with him because his peculiar clothes covered most of his body. The boy's trousers resembled one of his mother's patchwork quilts and his long sleeved shirt was more yellow than white, matching the color of his waistcoat.

"Can you move?" asked Charlie.

The stranger blinked his eyes, more from uncertainty of his surroundings than in reply.

"Are you hurt?"

The boy still did not reply.

"Where did you come from? Are you…"

A loud rattle resounded from the servant's hall, interrupting Charlie. He pulled himself to his feet once again and approached the door. The wood vibrated as thicker puffs of smoke funneled into the room. Like Hanna's door downstairs, pressure was building in the secret passageway, the door preparing to burst open. Charlie did not bother testing the handle, as his flight instincts were already urging him to move. He turned around, ready to grab Jimmy, but found his cousin staring at him, his chin resting on the naked mattress.

"Charlie, are we gonna die?" asked Jimmy.

Charlie wanted to reassure him, but he did not want to lie either. Their predicament was grave at best, because, without knowing how much of the kitchen the fire had devoured, it was hard to know the integrity of the crawlspace above.

"No, Jimmy," he finally answered. "We'll get out. I'm sure the others have already alerted the fire brigade." He gave his cousin a hollow smile.

Jimmy nodded, believing his cousin.

The boy on the floor, however, heard the lie in Charlie's voice. "Leave," he muttered.

Charlie glanced at the stranger as he returned to the floor. He met the boy's serious stare, his emerald eyes drawing him in as though to put him under some sort of spell. Charlie blinked and felt the boy grip his arm.

"You must leave," he repeated hoarsely.

Charlie nodded, his quest for escape rekindling his thoughts. "Jimmy, take his hand," he instructed. "We need to get him up."

Jimmy did as Charlie asked and together the cousins hoisted the stranger to his feet, finding he stood a foot taller than Jimmy. Charlie took the brunt of his weight as Jimmy simply held the stranger's hand. They managed to make it back into the hallway where a wall of fire welcomed them.

"I won't," said Jimmy, dropping the boy's hand and withdrawing back into the room.

"Jimmy!" Charlie lowered the stranger to the floor and propped him against the doorframe.

"Save him," said the stranger. This time his voice was clear and commanding.

Charlie hesitantly nodded and left to retrieve Jimmy from the dormitory, where he was crouched behind two mattresses leaning up against the wall. Charlie scooped up his cousin and cradled him in his burly arms. There was no getting around it. The appearance of the fire was just too debilitating for Jimmy. He had no choice but to carry him out.

"Let's go, Jimmy," he said.

Charlie coughed as he reentered the hall, black smoke finally engulfing every inch of space. He checked the stranger; his eyes were closed and his arms limp at his sides. Charlie felt a nagging urge to remain with him, but duty to his cousin came first. He would simply have to come back for him.

Baptized by Fire

"Oh Bartholomew, what a predicament you have gotten yourself into," murmured the boy as he coughed. His nose twitched uncomfortably from the competing smells of chalk, scorched wood, and sulfur.

Bartholomew rolled his eyes, disoriented, trying to reawaken his motor function. It took a few more seconds before his mind could comprehend everything he saw, although when he finally grasped his surroundings, he was not where he had expected. The last thing he remembered before escaping his prison cell was the tether between him and the Eden Wanderer, the wandering mortal soul known by the name of Stingy Jack. He had dedicated every ounce of his energy, hoping his exodus from Euxinus would draw him directly to the creature, but as things appeared, he had not quite found his target. Bartholomew tried to sense within him the magic that tethered him to Stingy Jack, but instead he felt hollow. It was an odd feeling and with it came a level of uncertainty he had not anticipated. Severing his ties with his masters, the Fates, appeared to have cost him more than the protection of their grace.

Bartholomew inspected his surroundings, the animated colors of flame and shaded hues of smoke advancing on his position. *All that effort to escape, and here I am, trapped by flames.* He sighed, knowing his act of defiance could have led him just as easily to Hell, where he would have been tortured endlessly for the information he possessed. *Maybe it is all for the best,* he thought. Maybe it was better his secrets died with him. Maybe dying a second time would not be so bad.

"Be swift, element of Flame," he said to the fire.

The fire moaned in reply, prepared to oblige.

Bartholomew closed his eyes and let the heat of the blaze warm his skin. He cleared his mind, ready to accept the punishment he felt he deserved, but in the recesses of his conscious, the single image of a young woman with soaked clothes and matted hair, the dramatic shade of a ripening cherry, appeared.

"I should never have let you die, fair lady," he said, his thoughts conjuring the face of the ill-fated Shepherdess. "I need more time," he added a few seconds later, as though the fire had the ability to grant his plea.

"Don't worry. I'll get you out," said a confident voice.

Bartholomew opened his eyes just as the older boy, who he knew to be Charlie, hoisted him from the floor and cradled him against his chest. The sudden movement made Bartholomew dizzy, the weight of his head too much to prevent it from leaning back. It bobbed limply, his eyes on what was left of the staircase railing. In the flames, a devilish silhouette appeared. An uneasy awareness stirred in Bartholomew, but he had not the energy to challenge the shadowy figure. It was no matter however, for in the blink of an eye it was gone, and with it, any sense of alarm.

At the end of the hall, Charlie searched for the familiar opening in the wall. He moved the drooping hibiscus-patterned wallpaper from the entrance and stooped low to clear the lip. He attempted to squeeze through, but did not account for the stranger's larger size and lost his balance. He dropped Bartholomew unceremoniously on a piece of plywood, then leaned over him.

"Now, I'm gonna need your help. I can't coddle both of you, so I need to know you're able to take care of yourself," said Charlie, letting out a few coughs.

Bartholomew fluttered his eyes, his haziness spilling onto his face and he felt the boy take hold of his chin.

"Are you with me?" asked Charlie, giving him a slight shake.

Bartholomew's eyes rolled into the back of his head, unsure if he was with Charlie.

"Are you with me?" repeated Charlie, with more urgency. The crease along his forehead rippled with the creation of three additional lines.

Bartholomew blinked in response.

"Fair enough," said Charlie, releasing Bartholomew's face. "Now just wait here," he added and slid him next to his petrified cousin.

Bartholomew altered his line of sight, unable to stare at the hypnotic rocking of the small boy. He looked up at the ceiling, the beams angling with the slant of the roof. Smoke lingered within the rafters, but then gravitated to the small opening above Charlie. He watched him crawl back toward them, the wooden planks positioned across the support joists.

"The boy first," coughed Bartholomew, when Charlie seized his waistcoat. He would rather face death again than watch another mortal perish in front of him.

"I can't," said Charlie, sensing the stranger's lack of motivation. "I told you, I can't coddle both of you. Here, I'll get you started."

Bartholomew felt his muscles spasm as Charlie flipped him onto his knees and placed his hands on the first plank. His whole body shook and he wondered if he could remember how to crawl.

"Now," Charlie began, "we can take it slow. We have to. I've done this enough times to know these planks aren't very sturdy.

And with the weight of all three of us," his voice rose to a shout as the unseen chaos beneath them escalated in volume, "be sure to stay on them or you'll fall right through the ceiling. I'll help Jimmy follow you. You think you can manage that?"

Bartholomew had no concept of what he could manage, his brain trying to remember each instruction. "I think I can manage," he mumbled. Charlie gave him a slap on the back, forcing him to lose his balance. He put one hand in front of the other to catch himself, his frail arms aching as he pressed his weight down on them. His body was not ready to move.

"One hand at a time, Bartholomew, one hand at a time," he repeated under his breath. He inched his palms timidly forward across the flimsy wood and, after the first two planks, he noticed his body slumping forward.

"Charlie!" he called and halted. His arms quivered as he waited, but he did his best to remain as still as possible.

"Hey, are you square?" said Charlie.

"What?" asked Bartholomew, unfamiliar with Charlie's choice of words.

"Are you all right?" said Charlie.

"No!" shouted Bartholomew, his eyes focused on the wood shavings and old newspapers imbedded in the troughs between the support joists on either side of him. "The plank is dipping and I am afraid the beam might give way if I go any further."

"Hold on," instructed Charlie. He moved onto the second plank before transferring the one behind him in front of him. He gave Jimmy a brief command to stay put and positioned himself on the plank next to Bartholomew. He leaned sideways and extended his left arm around Bartholomew's back, wrapping it across his skinny chest. "On the count of three—one, two, three." Charlie sat Bartholomew upright, causing the sudden weight distribution to plunge the plank dangerously against the makeshift insulation.

"Charlie—"

"I know. Mine's dipping too." He needed to act and he needed to do it fast.

Without warning, Charlie hoisted Bartholomew off the plank and sat him down in front of him.

"Now, I need you to get over to the fourth plank up ahead!" shouted Charlie.

A ferocious moan resonated through the crawlspace, accompanied by a chorus of hisses and a high-pitched whistle.

"We're running out of time," said Charlie. "We need to get beyond this weak spot or we're done for."

"As you wish, but you will have to help me across," agreed Bartholomew, his line of sight gauging the distance.

"I'll make sure you don't fall. All you have to do is reach out. I'll do the rest."

Bartholomew extended his arms, reaching for the fourth plank. It was only a few centimeters away, but to him, it seemed comparable to a ravine. He gripped the board of wood and felt the strain of the straddle in the tender arch of his back. Charlie's hands clasped his thighs, and, in a fluent motion, lifted him from the weak plank and placed him on the stable one. Bartholomew steadied himself as Charlie repositioned the weak plank ahead of him and joined him, removing all the weight from the sinking joist. Bartholomew watched Charlie advance along their path to the exit.

"Char-lie."

The voice chimed simultaneously with Charlie's turnabout.

Bartholomew witnessed the dread mount on Charlie's face, unable to see what was happening behind him. Over the crashes, the sizzles, and the hisses, Bartholomew distinctively heard the soft cries of the small boy. A piercing snap silenced all other sounds as though to scare the others into hiding. The joists behind Bartholomew began to collapse. The radiance of the fire from the kitchen below brightened the crawlspace as dark clouds billowed. All three boys coughed violently as their lungs filled with smoke.

"Char-lie," cried Jimmy. The weakening joists began to fall underneath his plank. Jimmy wrapped his arms around the slab of wood. "Now I lay me down to sleep, I pray da Lord me soul to take." Jimmy muttered the prayer, his speech lost in the boom of falling timber.

The front end of the board leaned forward.

"Oww."

"Jimmy!" It was all Charlie could say or do.

Jimmy stared at the beast below, its teeth ridged spikes of hungry flame. He knew the beast well, having met it the night his father died in their family home. Jimmy pictured his father's scruffy face and it comforted him to know he would see it again soon. Even the prospect of meeting his mother for the first time gave him reason not to be so scared, but it did not stop the tears, which evaporated quickly from the intensity of the heat.

Charlie watched as his cousin fell into the fire below, his body clinging to the plank, swan diving into the mouth of the growling beast until he was gone. No screams followed, and, with the little ability he had to think amidst his shock, Charlie was grateful it was swift. After a moment, he welcomed the sight of the fire and wished it to take him. The flames climbed into the crawlspace as his gaze fell upon Bartholomew. In the light, the boy's emerald eyes dazzled, and from them Charlie felt a calming influence, their subtle magic numbing his shock so he could press on.

Bartholomew coughed, breaking their trance, but he still felt Charlie's eyes on him. He kept his head lowered and dug his tired fingers into the wood, the back end of the plank sinking.

"Move!" shouted Charlie.

Bartholomew snapped to attention at the sound of Charlie's command and followed him as the flames began to consume the insulation. Charlie reached the ventilation spindle and pushed aggressively upward, dislodging it from its perch. It moved easily, and, with another push, Bartholomew heard it tumble down the slant of the roof. Charlie grabbed both sides of the opening, hoisted his body out into the night air, and propped himself on his stomach.

"Take my hand," Charlie instructed.

Bartholomew raised a limp arm and felt a strong grip secure his wrist. Charlie vigorously heaved him through the hole, the smoke coming with him. Beyond the confines of the roof, Bartholomew gasped as he breathed in the fresher air. His eyes wandered to get a sense of his new surroundings. From every crevice of the building smoke rose into the predawn sky. He tried to process everything, but urgent bells, the collapse of the crawlspace, and the rising hum of an awakening city pulled his focus in different directions. He felt disoriented and feared he might keel over, but his eyes found Charlie again.

The young man was still on his stomach, his attention on the fiery beast below. Whoever the little boy, Jimmy, had been to Charlie, it was clear to Bartholomew that the young man cared for the boy dearly. It was hard for him to understand the mortal connection, but he had a feeling it was similar to the love the Shepherdess had shown Stingy Jack. Bartholomew felt an unusual boil in his gut, angry at what had happened and at himself for being unable to prevent the boy's death. He wanted to say something, but he did not have the words to express his condolence.

"Charlie, I..." he stammered.

"This isn't the time," said Charlie, his demeanor overly alert. He stood, then lent a hand to assist Bartholomew to his feet. "We haven't yet escaped this beast," Charlie continued, "and I'll be damned if it thinks it's gonna get us both."

"What do we do?" asked Bartholomew.

"We need to get over the peak of the roof. It flattens out after that to the front of the orphanage. There's a drain spout we can climb down on the left edge."

Bartholomew's body went limp, his legs giving out. It was not entirely because he still did not have full control of his faculties, but more that there was something in the way Charlie said orphanage that struck him. Charlie caught him before he crashed against the warm shingles.

"Thanks," he managed.

"Don't worry," assured Charlie. "You can hold on to my back. You think you have enough left in you to do that?"

"I guess we will find out," said Bartholomew apprehensively. Charlie threw his arm over his shoulder to bear his weight. In the same stride, they inched their way up the roof, feeling out its integrity. At its crest, Charlie stopped and together he and Bartholomew gazed out into the predawn sky.

For miles, rooftops stretched in every direction. Smokestacks stood proudly as a testament to the modern age of industry. The calls of trains answered each other from east to west. To the north, the distant shrills of tugboats and barges floating along the river thundered through the air. The dark sky above blanketed every inch as far as the eye could see, the city lights hiding the stars. To Charlie, Chicago never looked that big, but tonight he felt small in its presence.

Bartholomew had never truly laid eyes on the like. Long ago, mortals had renamed their realm Earth, but he still preferred to call it by its true name, Eden. For him, the landscape of Eden had changed drastically since the early years beginning the Age of Enlightenment, and he could not fathom how much time had passed. In his prison cell, time had been a permanent state—a limbo, as mortals would call it—but Euxinus was more than that. It was the origin of the universe itself, and yet, its ancient rite paled in comparison to the ever-changing splendor of its paralleled eastern sibling, Eden.

Charlie released a faint breath as the anxious bells below chimed. He lowered his eyes to the street and saw the fire brigade doing its best to battle the flames, but knew their efforts were in vain. He searched the crowd for the nine boys and spotted them across the street huddled in blankets surrounded by a handful of adults, but no Hanna, at least not that he could see. Charlie smiled, glad to see they were being cared for.

"You still with me, kid?" asked Charlie, turning away from the commotion below and walking over to the side of the roof.

"I am still with you," sighed Bartholomew, although truthfully a part of him lay dormant.

"All right then, get on my back," said Charlie, as he crouched down.

Bartholomew climbed on the young man's back.

Charlie grabbed the spout and slid his body over the side of the roof, readjusting his grip before making his descent.

Bartholomew peered over his shoulder at the alley below and immediately felt a sense of vertigo. He swore in his head. *By the foolishness of mortals,* he scolded himself, having forgotten his aversion of heights. He shut his eyes, allowing his legs to slip from Charlie's waist. They dangled beneath him and he struggled to hang onto Charlie.

Charlie huffed.

"Charlie, are you all right?"

"I think…"

"Am I choking you?" asked Bartholomew, doing what he could to keep his arms from Charlie's throat.

"No. Now be quiet, I need to concentrate." Charlie placed his shoes on the braces holding the drain spout to the brick wall and cautiously resumed until his feet reached the ground. "Well, we made it, kid," he said, expecting the boy to slide down, but he did not. "You can let go now."

As worn as he was, Bartholomew clung to Charlie with a grip he did not think possible. And though he knew it was time to let go and be on his way and fulfill his promise to find the Eden Wanderer so they could together save the Shepherdess, something inside him refused. It was a strange sensation, almost as though he was obeying some untold command. Besides, if he let go, what would happen? Where would he go? Bartholomew fought the mounting urge to ask for help. Charlie had given him enough already, a complete stranger, and at such a cost. He lifted his eyes to the roof and shame washed over him. It was unfair, just as it had been unfair letting the Shepherdess die. He had never expected that his deliverance from Euxinus would come with such a price. Then it dawned on him—*what if they come looking for me?* Bartholomew's guilt gave way to fear. He had no choice but to ask for Charlie's assistance a little longer.

"If you would not mind," Bartholomew spoke with every ounce of courage. "I know what I am asking of you, but…"

"It's all right, kid, I can carry you for a while," said Charlie selfishly, the kid's presence the only thing preventing the gaping hole in his chest from crushing him completely as he feared being alone with his grief. Charlie grabbed Bartholomew's legs and entered the commotion on the city street, not bothering to let the other boys know he was alive. Better they think he was lost in the fire with Jimmy, because nobody chased the dead.

Bartholomew rested his head on the nape of Charlie's neck as a spring breeze soothed his seared skin. He watched the metal poles of the streetlamps pass by, inspecting the fire-less glow trapped in the transparent oval-shaped cages. A faint cadence danced in the space around him, the heartbeat of the industrial city. It wafted through the air as if to welcome him home and oddly enough he felt eased. Bartholomew let out a faint yawn and fought the heaviness of his eyelids, his body digressing back into a state of rest. He felt tired, but did not want to sleep, afraid he might reawaken in the darkness of his prison cell. That somehow everything he had just experienced was simply a nightmare.

A Mother's Kindness

The lamps finally yielded to the brightening sky as a loud horn blew in the distance, signaling the start of a new day. The streets became rich with voices and the putt-putt of vehicles, particularly freight trucks that moved along Halsted Street, an artery to the Chicago Union Stockyards and the Central Manufacturing District. Bartholomew was somewhat oblivious to the ongoing bustle, his left ear pressed between Charlie's shoulder blades, the whisper of the boy's heart vibrating through his skin. He took stock, however, in the things he saw, his eyes soaking up his surroundings despite their heaviness. Eventually, the red brick buildings began to mix with structures of gray stone, each one a carbon copy of the last. They had an eerie feel about them and reminded him of the row houses in Euxinus, which rested like coffins along the streets of igneous black stone that lined the valley from mountain peak to mountain peak. Bartholomew twisted his fingers into the thin cloth of Charlie's shirt until the memory passed, hoping he would never have to see those darkened streets ever again. He inhaled the dry morning air to release a sigh and nearly gagged on a foul stench, which smelt of iron laced with a hint of liquor and the aroma of bacon.

"Hey kid, you awake?" Charlie's voice was even and patient, but beneath it, tentacles of despair bled through. He cut across the block to the less busy Morgan Street.

"Yes," replied Bartholomew, as the reflection in a large picture window revealed the image of a group of mortals lining in front of an enormous white tent. He rotated his head and saw the line was much longer than the reflection had allowed. "Charlie, what is that?" he asked.

"The breadline," replied Charlie, halting his stride. He relaxed his hold around the stranger on his back.

Bartholomew slid down, landing on unsure footing, but he managed to keep himself upright. He looked up at Charlie, waiting for him to give more of an explanation, but it was clear he was lost in thought.

Charlie stared somberly across the street, his adrenaline still high enough to prevent the numbness of his shock. He stuffed a hand in his pocket, his fingers curling around two priceless trinkets: Jimmy's marble and the bottle cap. The size of the tent reminded him of a circus big top, but he knew there was no spectacle within. Instead, several tables sat side by side with large wicker baskets on top where, behind them, people with white shirts and red sashes stood handing out bread to those in line.

"The breadline is a service the government established for people who have no means of getting food," explained Charlie, greedily licking the corner of his lips, his stomach rumbling. "They don't get much, just some bread, but it's the best most can do right now." He placed his hand over his side in an attempt to tame his hunger.

"And what about that?" asked Bartholomew. He pointed to the bronze seal posted on a set of stilts. He squinted to make out the words arched above and below: CITY OF CHICAGO + INCORPORATED 4th MARCH 1837.

"That's the Great Seal of Chicago," said Charlie with a hint of reverence in his voice, though he claimed no loyalty to the city.

"Urbs in Horto?" recited Bartholomew, reading the words bannered in the center circle. "City in the Garden," he added, translating. He looked at Charlie to find puzzlement on his face. "What?"

Charlie did not respond and looked away. It was not uncommon for people to know Latin, particularly the educated or Catholics. And yet Charlie had an inkling the stranger was neither of those, and was mildly curious to know the boy's story.

"So, what's your name, kid?" asked Charlie, tucking in his shirt.

Bartholomew's cheeks burned. How could he have forgotten to introduce himself? His lapse was excusable, as they had been dodging death and fire at the time, but Bartholomew, a slave to ceremony, always honored such formalities.

"Pardon my manners," he said. "Bartholomew, at your service." He bowed his head low, a gesture he was accustomed to.

"Why are you bowing?" asked Charlie, taken aback by the lad's old-fashioned gesture. He looked around to make certain the kid was not making a scene.

"It is a sign of respect where I come from." Bartholomew pressed his lips together and lifted his eyes to see a sour look on Charlie's face.

"Get up," said Charlie. He did not need any passersby to take an interest in them, not in this neighborhood. Too many crooks looking for an easy mark.

Bartholomew stood up straight. "Is something the matter?"

Charlie did not reply, his attention scanning every face in the breadline, making sure they were clear of curious eyes. He did not need any more surprises or another casualty. His adrenaline kept him alert despite how heartbroken he felt, but he feared the inevitable moment when he would crash.

Bartholomew resumed his observation of the mortals inching through the breadline, but eventually his mind wandered onto other things. Out of all the mortal cities in Eden, his death had spirited him to the one that proclaimed to be the City in the Garden. His instincts told him such a feat could not have occurred by chance, but by design, and he could not help but wonder if he had been able to choose this place because his tether to the Eden Wanderer had led him here. That somewhere in this city he could find his proverbial needle in the haystack. But, without the magic to tether himself to the Eden Wanderer, his needle would remain hidden to him, even if the wandering mortal soul were standing right in front of him. He was tempted to ask Charlie if he had heard of Stingy Jack, but his eye caught sight of a little girl with braided pigtails, standing near the curb just outside the front entrance of the tent. She clung to the skirt of a middle-aged woman, teetering on skinny legs. She lost her balance and to prevent herself from falling she tugged on the woman's skirt. The middle-aged woman grabbed the little girl and scolded her, her voice loud enough for all to hear. The little girl nodded, obeying her mother, and settled her body, turning her attention to the street. She spotted Bartholomew and waved at him with a bandaged hand, the innocence of her baby doll face beaming at him.

Bartholomew stared back at the little girl, baffled. Her eyes were big with wonder, and for a moment he thought she saw him as more than his outer mortal appearance. But he noticed she was not looking straight at him. Instead, her eyes were on the sky. He rotated his head to get a peek at what would generate such a reaction, but before he was able to spot it, he heard the little girl's voice.

"Mama, look," she said, her voice carrying across the hushed street.

Behind him, Bartholomew saw a mass gathering of small birds perched on the rooftops, their hungry eyes engaged on the tent. Atop the highest point, a harpy eagle curled its lethal talons around the brick of a chimney, its double-crested crown of grey feathers ruffled like a lion's mane, as though to give proper warning of the imminent attack. Bartholomew heard the gasps of awe, certain none of the mortals had ever seen another creature quite like it, but he knew this "winged wolf" was no ordinary bird.

"Well, I'll be a monkey's uncle," said Charlie matter-of-factly. "I ain't seen an eagle of its like before."

The harpy eagle screeched, and on command, the small birds dove, their numbers fanning out for half a city block. There were several screams from those in the breadline and Bartholomew threw a glance over his shoulder to watch the middle-aged woman drag the little girl into the safety of the tent. The onslaught of the flock forced everyone to scatter or duck where they stood. The birds swarmed, changing patterns deliberately to prevent the mortals from witnessing whatever was about to take place. It was a notable and well-calculated distraction, which even had Charlie diving into a hedge for cover.

The harpy eagle screeched again, although this time it was much closer as the bird's magnificent wingspan extended and soared towards the center of the street, casting a commanding shadow. Bartholomew turned as the eagle circled sharply and landed on the concrete in front of him. The bird folded its wings, the downy feathers of its breast puffed out. The street became still. The screams and chirps faded away in order to give the two supernatural creatures a moment of privacy, for though neither had the power to stop time, the eagle had the ability to slow it down.

"Greetings, Master Herald," said Bartholomew, presenting a brief yet courteous bow. His thoughts were concerned by the creature's presence.

"Greetings, Master Breedling," said the harpy eagle, its sharp, high-pitched voice a direct reflection of its screech. It nodded its regal head. "I bear a message," it added, setting its left talon out in front, a rolled piece of parchment tied to its leg.

Bartholomew removed the scroll and instantly the harpy eagle took to the sky, the flock of birds following in kind.

"Wait," he objected, turning skyward.

The eagle twirled and flapped its wings in suspension, its wide eyes fixed on the Breedling.

"How did you know I was here?" asked Bartholomew.

The harpy eagle paused, debating whether or not to entertain the Breedling's question, its temporary magic already lifting from the street.

"Please," said Bartholomew, his hands clutching the parchment. He knew the Fates' messenger seldom answered questions outside the parameters of its intended correspondence, but he needed to know if the Fates knew his whereabouts. "Do they know I am here? Did they send you? Are the Retrievers far behind you?" Bartholomew felt a paralyzing shiver freeze his veins at the thought of the Fates' bounty hunters.

"Master Breedling," screeched the Herald. "The Fates bear no knowledge of your escape, and at present, only my sender knows of your miraculous feat."

"Your sender?" said Bartholomew. "But I am no longer bound to the servitude of the Fates' power or influence, no one should know I am here."

"As you know, Master Breedling, my sender is a creature of great power himself and has gone to great lengths to get you here.

Well, in a manner of speaking, as it was by your will you escaped, not his. Nonetheless, he was confident I would find you here in the City in the Garden."

Bartholomew was stunned by this news and though he had had a feeling his arrival was not by sheer happenstance, to think any Euxian creature could have orchestrated the location of his arrival was beyond perplexing, while at the same time diminished his hope that Stingy Jack was in fact somewhere present in the city.

"The council is with you, Master Breedling," added the Herald.

Bartholomew lifted his gaze as the eagle took its leave. There were so many questions he wanted to ask, but the Herald did not give him the chance. He looked at the scroll, certain it could only be from the sole Euxian that held as much authoritative sway in Euxinus as the Fates. A creature of great wisdom and prestige, the eldest of them all, the Apothecary.

The sounds of the city began to resume and the mortals across the street gossiped about the phenomenon they had just witnessed. The neighborhood was absent of all the birds, save for two red-winged black birds tucked out of sight in the branches of the nearest tree, their eyes watching the Breedling.

Charlie crawled out from behind the hedge, brushing off the leaves sticking to his clothes. He looked about the street then at Bartholomew and studied the boy for the first time. Judging by the outdated nature of his clothes and their deterioration, he had been clothed in them for quite some time. His golden waistcoat drooped, drowning his weak frame. His dirty blond hair lay flat on his scalp, glued down by sweat. His round face resembled that of a young child, but his stance suggested a boy coming into his own. Charlie inspected him for scratches, but luckily his ivory skin was untouched. He noticed the scroll crinkled in the boy's hands and contemplated an outlandish scenario about homing pigeons and circus performers, which would explain the bizarre clothes and the bird performance. However, what remained unanswered was how Bartholomew managed to appear in the second-floor dormitory out of the blue. Plus, he had only heard about kids running away to join the circus, not running from one.

"You got any family?" asked Charlie, engaging in conversation.

"Family?" said Bartholomew, lifting his chin. "A sister. Why do you ask?"

Charlie shrugged. "Just thought she might be the one who would send a message via bird. Are you meeting your sister somewhere?"

"That is not possible," said Bartholomew.

"How come?"

"I do not know where she is."

"You lost your sister?"

"No, I did not lose her." Bartholomew paused. He had not seen his sister, Miriam, since his trial. She had passionately spoken on his behalf, and, after his imprisonment, he feared she too had fallen victim of the Fates' wrath, having not once visited him. "My sister and I were separated by our masters and have been now for quite some time."

"Masters, what about your parents?" asked Charlie, his mind conjuring fantasies about how Bartholomew and his sister had been sold to a traveling circus and were indentured servants.

Bartholomew delayed, pondering an answer. "Um, I do not have any, parents I mean. I only had masters. Besides, now that I have escaped, I do not even have them."

"Why did you run?" asked Charlie.

Bartholomew lowered his head. The answer was obvious, but one that warranted explanation. "Someone died," he muttered.

Charlie stared in amazement as his stomach burned with a

familiar sentiment that happened whenever an abandoned youth crossed his path. Call it a hero complex, but Charlie knew better than to label the empathetic gift his mother had nurtured in him, even if some days he saw it as a curse.

His darling mother, Adele, rest her soul, had been the kind of person to never turn anyone away. Even after her parents disowned her, she had made it her life's goal to help others any way she was able. One day, when he was six, while the two of them were riding along the South Branch Forked Creek through Peotone Township, they had come across a group of teenage boys surrounding two smaller ones. The teenagers he knew from school—a pack of bullies, hell bent on beating those smaller than them, but the two standing in the water, he did not. His mother had dismounted from her horse and instructed him to stay put while she went to break up the fight. He had insisted on helping her, but she smiled and said, "When you're older, love." Charlie had sat anxiously on his horse, Taurus, as his mother approached the taunting boys. She had spoken to them in her usual gentle voice and won them over, but back then, he just figured she had threatened to speak with their parents. She had sent the bullies on their way, helped the other two boys onto her horse, and walked them into town. Later, on their return home, Charlie and his mother had come across a young spotted fawn caught in a section of barbwire fence. His mother had pulled on her reins to stop and assist the creature, but Charlie had hopped down from his horse first.

"I can do it, Maw," he had assured her and proceeded to untangle the fawn. Once he had freed the small animal, it limped away across the field. Charlie had kept his eyes on it to make sure it reached the thicket up ahead and before it disappeared, the fawn paused, looked at Charlie and bowed in gratitude. He didn't know whether to return the gesture, his young mind baffled by the peculiar display. Charlie looked to his mother for guidance, but before he could ask, she placed a tender hand on his shoulder.

"I'm proud of you, Charles," Adele Reese had said. "One day, you will do something greater than even the stars themselves are capable of."

Charlie sighed at the memory, sensing the presence of her touch even now, her prophesized expectation still in effect. He felt his eyes glaze, but held in his emotions, suppressing them even further. His chest tightened, his adrenaline in a lull. He slicked back his dark brown hair, revealing a streak of soot on the ridge of his wide cheekbone.

"So, did you live at the orphanage?" asked Charlie, digging deeper into the mystery of the stranger.

"Um, not exactly," said Bartholomew sniffling, grateful that Charlie did not ask to know more about the death he had witnessed. "I snuck in."

"I had a suspicion you were out of place, but then again, the orphanage can house twenty-four boys at a time, sometimes thirty. I try not to get too attached to anyone as the older boys often run away and younger ones are always waiting to take their place. There were twelve of us on my last count, waiting on a thirteenth." Charlie paused. He wiggled his nose to deflect a mounting suspicion. "How did you end up on the second floor?"

"I am not quite sure," said Bartholomew, stretching the truth and unwilling to explain to Charlie that, unlike him, he never aged; or that after thousands of years of obedient service he had disobeyed his masters. Or that because of his actions his masters threw him in prison. Or that through his suffering he decided to take his life in an attempt to escape.

Charlie lifted an eyebrow, unconvinced. Clearly, the kid had been through some sort of ordeal and was hiding something. His flight instinct told him to get as far away from the strange boy as possible, but it was not strong enough to combat the legacy of his mother's kindness, at least not at the moment. Charlie grappled with the urge to ask several intrusive questions, ones he had never thought to ask anyone, but he bit his tongue. If there was a chance he could get some answers, he needed to ask his questions at the right time. That is, if the kid stuck around long enough.

"So what's the message say?" asked Charlie temporarily diverting the subject.

Bartholomew unrolled the parchment, not giving any thought as to the sensitivity of the message or how it would affect Charlie. Immediately, the calligraphy letters of the Apothecary's hand appeared in quill-tipped ink. *The mortal will lead you to the mortal Damek who alone has the power to reaffirm the tether of your charge. Take heed, Master Breedling, the mortal knows not of this plan, and therefore must remain innocent.*

"It's blank," said Charlie, looking over Bartholomew's shoulder. "Why would anyone send a blank message?"

Bartholomew crumpled the note, not at all surprised Charlie could not read the enchanted ink, his mind not in tune with the supernatural. He had no way of deciphering the Apothecary's message further and had no choice but to do as it suggested.

"Charlie," said Bartholomew. "I know it is a lot to ask of you, because you have done enough for me already, but I know nothing about your grand city or how to survive here."

"It was a warning, wasn't it?" said Charlie, sucked in by the sudden urgency mounting on the boy's youthful face. "They're after you, your masters."

Bartholomew found Charlie's intuitiveness refreshing, as he had always been under the impression that mortals lacked keen observation skills. And though Charlie was wrong, he was right, too. For once the Fates discovered his absence, he had no doubt the Retrievers would be on the hunt to find him.

"It is only a matter of time, I suppose," said Bartholomew with a shrug. "So, if you would be so kind to help me at least through the next day or so, I would be eternally grateful."

Charlie looked again at the breadline as he contemplated denying the youngster. It would be best to leave him with one of the volunteers, but staring at the opening to the tent, he noticed a bean pole of a man standing next to a dandy, their eyes watching him. Charlie knew the two men well—snitches for the Polish gang. He was not surprised to see them loitering, for nothing happened on Morgan Street without Frankenstein knowing about it. He cringed at the thought of what story they might tell, his friendly exchange with the kid and the bird attack noteworthy news. Charlie quickly withdrew his gaze and returned his attention to Bartholomew. There would be no leaving him here, not without consequence, and with everything that had already happened, he felt somewhat responsible for the kid. Charlie sighed, knowing he would just have to bring him along, but better he look out for the kid than worry what tragedy had befallen him.

"Very well, Bartholomew, if you're gonna tag along with me, I can show you the ropes of Chicago, but there is a matter of urgency that needs my attention right now, so be sure to listen well and do exactly what I say."

"We have an accord, Charlie," said Bartholomew. He cracked a small smile as he stuffed the crumpled note in his pocket for safe keeping.

Charlie smiled back, as an unsettling tingle brushed the back of his neck, part of him knowing something was off about the kid and his story. The sensation gave him pause, but was overpowered by his grief, his raw emotion latching himself to Bartholomew as though they were two soldiers having miraculously survived the hardships of a foxhole. The internal struggle twisted his gut and his palms clammed, but he did not fight it. The best he could muster was to put forth a shard of hope that he would not regret taking this stray under his wing.

BREAKING ICE

"All right, Bartholomew," started Charlie, as they walked further along Morgan Street. "First lesson: we don't bow to each other. Bowing is old hat and we ain't Europeans. We Americans shake hands." He extended a hand to the kid.

Bartholomew looked at it for a second and reluctantly extended his own hand toward Charlie. They shook hands and Bartholomew chuckled with delight, finding the action quite enjoyable. After a few shakes, one too many for Charlie's liking, he weaseled his hand away.

"Secondly," said Charlie, "Bartholomew just won't do. It's too old fashioned and only adults go by their given names. Here on the streets, a good rule of thumb is to use a name that is convenient and easy, and never, and this is important, never give anyone the same last name twice."

Bartholomew cocked his head.

"Hold on a spell," said Charlie, taking note of the lad's confusion. He lingered on the corner of the block to survey the street, his eyes first catching sight of a group of school kids walking with their teacher. His eyes drifted to an elderly couple walking a red-grizzle border terrier before finally watching some middle-aged men in overalls with thermoses hopping on the back of a Stake truck. In all the ongoing commotion, he could not find what he was looking for, so he turned his eyes upward.

Bartholomew followed Charlie's gaze to the rooftops, where an illustrated billboard stood out against the canvas of a clear sky. The picture was in excellent condition, though a little faded from being out in the sun. In the center of the massive rectangle, a large clean pig sat on its hind legs next to an egg-shaped can; beneath them big letters spelt the word HORMEL.

"There, Hormel, that'll be your last name for now," said Charlie, looking back at the kid. "And as for your first, well, you don't strike me as a Barty. How about Buck? I had a schoolmate named Buck. You resemble him a bit, your round face anyhow. It's much easier to remember than an old hash of a name like Bartholomew."

"Buck Hormel," said Bartholomew. The sound of it was rather odd and he did not care for it. "Buck," he pondered further, the name resonating comfort. He tried the name again and this time he felt a sense of change, but was unsure of the extent. He agreed to "Buck" nonetheless and thanked Charlie.

"Charlie, what are those?" he asked, pointing at the bizarre procession of horseless carriages.

"Those? Those are automobiles." Charlie looked at the kid sideways, unable to conceal his surprise. "You act as if you've never seen one."

"Well, of course, automobiles," repeated Bartholomew, with little confidence. The faint smell of rotten eggs and exhaust forced him to sneeze. He sniffled, sneezed again, then rephrased his question so as not to rouse the mortal's suspicions further. "What I meant to ask is, what kind are they?"

"Well, those black ones there sitting in front of the apartment complex are the original Model Ts. My pa and Uncle Gert had one back on the farm. That blue one parked in front of the white house with the long nose is a Cadillac, and of course there are the freight trucks. You'll see a lot of those 'round this neighborhood."

"Fascinating," said Bartholomew, as he watched the Ford Model T pass them. He wanted to know more about the metal beast. "How do they work?" he inquired, as they walked across the street.

"What?" Charlie raised an eyebrow, his instincts already second-guessing the rationale of his mind, though they were not yet prepared to write off the kid.

Bartholomew looked back at Charlie. "What?"

Charlie halted on the opposite corner below the Thirty-Fourth street sign. "Did you just ask me how automobiles run?"

Bartholomew paused as a slender woman with a basket of linen collided with him.

"Excuse you," she snapped.

Charlie stepped aside. "Ma'am," he expressed.

The slender woman flicked up her nose in disgust and continued on her way, the scent of lye soap leaving with her.

"How old did you say you are?" asked Charlie, his eyes scrutinizing the kid's boyish face.

Bartholomew shied away as though embarrassed, but really, he did not have a believable response. He could not tell Charlie he was over five thousand years old, nor could the mortal know that his appearance of a young teenage boy was simply an immortal shell. Regardless, Bartholomew never had to deal with time the way mortals did, and wondered how old he appeared to Charlie. In all his studies with the Apothecary or in the Tales Teller's library, the topic of age had never come up in conversation. Nor had there been any need. As a soulcatcher, Bartholomew had moved through Eden more like a shadow and had had very little personal contact with mortals. Aside from the Shepherdess, Charlie was the first mortal he had ever engaged. With that in mind, he wondered what Charlie would believe.

"How old are you?" Bartholomew asked, moving the spotlight back onto Charlie.

"I asked you first," said Charlie.

"Well, I asked you second," said Bartholomew.

Charlie rolled his eyes, not fond of the game Bartholomew was playing, particularly because he never won when it came to verbal contests with anyone younger than him. The exchange made his heart skip, and for a brief moment he pictured his cousin's cheerful expression as though he were arguing with Jimmy and not some stranger. Charlie smiled at the mirage, but with a blink of his eyes, it evaporated.

"I just turned seventeen a few days ago, on May second," he said, disheartened, his fingers again finding the bottle cap in his pocket.

"Well, to be honest," said Bartholomew, "I am not sure how old I am, but if I have to guess, maybe fifteen?"

"And you don't know how an automobile works?" said Charlie, his words bearing an onset of irritability.

"Not really," said Bartholomew, plotting his next words carefully. "My masters never gave me the opportunity to be around them, to be honest. So no, I do not know that much about them."

"Are you sure you're not some Amish runaway?" asked Charlie, remembering a visit to an Amish village in Wisconsin when he was ten. His mother had insisted on taking him and his siblings in order to teach them how to appreciate a different way of life.

"Beg your pardon, Charlie, but I do not even know what you mean by Amish," said Bartholomew. "My masters did not allow me to see the world as you see it, so if I ask queer questions it is not my intention. As I said, I ran away from them and after what happened…" Bartholomew became quiet and turned away. The Shepherdess' death was on his mind and, for a fleeting moment, he wished he could share his horrible secret, but the Apothecary's warning weighed on him.

"Well…" said Charlie, disappointed. He had hoped Bartholomew would have divulged more about himself. "Each car has an engine that runs on gasoline, and quite frankly, I don't know that much about automobiles either." Charlie laughed at himself for trying to sound smarter than he was on the matter and felt bad for giving Bartholomew such a hard time. "What do you say, Buck, water under the bridge?"

Bartholomew smiled. Charlie calling him by his new name reminded him of a question he had before being distracted by the vehicles. "Do you have a last name?"

Charlie chuckled and smacked his hand on Bartholomew's back, ushering him forward. "You certainly have a crafty way of steering a conversation, Buck," he said then proceeded to tell the Breedling his last name was Reese, but that he had not gone by it in quite some time.

"And what happened to your family?" asked Bartholomew, not realizing how much his inquiry would affect Charlie.

Charlie's cordial expression lapsed, and he instinctively deviated from the sidewalk into an alley, away from prying eyes. He stood stoic for a moment before crossing his arms and leaning uncomfortably against the bricks of a bungalow. He let out a sigh, unsure if he felt comfortable talking about his family, as a vice gripped his chest, forcing the air from his lungs. He took a deep breath that filled him all the way to his gut, and before he could make a conscious decision, his mouth opened and he started talking.

"This really isn't the place for such talk," Charlie said, not analyzing why he was opening up to a complete stranger. "It would be better suited in the dark corner of a tavern, with a good drink in hand. To start, I must first speak about my mother. She was born in Bohemia, or Czechoslovakia, as it's known now, to wealthy parents who catered to her every whim. She met my father, a German man with no social standing, in New York City and fell fast in love. Her parents were furious when she wrote them of her plans to marry, and threatened to disown her should she go through with it without their blessing, but she didn't care; she wasn't seeking their approval. She had all the family she needed, my father and my Uncle Gert, Jimmy's father."

"Jimmy was your cousin?" exclaimed Bartholomew, wondering how Charlie could have allowed himself to choose a stranger over blood.

"He was," said Charlie, his voice cracking, his chest tightening again. "As I was saying," he continued, clearing his throat, "just before I was born, my pa bought a farmhouse on the outskirts of Chicago in Peotone Township and moved the family here to the Midwest. In short, one night a fire ravaged our home, killing my family. I only survived because I had fallen asleep in front of the fireplace."

"And Jimmy?"

"I managed to get my Uncle Gert's attention by breaking his bedroom windows with some rocks. He left to retrieve Jimmy, but only Jimmy came back. After that, we were shipped up here to Bridgeport with some other orphaned kids." Charlie tapped his fingers on his thigh as though he were playing the piano, a nervous tick he used to hold back his rising emotions. "Jimmy and I were given over to the care of Father Van Lewen, the pastor of St. John Nepomucene Church. The other kids went to various boarding houses, but Father Van Lewen took a liking to Jimmy and me, so he let us stay for a while. We did all sorts of errands and chores for him, but soon more people began to seek refuge in the church, looking for food or alms and so we were placed in the orphanage."

Charlie took another belly filling breath, as a warm wave of vulnerability coursed through him, tempting his sensitive eyes to cry.

"I begged Father Van Lewen to let us stay," he resumed, "but he was insistent and I had no right to question his kindness. He had done so much for Jimmy and me already. It worked out well enough in the beginning, though. Father Van Lewen had introduced me to his Polish acquaintance, Grocer Pawlak, whom I've been working for in his market for the last several months. He has been quite generous with food credit, all of which I shared with Jimmy." Charlie paused again and looked at Bartholomew. "So that has been the last year or so. You already know the rest."

Silence fell between the two boys as the sunlight temporarily dimmed and the smell of chicken potpie wafted through the air on a weak gust of wind.

"What of the fire?" asked Bartholomew, still holding back from Charlie.

"A week ago, I overheard Miss Schwarman talking with a traveling salesman in her study about insurance claims. I don't know exactly what he was telling her, but it sounded like he was trying to get her to collect damages on the property in case of fire." Charlie's eyes grew grim, unable to mask his anger. "I figured they were up to something, but it wasn't until Hanna came waltzing into the dormitory with her guest that I realized Miss Schwarman was in cahoots with the traveling salesman to burn down the orphanage." The back of Charlie's throat warmed and he sensed the strength of his control falter. "Luckily, I was able to get all the other boys out before searching for Jimmy, but we both know how that turned out."

Poor Jimmy, Bartholomew mused, knowing well what awaited Charlie's cousin. No doubt the Fates had already dispatched one of his fellow kin to retrieve Jimmy's soul.

Typically, deaths in an orphanage would not warrant such intervention, but in this case, his mere presence had kissed Jimmy's demise with a touch of the supernatural. All mortal souls claiming this distinction were retrieved by Breedlings and ferried to Euxinus, where they stood trial to determine placement in the afterlife. The mere thought of it sickened Bartholomew and he felt the need to tell Charlie the truth about his cousin, but his slight window closed as Charlie resumed.

"If only there was something more I could have done," said the mortal, as though to make a case for himself, regret present in his voice. His eyes stung as water pooled, his knees giving out; his body folding like an accordion to the ground. He dropped his hands into his lap. "I couldn't do anything," he said with a gasp, his grief overwhelming him. "I couldn't reach…"

Charlie's breakdown stirred Bartholomew from his thoughts, uncertain how to react. He recognized the mortal's grief and somehow, within it, he saw a reflection of himself. It was a brokenness he too had endured, the time spent in isolation having taken its toll. Bartholomew stooped down in front of Charlie and set a hand on the young man's shoulder with all the genuine care he could muster. He tried to think of the right words to speak, but again they eluded him, so he said nothing.

Charlie lifted his head, the chiseled features on his face more prominent than before. The tears washed away the grime from his copper tone skin, leaving streaks. He felt embarrassed by his vulnerability, and yet there was a sense of peace about it, as though he could tell the stranger anything. Through glistening eyes, he searched Bartholomew's somber expression, the boy's emerald eyes revealing the old soul behind the youthful exterior. He wanted to hate him, place the blame for Jimmy's death at his feet, but he could not summon the emotion. He lowered his gaze to his lap and concentrated on the cool pulse emanating from Bartholomew's touch. With each breath he felt lighter, his conscience clearing, his breath returning. His grief shrank and without questioning the instantaneous relief, Charlie stowed it away.

"Thank you," Charlie managed.

Bartholomew smiled and returned to his feet. He took a few steps back to give Charlie some space. He felt oddly drained from the ordeal and wondered if mortals experienced the same when giving comfort.

Charlie rose and released a steady breath, the hole in his chest still present, but again, at least for the moment he was numb to it. He wiped his tears with his shirtsleeve and when he was ready, he cleared his throat, prepared to press on until he crashed.

They returned to the sidewalk and moved off the topic of death, allowing Bartholomew to ask questions about New York City, which in turn led to discussion on America. Charlie told him everything he had learned about the world from his schooling and the books his mother had forced him to read. The scope was grander than Bartholomew was expecting, but it was clear that in mortal terms of years, he had been in prison for about two centuries. He hung on Charlie's every word and was interested in America's mystique as a place of opportunity, where dreams came true; a place to start anew. When Charlie could not think of anything more worldly to account, he turned his focus to their Chicago surroundings.

"Now this part of Chicago, Buck, is known as Bridgeport. It's made up of many different cultures. For instance, the Polish neighborhood is here to the left of Morgan Street and the Lithuanian neighborhood is to the right. "

"What about the orphanage? I mean..." Bartholomew stumbled for more words to frame his question.

Charlie lowered his gaze and could tell Bartholomew was concerned about upsetting him. "It's all right Buck," he said. "And to answer your question, the orphanage is located in a predominantly Irish neighborhood south of Bridgeport most folks call Canaryville, which is funny, because a German broad acted as warden. Then again, it is financed by the city, so in a way I guess it works. Although Hanna, the assistant caretaker, is at least half Irish, but that is neither here nor there."

Bartholomew nodded and bit his lower lip, hesitant to ask another question.

Charlie noted the apprehension. "Buck, there is no need to hold back; it is what it is, and there ain't no changing it. You can ask your question."

"Um, well, after leaving the orphanage, there was a putrid smell in the air."

"Ah yes, that would be the Union Stockyards, which are south of us now as well. Thank goodness too. There are quite a few foul smells that come from the killing floor."

"Killing floor?"

"The slaughterhouse, you know? Where they butcher the animals. But to be fair to the animals, the Back of the Yards, which sits on the stockyards' eastern border, is littered with ill-kept wooden buildings and disease-ridden streets and—" Charlie shivered, his words conjuring the poor conditions. "I've never been as far as the front entrance and I plan to keep it that way.

There is no need to enter that part of the city if you don't have to. Good thing the smell doesn't carry as heavily this far north—well, unless a warm breeze blows in from the south."

"Extra! Extra! Read all about it!" said a lanky boy dressed in brown knickers and a heather grey vest, his arm thrown in the air with a stack of papers in hand, his voice booming like a herald. "Dust storms continue! President Roosevelt urges all citizens to be prepared. Black Blizzards spotted moving towards Chicago!"

"Charlie, what is a Black Blizzard?" asked Bartholomew, keeping an eye on the lanky boy as several individuals flocked to him, exchanging a few coins for a sheaf of papers.

"It's a blizzard, but without the snow," said Charlie. "From what I've heard, they are huge dust storms that darken the sky, have treacherous winds, and cover everything in their path with blackened ash."

"Where do they come from?" Bartholomew faced forward in order to prevent himself from tripping over his feet.

"The farm fields of the Great Plains, supposedly. I don't know all the scientific mumbo jumbo. All I know is that the soil is being blown away and farmers can't plant crops. I've heard many people say it's a bad omen."

"An omen of what?" Bartholomew crinkled his nose at the word, knowing mortal superstition meant supernatural involvement.

"Well, there are some who say the Blizzards are the work of the Devil and that Judgment Day is upon us. Lots of folks have lost hope things will get better."

"And what do you think?" asked Bartholomew, aware the notion of Judgment Day was a seed the Devil planted in the heads of mortals thousands of years before.

"Everything happens for a reason, Buck, and I was raised to believe in the impossible. My mother encouraged it. So it's hard for me to deny the possibility that there may be forces at work beyond my understanding," said Charlie with a sigh. "Nowadays," he continued, "the loss of my family has jaded my openness to greater forces. Not unlike that gentleman—he wholeheartedly believes the hype."

Charlie pointed to a bearded man with a leather face and mangy salt-and-pepper hair sitting on the boulevard under the shade of a tree. In his hands, he held a sign that read, REPENT, FOR THE END IS AT HAND.

"And you do not?" asked Bartholomew, looking away from the hideous man. "Believe in the hype, I mean?"

"No, Buck, I have to believe there is hope for all of us. Otherwise, what's the point?" said Charlie, turning the corner away from Morgan Street. "Suffering is a cruel mistress and it never affects us the same way twice, so sometimes all we can do is keep going, even though all we feel is gutted inside, but eventually we are able to release ourselves of its burden. Do you understand?"

Bartholomew nodded, even though he only had a small inkling of what Charlie was saying.

"Good," said Charlie, straightening his appearance.

"So, where to?" asked Bartholomew, after a brief pause to allow a milkman to hurry around them.

"To meet a friend of mine; well, he's more of an acquaintance, you might say. On the street, people call him Frankenstein, which is a horrible misconception, because he resembles Frankenstein's monster," said Charlie, not catching Bartholomew's puzzlement. "He's a particularly important fellow in this neighborhood, the leader of one of many street gangs in the area."

Charlie halted his stride, forcing Bartholomew to do the same.

"There are a few things you should know," he said, the serious expression on his face exaggerated by his fatigue. "Frankenstein cares about only two things, his family and his reputation. A while back, he had an altercation with one of his rivals and the hostilities between them have escalated beyond boyish fisticuffs."

"What does that have to do with you?" asked Bartholomew.

"I've been asked to broker a truce between the two gangs, which is why I need you to do one thing for me."

"Anything," said Bartholomew.

"Keep that politeness close to the vest," said Charlie.

"What?"

"Don't overdo it," warned Charlie. "Frankenstein has no tolerance for smart alecks and your proper manners will only set him off. The conflict you are about to walk into is not something to be taken lightly."

"Then what should I do?" asked Bartholomew, his curiosity filling in the blanks, wondering if this Frankenstein was the mortal the Apothecary had written about.

"Keep your head down," instructed Charlie, his tone stern.

"My head?"

"I'm serious, Buck," said Charlie. "No one has died yet from this feud and I'd like to keep it that way. I'm keen to avoid taking you with me."

"No!" said Bartholomew. "I will keep quiet."

"All right," said Charlie, rounding back his shoulders, grateful there would be no further argument on the matter. "Just remember to let me do the talking. Now keep up, Frankenstein lives close by."

FRANKENSTEIN

Charlie held the bronze knocker and gave it a few taps. He kept his eyes on the door, trying to ignore the warning that pulsed from his subconscious mind, uncertain how the Polish gang leader was going to react. Frankenstein, as he was nicknamed on the streets due in part to his gigantism, did not do well with surprises. The monster used his appearance to his advantage, striking fear into his adversaries with his brutish demeanor, but under his physique, Charlie saw the paranoid young man, a character flaw he had witnessed behind closed doors. If he played his cards right, he would be able to convince the brute into letting his new tagalong accompany them.

Charlie knocked on the door again, this time with the side of his fist. After the third rap the door opened and through the crack, Charlie saw a bouquet of yellow daffodils covering the face belonging to two little eyes. He bent low to address the flowers.

"Morning Tabitha," he greeted Frankenstein's seven-year-old sister. "Is your brother in?"

The daffodils bobbed with her nod.

"May I speak with him?"

Instead of nodding, the little girl closed the door, rattling the etched glass.

Charlie uncurled his spine and stood upright, his eyes falling to the welcome mat beneath his feet. He sighed, mentally preparing himself for Frankenstein's temper and hoped he could catch the twenty-one-year-old monster in good spirits.

The lock on the door clicked and swung open with a creak.

Charlie elevated his gaze to address Frankenstein, whose monstrous frame filled the doorway. He swallowed hard at the sight of the brute's features, still taken off guard by them. Frankenstein's shoulder-length black hair covered most of the scars and the deep crevices on his flushed cheeks. His nose, which had been broken twice, sat crooked on his face. His physique, a close relation to Dr. Frankenstein's monster, was both intimidating and nightmarish, his height a freakishly accurate seven feet. Unlike the monster in Mary Shelley's novel, however, his eyes did not glow, nor were his mischievous thin lips black.

"Charlie, my boy," said the Polish gang leader, in a shrewd baritone voice. He extended a large hand, his fingers the size of kielbasas.

Charlie took hold of Frankenstein's hand without hesitation and did his best to ignore the crushing of his bones by keeping a pleasant expression on his face. "Morning Frankenstein, good to see you," he said through clenched teeth.

Frankenstein grinned, the crest of his lips accentuating the sharp scars around his cheekbones and yellowed teeth. "That it is, a fine morning. A very important morning, one too important to be running late." A hint of disappointment underlined his comment. "And where is that small sprout of a cousin of yours?" he continued, releasing Charlie's hand. "Tabitha hasn't stopped badgering me about seeing him again."

Charlie choked on his saliva. He had hoped to leave Jimmy out of conversation, but the Polish gang leader's frosty eyes grew instantly perturbed by his hesitation and with an easy glance over his head, looked past him to the boy at the bottom of the stairs.

"Charlie, what in tarnation have you been feeding this boy?" teased Frankenstein, taking note of Bartholomew's baggy clothes. "And what is that getup you have him wearing? He looks like an English pauper. I swear, Charlie, the ridicule that is going to follow..." Frankenstein moved around Charlie and took a step down the stairs, but paused midway when his weak eye-sight realized the ivory-skinned boy was not Jimmy.

Charlie took a deep breath, preparing himself for the backlash. *Steady, Charlie, steady.*

"What's this?" said Frankenstein, the enthusiasm in his tone turning venomous. "Charlie, I said..."

"I know," said Charlie, as he rushed down the steps to stand in front of the kid. "I know what you said." He leaned into Buck and whispered, "Stay behind me."

"Charlie, this is my territory and I said no outsiders," said Frankenstein, his mangled facial features growing more defined by his anger. "And outside my home..." He flung one of his long arms toward his house. "Do you know how serious your infraction is?"

Charlie eyed the dank row house, then looked back at the giant. "I know you'd punish one of your flunkies for less, but you don't understand."

"Don't get wise with me, Charlie," threatened Frankenstein. "I don't have to understand."

Bartholomew grabbed Charlie by the arm, startled by the fury in the giant's voice, the tone of it producing a similar tremor that reminded him of the Spirit of Flame. And yet, in all his dealings with the Master of Hell, he had never found him to be as intimidating as Frankenstein.

"Buck, it's all right," said Charlie, feeling the squeeze of the boy's grip.

"No, Charlie, it's not," said Frankenstein, and he pulled back black bangs from his eyes to ensure Charlie took him seriously. "He could be a Bogeyman spy for all I know."

"Frankenstein, please, I can assure you he's not," said Charlie, preparing to walk a proverbial tightrope. "The kid has been through enough. He doesn't need you bullying him, and neither do I."

Frankenstein glared at Charlie, his nostrils flaring. No one spoke to him like that and walked away without at least a bloody nose, not in his neighborhood. And yet, Frankenstein was no fool. He knew Charlie's brains were too rare a commodity to have them scrambled. He needed him sharp if he was going to get the chance to exact his revenge against his clever rival, the Bogeyman. Charlie had fallen in favor with the Lithuanian gang leader after saving him from a beating that nearly cost him his life, and he was going to use that to his advantage. Frankenstein puffed out his massive chest, mostly for show, but it was enough to keep Charlie in check—well, at least he made it appear that way to the people watching from across the street. He had a reputation to uphold after all.

"Frankenstein…" Charlie steadied his voice to be more diplomatic. "I can assure you the kid's no spy."

"And what of Jimmy?" asked Frankenstein. His large fingers curled into threatening fists.

"Jimmy's gone," said Charlie.

"I see." Frankenstein eyed Bartholomew, satisfied that the kid was at least scared of him. He was no Jimmy. Charlie's cousin had been easy to manipulate, but this new kid, there was something off about him. "Fostered out, then, was Jimmy?" he added.

"No," said Charlie, his upsurge of adrenaline preventing his voice from shaking. He refused to break down in front of the brutish giant. "He's dead. Swallowed up by the inferno that gutted the orphanage, which is where I saved the kid. He owes me, Frankenstein."

Frankenstein inspected Charlie's figure more thoroughly and saw the traces of ash on his shirt. He inhaled and finally understood where the heavy smell of smoke was coming from. It did not excuse Charlie from bringing a stranger to his front door, but he did understand the recompense and importance of paying one's debts, a fact that was still binding him to Charlie.

"I grieve with you, Charlie," Frankenstein offered, in a moment of rare concern. "If there is anything I can do," he added halfheartedly, his thin lips pursed into a weak smile.

"If you want to do something, stop intimidating the kid," said Charlie, not wanting the Polish gang leader to gain the upper hand regardless of whether or not he was being sincere.

"You trust him?" asked Frankenstein, giving Charlie an ample piece of rope to hang himself on later if things went sideways.

"I do," said Charlie, his quick answer giving him pause. He hardly knew the kid, let alone had had enough time to build trust, but in saying it he believed it, for he had no reason otherwise not to trust him—not yet anyway.

"Very well," said Frankenstein, accepting Charlie's assurance, "but see it as a favor Charlie, not charity, for I will hold you responsible if anything goes awry."

"Agreed," said Charlie, adding another shard of hope that his actions would not betray him. "I claim full responsibility for the kid, just as I would've for Jimmy."

"Right then, who is your new friend?" Frankenstein eyed Bartholomew's clothes again with disgust.

"This is Buck, Buck Lipinski," introduced Charlie, knowing the Polish gang leader might warm up to the lad much faster if he thought he was Polish. "Buck, this is Frankenstein."

Bartholomew stepped out from behind Charlie, exposing himself to the giant. He felt it necessary to bow, but he refrained as he remembered what Charlie told him—*we Americans shake hands*. Bartholomew put out his hand to Frankenstein. His stomach somersaulted as Frankenstein's hand swallowed his fingers. It was no different than shaking hands with the Master of Hell, whose long, bony fingers would consume his hand as well, but instead of a fiery grasp, the giant's grip was strong enough to crush bone. Bartholomew's expression mirrored his discomfort.

"Buck Lipinski... Polish, are ya?"

"Possibly," offered Bartholomew, his voice a bit insecure.

Frankenstein laughed.

Charlie chuckled along, but he was anxious as to whether Frankenstein had discovered his bluff.

"Charlie, you sure know how to pick 'em; always entertaining these strays of yours. But this one here—finally you got your head on right and found a good one. Not like those potato-eating Micks."

Charlie bolstered his laughter as best he could to play along, but truthfully, he had no qualms with anyone based on where they or their parents were born. It was simply one of his inherent traits not to judge, or as Father Van Lewen had once told him—*we are all members of the same house, Charlie. Believe in the heart of a person, not the shell they wear.*

Frankenstein's laugh waned and his expression tightened to sternness. "Well, boys, I believe we have ourselves a reckoning to attend," he said. "But first, I must see to Tabitha before I leave. I won't be but a moment or two." He withdrew up the stairs and back inside the house.

Bartholomew stared at the front door of Frankenstein's house, as Charlie took a seat on the steps, his energy exhausted. His eyes caught sight of movement at the window, the lacey curtain drawn enough to see two tear-filled eyes staring down at Charlie. When Tabitha noticed he was staring, she darted away, disappearing behind the cloth. Bartholomew lowered his gaze, his instincts gnawing at him, pulsing a steady warning. There was no possible way the brutish monster was the mortal the Apothecary had alluded to in his letter. The giant's spirit was too jagged, villainous, and unpredictable; at least that was what he had felt when they shook hands. Bartholomew maneuvered his gaze to spy on Charlie, debating whether he should express his concern.

"Buck, stop staring. You're making my head ache," said Charlie with a groan. He dug his fingertips into his temples and massaged them.

"Charlie, what are we doing here?" asked Bartholomew.

"Buck, not now," said Charlie, rubbing his hands down his filthy face.

"But, Charlie, I do not trust him," Bartholomew said.

"Buck…"

"Charlie, you cannot honestly want to help him, he…"

"Buck, I said that's enough!" said Charlie under his breath. "Frankenstein has been nothing but generous to me and Jimmy. A thing like that is hard to come by nowadays and you do what you can to protect your own. You only get one family, Buck, and once they're gone…" Charlie shook his head, trying to shake the real reason why he had planned on bringing Jimmy with him and how, in some way, it was the actual reason why he had brought Buck along. "Listen, Buck, you said you would do as I say, so if you're still planning to tagalong, this is the way it's gonna be."

"But why? Why do you feel obliged to help a monster?"

"Buck…"

"Please, Charlie, help me understand."

Charlie sighed, unwilling to make a scene. "Fine, but you can't give me any more guff, understood?"

Bartholomew nodded and took a seat next to him.

"One day, a few months back, I was finishing up my shift at Grocer Pawlak's market, I witnessed Frankenstein being pummeled by three men even larger than him. It wasn't any of my concern and I was tempted to retreat into the market and head out the front door. But if there is one thing you need to know about me, Buck, and know well, my conscience tends to get the best of me. So, I approached the assailants. Judging from their tailored pants, I figured they were members of the Lithuanian gang. I introduced myself, but the ogres didn't seem to care. One even knocked me to the ground, but I got back on my feet. It was stupid on my part to demonstrate moxie, for it just invited them to teach me not to get involved in matters that didn't concern me. They started in on me with a punch to the face then a blow to the gut. Before they could get in a third shot, I distracted them with the earnings Grocer Pawlak had given me. I offered it to them to take back to their boss and though they gladly took it, they gave me that third shot to the ribcage."

"Then why help him now?" asked Bartholomew. "You owe him nothing."

"Because, Buck, when you save someone, you form a special bond with that person, and it's something you can't turn your back on. Well, I could've, but Jimmy and I wanted for nothing the past few months and we've always been protected in this neighborhood. Besides, it's hard to collect on a debt if you run from it."

Bartholomew opened his mouth, but found nothing useful to refute Charlie's logic even though he was having trouble grasping it. "Then what happened? I mean, they must have come back, if you stepped into the middle of this feud."

"You're quite perceptive, Buck," said Charlie. He rubbed his fingers on his pants, drying his clamming palms, hiding his apprehension. "Sure enough, a few days after the incident, the three Lithuanians returned to this side of Morgan Street looking for me."

"Did Frankenstein not protect you?" asked Bartholomew, scooting to the edge of the step to gauge the mortal's expression.

"He surrounded me with a posse of his men and was prepared to throw down in front of his house," said Charlie. "But the three Lithuanians were not interested in blood. First, you need to understand, Buck, that the two gang leaders come from very different schools of thought. Frankenstein, while intimidating in stature, is all about brash action and brute force. His well-educated Lithuanian rival, however, is calculated in his actions, which is why people say his name in whispers—Bogeyman, for you never know when he might be coming for you."

"What did they want?" asked Bartholomew, wondering if the Bogeyman could possibly be the mortal Damek.

"They were sent on an errand to fetch me as though I were some dog," said Charlie bitterly. "Apparently, the Bogeyman was requesting my audience and despite Frankenstein's reservations about my safety, I was certain the Lithuanian gang leader meant me no harm."

"What did the…" Bartholomew lowered his voice, "Bogeyman want?"

"My help," said Charlie, envisioning what the Lithuanian gang leader was going to think about Buck's presence at the summit.

"With what?"

"Frankenstein, naturally," said Charlie. "As I have already

alluded to, their feud has escalated since the Bogeyman's three ogres pummeled Frankenstein."

In all truth, the feud was not the sole reason behind the attack, at least as far as Charlie was concerned. The rivalry festered because Grocer Pawlak sold Frankenstein down the river, giving the Bogeyman god only knows what secrets on the Polish gang leader. Charlie had had an inkling about the greedy grocer's seedy dealings and was proven right after he spotted the man consorting with one of the Bogeyman's goons. Two days later, after Frankenstein was viciously attacked, he saw the same man paying the grocer off in the alley behind his store. Charlie scrunched the fabric of his pants. He needed to be careful not to give his ace in the hole away, not until absolutely necessary, although he secretly hoped he would not have to stoop so low and use it.

"Fights were beginning to break out anywhere between the neighborhoods, even to the detriment of civilians. Things had gone on long enough and the Bogeyman needed them to stop. Rumor has it that was because his older brothers offered him a spot in their criminal empire on the north side if he demonstrated his diplomacy and settled his conflict with Frankenstein. It hadn't occurred to me then, but apparently I was gaining a reputation as a trustworthy party and the Bogeyman sought to enlist my skills."

"Why would that matter to a phantom?" asked Bartholomew, mistaking the Lithuanian's nickname with a creature in mortal folklore.

"Buck, do not mistake the power of the Bogeyman's nickname, for he is no more a phantom than you or me. He is a man of flesh and bones. Secondly, agreeing to assist the trickster is not so cut and dry. There were extenuating circumstances that forced my hand to say *yes*," said Charlie, wiping the top of his brow. "I made a promise and gave my word to act as intermediary between him and Frankenstein. Had I refused, the Bogeyman would have threatened Jimmy to force my hand, and I couldn't let that happen. And there you have it, Buck. I can't put it any clearer than that."

"But Jimmy…" started Bartholomew then held his tongue. He shied away from Charlie.

"Buck, I understand what you're trying to say—I do," said Charlie. "I'm not a damn fool. But I also know I can't be looking over my shoulder for the rest of my life either. The meeting is today and regardless of my grief or what has already transpired, I'm not afraid nor should you be. It's like my mother used to say, *fear the man who does not keep his word, for he is the truest of tricksters and cannot be trusted.* Can you remember that?"

Bartholomew nodded. He stuffed his hand in his left pocket and curled his fingers around the crumpled parchment, his thoughts on the promise he had made before escaping his prison cell—to find the Eden Wanderer, Stingy Jack, and save the Shepherdess. And yet, he alone could not see his promise fulfilled. He recited the Apothecary's note: *The mortal will lead you to the mortal Damek, who alone has the power to amend you to your charge.* Bartholomew sighed. His tactic to sway Charlie from his current course had proven unsuccessful and despite what his instincts were telling him, he would have to stick with Charlie if he was going to have any hope of resuming his mission.

"Ready, lads?" boomed Frankenstein's voice, returning outside.

Bartholomew jumped as a nearby pair of red-winged black birds were startled into taking flight.

Charlie rose from the step and winced from the fatigue in his legs. His muscles screamed at him to remain seated as they wobbled, but he gained his balance.

"Here Charlie, put this on," said Frankenstein, throwing a

piece of fabric at Charlie as he made his way down the stairs, dressed in what was probably his finest clothes, a pin-striped suit with a matching black fedora. It was a little overkill for a street hooligan, but appearance was everything. "I can't have my, what'd you call it, my liaison looking like he just got back from working in the stocks," he added.

Charlie did not need telling twice and took off his stained shirt. He used it to wipe the rest of the grime off his face, then tossed the rag onto the sidewalk and buttoned up the navy blue shirt. Charlie's fingers trembled as he fiddled with the buttons, his body acknowledging the nerves his brain refused to address.

"There, now you look halfway presentable," said Frankenstein with a snicker and stepped onto the sidewalk, his buffed shoes gleaming in the sunlight. He headed down the street without another word, his stride flanked by Charlie.

Bartholomew lagged behind, giving him the opportunity to take in more of his surroundings. As he crossed the street, a gust of wind blew across the back of his neck. Everything around him slowed down as it had before when the Herald had appeared. This time, however, it made the tiny hairs on his arms prickle and an unsettling sensation that something was watching him rushed over him. He halted abruptly and about-faced, but no one was there. He scanned the opposite side of the street where a few kids kicked a ball back and forth to each other. He spotted a woman sitting on a bench beneath an elm tree, her nose in a book, and a reddish-brown tabby cat scurrying down a set of steps, disturbed by a mustached man coming out of his front door in a hurry. He half-expected to find another otherworldly creature, but it appeared none were in the vicinity. Bartholomew's skin crawled. He shivered and brushed his hands gingerly against his arms, taking the sensation as a warning to be on his guard.

"Buck!"

Bartholomew averted his attention and saw Charlie waiting up the next block. His stomach fluttered in a panic before darting after him, not bothering to look both ways before crossing the street. He dodged one of the horseless carriages, its horn shouting at him.

"Charlie, where did Frankenstein go?" he asked through puffed breaths.

"He went inside Harry's Hall." Charlie pointed to the yellow sign hanging above the green doorframe overhead. "Honest Harry, the proprietor of the joint, is allowing us to use his pool hall to settle the dispute. It was the Bogeyman's idea, and oddly enough Frankenstein agreed to it." Charlie stalled beneath the sign, his eyes looking through the open door at the wooden staircase leading up to the second floor above the laundry. "Kinda silly to leave it all riding on a game," he added. "But better it be on a game of skill than a game of chance."

Bartholomew stood quietly next to Charlie. It was obvious the mortal was preparing himself for the task at hand, though he still was not sure what exactly it was Charlie was getting himself into. He had the sudden urge to talk him out of the endeavor again, the lingering chill he felt still pressing him that something was amiss. He inspected his reflection in the picture window of the laundry in front of him, alarmed by his thin, disheveled physique, not having realized the dismal state he was in. He inspected himself from head to foot, finally realizing how much his emerald eyes contradicted the young teenage face of his mortal exterior. As his eyes shifted, they caught sight of the reddish-brown cat stalking along the sidewalk on the opposite side of the street.

"All right, Buck," said Charlie, finally ready to head upstairs. "Buck?"

Bartholomew ignored Charlie, his attention focused on the cat. He felt the tiny hair follicles on his skin bristle and his body involuntarily shuddered. The cat paused and perked its ears, turning its head until its eyes were staring directly at Bartholomew's spying reflection. Bartholomew's heart skipped at the sight of its pink eyes and he quickly pivoted towards the street, but, in doing so, lost sight of the cat. His heart raced, paranoid he was being followed.

"Buck," came Charlie's voice, followed by a nudge.

"What?" Bartholomew looked up at Charlie, doing his best to cover the frazzled reaction.

"Ready to go inside?" asked Charlie.

Bartholomew returned his gaze to the street, avoiding Charlie's perceptive eyes. He surveyed the street again, but found no sign of the feline. The chill in his body thawed and the tempo of the street resumed its rhythm. Whatever otherworldly creature had been near was gone. Bartholomew sighed and turned back to Charlie.

"Ready," he said.

Charlie hesitated, for it was not hard to deduce the kid had something else on his mind. He wanted to ask if he was all right, but instead, he put an arm around Bartholomew's shoulder and made a mental note to broach the issue after the truce was settled.

Bartholomew gave a quick glance behind him as Charlie ushered them up the stairs to Harry's Hall. He found no sign of the reddish-brown tabby and could not sense the presence of another otherworldly creature, but still, he could not shake the feeling of being watched. His thoughts ran rampant, speculating what would be waiting for him when it was time to leave.

Pocket Billiards

At the top of the stairs, Charlie and Bartholomew rounded the mahogany banister to the openness of the second floor. Several lights hung low from the ceiling, spotlighting ten tables, each equipped with a triangular rack and sixteen colored balls. Along the opposite side of the room, four double-paned windows facing the street brightened the room with an offering of the day's sun. Away from the billiard tables, a gangly man sat on a stool at the high counter and beside the man, five other four-legged stools stood vacant. His hands clasped a coffee cup, and his narrow eyes glanced over at Bartholomew and Charlie before going back to his conversation with a stout fellow behind the counter, dressed in a white crewneck t-shirt with an apron around his pudgy waist. On his elongated face, bristles gave him a five o'clock shadow and behind him, a striking mirror drew attention to the back of his bald head.

On the other side of the stairwell, a thin walkway housed the equipment of the hall. Tacked to the wall was a row of long wooden sticks hanging from a special mantel. Their thin ends pointed towards the checkered parquet floor where flecks of blue dust gathered. The room filled with a thunderous roar, startling Bartholomew from his inspection. As the commotion settled, a pleasant voice sang from somewhere in the room over the light hum of lily-shaped electric fans. Bartholomew focused on listening to the music for a moment, trying his best to drown out the vociferous men, but all he was able to catch was one phrase.

In the lemonade springs, where the bluebird sings, in the Big Rock Candy Mountains.

Bartholomew turned his attention to the center of the room where a dozen men the same build as Frankenstein, but not nearly as tall, stood around one of the tables. The men were not dressed as respectably as the Polish gang leader, but were presentable. Bartholomew judged each man, trying to sense if any of them might be the *mortal Damek,* but he felt no connection to any of them. He watched Frankenstein circle the rectangular table, before thrusting a stick against a white ball. The ball sped across the rose-colored surface, bouncing off the lip and into a solid yellow ball. The yellow ball proceeded to the far left hole, but did not go in. Frankenstein roared a curse and threw his stick onto the table in disgust.

"Brava," said a sarcastically dry voice accompanied by drawn out claps. "I see your skills have not improved, Wiktor."

Frankenstein scowled at the sound of his name, his eyes passing over Bartholomew and Charlie at the short man standing behind them, whose face leered at him. Frankenstein puffed out his cheeks, ready to release a volley of hot air across the pool hall, but his crafty rival looked away to address Charlie.

"Morning Charles," greeted the man, his square face holding a rather pleasant but indifferent expression.

Charlie shivered, his reaction less subtle than Wiktor's response. No one, except for his mother, called him by his given name, but under the circumstances, he was willing to accept the Bogeyman's use of it a little longer.

"And morning to you," Charlie replied. "May I introduce my friend, Buck Lipinski?"

The Bogeyman turned his gaze to Bartholomew, unsure what to make of him. He was taken aback by the centuries-old Englishman garb and his thin physique. His first impression was to write him off, but his intellect proved more curious to discover the boy's worth, since anyone who was important to Charlie was even more important to him. The Bogeyman smiled and extended his stubby hand.

Bartholomew shook the man's hand and instantly knew he was standing in front of an untrustworthy mortal. There was something quite charming about his disposition, but surely he could not be the mortal to whom the Apothecary had entrusted to assist him.

"Call me Kalvis, please," replied the man. "After all, here the Bogeyman and Frankenstein are but men." He lifted his eyes for a brief second to Wiktor.

"Um," stumbled Bartholomew. "Pleasure to make your acquaintance then, Kalvis."

Kalvis laughed, letting go of Bartholomew's hand, the boy's natural politeness an unexpected delight.

"I see things haven't changed, Kalvis. Still heckling those shorter than you," challenged Wiktor as he approached the banister, his men closing in ranks behind him.

Kalvis' face morphed instantly into an apologetic expression in an attempt to admit his error. "Excuse my rudeness, Buck, Charles. I only meant it in good humor, no harm."

"Certainly Kalvis, no harm," said Charlie and scrutinized Kalvis, as the Lithuanian's curious gaze lingered on Buck, uncertain of the Bogeyman's intentions.

"Well then," said Kalvis. "I believe there is a matter of recompense to address."

"Right," said Charlie, glad Kalvis was not questioning the stranger's presence. A warm sensation gurgled in his throat then he steadied his nerves, and brought forth his confidence, shutting out everything dismal about his life, transforming himself. "We're all here this morning to settle a dispute," he said. "As I have taken each party aside to assess the grievance, I've determined Kalvis' men were indeed acting alone when they assaulted Wiktor."

"Like bloody hell!" objected a blotchy-faced young man, standing beside Frankenstein. The rest of the Polish gang voiced their disapproval towards Charlie's finding.

"That being said," added Charlie, raising his voice over the grumbles. "It was agreed upon to settle this issue in a more civil manner. Honest Harry..." Charlie shot a wave to the bald man at the counter and received a nod of acknowledgement, "has so generously allowed us to use his establishment for a match of pool. Now, seeing as Kalvis is a seasoned pool-hall junkie, it's only fair he not defend his position."

"That's right, Wiktor wouldn't stand a chance," voiced one of the Lithuanians.

"Yeah," agreed another. "He'd be breaking his cue in frustration after he botched the first shot."

"At least he'd be able to bloody your short man with his fists if he wasn't such a coward," said one of Wiktor's men, removing a lead pipe from his pocket.

The Lithuanians responded in kind and produced their own weapons: brass knuckles, knives and chains. They fanned out, blocking any access to the stairs. Kalvis stood coolly, his disposition immovable.

The Poles scrambled to show the same force, but several of them had not brought a weapon.

"Gentlemen," said Charlie, positioning himself as close to

Buck as possible and holding out his arms to halt the tension from escalating.

Wiktor snorted. "I told you, Charlie," he said with an accusatory tone. "I told you; Kalvis wouldn't honor the arrangement." He glared at the short man. "Don't underestimate me, Bogeyman. I'll have satisfaction, even if I have to take it by force."

"Wiktor, I can't just let you…" started Kalvis.

"You will, Kalvis, or I'll take it by force." Wiktor removed a jagged blade from his coat pocket.

Kalvis did not answer and looked at Charlie.

"Don't look at Charlie, Kalvis, this is between us!" shouted Wiktor.

Charlie's eyes widened, confused by Kalvis' sudden lack of interest. He stared at the Lithuanian and tried to unlock his stratagem. It was unclear at first, but after a moment, Charlie understood why Kalvis was stalling. He wanted him to tame the beast.

Frankenstein took an intimidating step forward.

"Wiktor, wait," said Charlie, his voice not particularly strong, his adrenaline waning again. All he had to do was hang on a little longer. "You don't want to end up killing each other like The Rats and The Jellyrolls in St. Louis, do you?"

There was a lengthy pause, the thought of the two ill-fated St. Louis gangs conjuring images of a deadly blood bath. For a moment, Charlie feared the mounting tension would come to a head, but in a surprising twist, Wiktor withdrew, stowing his blade in his coat.

"All right, Charlie, a game of pool then," said Wiktor.

"Then name your champion," said Charlie.

"Hardly," sneered Wiktor. "I'm a gambling man, and I don't see much sport in choosing my own man. I say we raise the stakes and pick the other's champion. Anyone, except for Charlie, of course."

"Kalvis, what say you?" asked Charlie.

"I will see that wager, Charles," said Kalvis, as a wave of his hand instructed his men to conceal their weapons.

"Very well," said Charlie, lowering his arms. "If Wiktor's champion wins, he will be able to exact his revenge on those who did him harm, and if Kalvis wins…"

"I reserve the right to call upon Charles as I wish without question," said Kalvis.

Wiktor glared at Charlie as though he had had something to do with Kalvis' unanticipated request, but agreed.

"Then pick your poison, Wiktor. Who will it be?" asked Kalvis.

"I pick your man, Link," replied Wiktor. "He's brainless enough for a giant." He laughed, pointing at the man standing behind Kalvis, a man who stood a few inches taller than him. "So, who will it be, Kalvis?" he said smugly.

Kalvis' expression did not change, in spite of Wiktor's small self-indulgent victory, but his clever mind had a plan. He did not need to win, he simply had to appease Wiktor, and since there was no other motivation, he was going to use this opportunity to test Charles' attachment to his new mate.

"I choose Buck," he announced.

A look of bafflement plastered Wiktor's face. "You can't choose Buck," he said, his voice cracking.

"And why not? You wanted to raise the stakes," said Kalvis. "You said nothing about Charles' friend."

Wiktor's jaw dropped, but he closed his mouth, unable to refute Kalvis. He cursed under his breath, but he kept a level head and instructed Charlie to fix the boy with a cue. He stormed off, pushing through the cluster of his men, and proceeded to set up the pool table. Kalvis snickered as the Poles followed their leader like sheep. He gave Charlie a pat on the back as he passed, his men following close behind him.

Charlie stood dumbfounded. What was Kalvis playing at? If Buck lost, Wiktor would blame him for bringing the kid and they would not make it out of the pool hall unscathed. Was that the reason Kalvis chose Buck? To ensure such an outcome, to force him to ask for help. To be in his debt. Charlie pulled at his hair. The situation was spinning out of his control, and after rescuing Buck from harm's way all he had managed to do was lead him straight back into it. He felt a clasp grip his arm and he looked at Buck, the boy's eyes fixed for flight.

"Charlie, we should leave," said Bartholomew.

Charlie blinked, coming to his senses. He should have known better than to involve the kid, but there was nothing to do about it now. Buck would have to play the game whether he wanted to or not.

"Buck, it will be fine." Charlie attempted to keep his tone reassuring. "It's just a game of pool."

"But, Charlie, I do not know how to play pool," said Bartholomew, keeping his voice to a whisper.

"Naturally…" Charlie ripped his arm away, anger replacing every other emotion. "Well, I'm sorry Buck, but you have no choice in the matter," he added.

"Of course I do," said Bartholomew, wondering if he somehow had misunderstood the meaning of free will.

"Buck, did you or did you not ask me to show you the ropes?" asked Charlie, too upset with himself to coddle. "Well, here are the ropes, Buck. This is the way things are in the big city. People here do plenty of things they don't want to do." He stuffed his hands in his pockets, his fingers running into the hard sphere of Jimmy's marble. They were in a serious jam and despite the option of escape down the unguarded stairs, he knew they would not get more than a few blocks, a mile at best.

"But why?" asked Bartholomew.

"Because, Buck, you do things you don't want to do to survive, pure and simple. So, you ain't got a choice in the matter."

"But I do have a choice," said Bartholomew, annoyed with Charlie's new tone. He crossed his arms in protest and motioned towards the stairs, but Charlie grabbed his arm and spun him around.

"Fine, let's say for argument's sake you do have a choice. Say no, and see what happens. A week from now the coppers will be pulling you out of the river dead—dead, Buck, do you understand?"

Bartholomew nodded. He knew what Charlie meant and understood now what he had said about Kalvis using Jimmy as leverage. Bartholomew glanced over at the men waiting around the pool table and weighed his options. He could either play or risk having the Bogeyman or Frankenstein toss him into murky water, the second of which stirred an unpleasant memory. Like Charlie said, he had no choice.

"Listen, Buck," said Charlie. "I know you're out of your element here, but I know you can pull this off."

"What makes you so sure?"

"Because," Charlie placed his hand on the kid's shoulder, "you're a survivor, Buck. You'll find a way."

"As you wish, Charlie," said Bartholomew, Charlie's cool demeanor calming his nerves. "I will do it your way, but I have just one request."

"Name it."

"Can you show me how to hold the stick?"

Charlie chuckled. "Sure thing, Buck, but they're not called

sticks, they're called cues." He wrapped his arm around Bartholomew's shoulders and led him around the banister. He pulled the shortest one off the cue rack then demonstrated how to hold it, using the banister as a prop.

"Okay, Buck, you hold the end of the cue like this between your fingers." Charlie leaned over a little. "With your other hand you'll hold it somewhere in the middle, near the end, whatever feels natural. Are you a righty or a lefty?"

Bartholomew put his hands out in front of him and inspected them. "Left, I think," he replied.

"Well then, you'll hold the cue like this," said Charlie, switching hands before handing off the cue.

Bartholomew gave it a try, his stance awkward. "All right, now what?" he asked. "What do I do with it?"

"Well," began Charlie, and he proceeded to explain the rules of the game. Though the kid seemed to understand everything, there was a hint of unmistakable fear behind his gaze.

"Charlie!" shouted Wiktor.

Charlie acknowledged the gesture and quickly finished. "And one more thing," he said. "Don't sink the black ball 'til the end. Now what do you say you unleash David on that Goliath?"

Bartholomew's nose scrunched.

"You're a tough egg to crack, Buck," said Charlie, his brief attempt to lighten the mood failing miserably.

They joined the two gangs in the center of the hall, each side taking up residence on either side of the table. Charlie withdrew a silver coin from his pocket and instructed Wiktor to call. The coin revealed tails, giving Bartholomew the break.

"All right Buck, you're up first," said Charlie, pointing the kid in the right direction.

Bartholomew made his way to the head of the table, reminding himself of Charlie's instructions. He stared at the red surface, the racked balls sitting opposite the white ball. He placed the cue between his fingers, glanced at the triangle to line up the shot, and in an overpowering thrust, struck the ball. The white ball flew over the top of the triangle and the rim of the table. It landed on the floor with a loud *crack*, bouncing several times, then rolled across the checkered floor.

"Well now, that was brilliant," mocked one of Kalvis' men, retrieving the escaped ball.

"My, my, what luck," said Kalvis with a devilish grin as he passed along the ball to his associate. "Link, I believe this is your break."

Link lugged to the top of the table and placed the ball on its starting position. He bent with a level of difficulty, his hand nearly pulverizing his cue to dust. But the giant took a breath and cradled the wooden stick as though it were a newborn. He lined his shot with the point of the pyramid. Then, with the tip of his tongue sticking out the corner of his mouth, Link pulled back and hit the white ball. The strike sent a tremor through the pyramid, scattering it. A thunderous applause erupted from Kalvis' men as the yellow-striped ball fell into the corner pocket.

Bartholomew felt a nudge as Link bumped him with his elbow, the giant's smirk glowering at him. He let out a pitiful whimper and rubbed his pulsating muscle. He stole a glance at Charlie; the mortal's complexion was draining of blood, his worry appearing noticeably in his stance. Bartholomew shook his arm and knew he was going to have to do better if he was going to beat the Goliath. He studied his skill, memorizing every inch of motion. He did not know if he still had the ability, now that his ties to Euxinus were severed, but if there was a chance he still possessed the skill of Adaptation, he would be able to imitate Link's actions.

Granted, the giant was not a suitable subject, but the ability had proven useful in the past.

Bartholomew's muscles twitched as he activated each one he saw Link use as the giant proceeded to sink three more balls. By his fifth turn however, the white ball fell into the hole. Link moved away from the table as Charlie retrieved the ball and rolled it across the table to Bartholomew.

Tension shifted as Bartholomew lined up his shot, aiming for the middle pocket. He took his stance and cradled the cue, visualizing the strike. He pulled back, and with more control, struck. The solid green ball fell short of the hole and with a disappointing sigh he relinquished command of the table, allowing Link to sink two more striped balls. The objective to win seemed fleeting, and yet, with a stroke of luck, Link's blunder shifted the course of the match.

"I'll take it!" shouted Wiktor as Link's shot accidently sank the solid red ball.

Bartholomew looked at Kalvis and found the short man unmoved by the minor setback—his confidence intact. He then caught Charlie's eye, who mouthed at him to go *ahead*, his eyes flashing to the table to signal it was his turn. Bartholomew took his position, sucking in a calculative breath. He firmed his feet and sensed the pressure of air in his throat. He held it for a few more seconds, eyed the purple ball then the white, and in a burst he simultaneously exhaled and struck the ball, which somersaulted with circular speed, kissing the purple ball enough to push it into the hole.

Wiktor's men hooted their applause.

"Way ta go, kid, sink them all!"

Bartholomew repositioned along the table and set his sights on the yellow and brown. He took in another breath, held it, and with a much quicker release both balls rolled in a precise line to the corner pocket. The white ball balanced on the rim. Bartholomew cracked a smile as the energy in the room shifted into a collective sense of awe, even from Kalvis' men.

"Da kid's cheaten!" shouted one of Kalvis'men.

Bartholomew stole a glance at Kalvis, his confidence flickering.

"Yeah, he can't get that good all of a sudden," voiced another.

Grumbling ensued and Wiktor's men verbalized their support in a shouting match until Charlie reprimanded them. When the commotion settled, Charlie winked at Bartholomew, vibrancy returning to his face.

Bartholomew circled back to the top of the table, only to discover his remaining balls were at the far end. He eyed the green ball, visualized, and with a sharp jab, sailed the white ball across the table.

"Go, go, go, go," chanted Wiktor's men in hushed voices, pumping their fists like maracas.

The white ball collided with the green ball. The green ball sank into the nearest hole, but the white ball ricocheted and settled next to the black ball.

There was a collective gasp as the yin and yang of pool teetered precariously on the rim of the corner pocket.

"Please, please, please..." mumbled Buck, wishing he had the Master of Hell's power to stop time.

The balls stilled, the game still in play.

Link gaped at his predicament, dread filling his droopy face. He approached the table and lined the tip of his cue, pressing down hard on the inner edge of the table. He lifted his right elbow high, angling the stick. Link twisted his right hand on the center of the cue, and with too much force he broke it in half. The point hit the white ball, sending it over the table, the black ball falling into the pocket.

Link threw the two halves of his cue across the room, interrupting the conversation of the men at the counter. The billiard room grew silent, except for the sizzling sound of the hot grill, the hum of the electric fans and an upswing, jazzy tune with a comical male voice—*you're much sweeter goodness knows, you're my honeysuckle rose.* The tune faded into the background as an explosion of cheers erupted from Wiktor's men, each charging Bartholomew to shake his hand, pat him on the shoulder, or rub a hand through his hair.

"Atta boy!" shouted the blotchy faced young man.

"Ey, you sure showed that buffoon," said another.

Bartholomew was not prepared to receive such praise, but he found it rather agreeable. The tension in his shoulders fell away—he had won! A smile broke across his face and he joined in the delight of the other young men around him, even shook a few of their hands. Every shady thought he had had about any of them dissolved.

"You got some guts, Charlie," said Wiktor, giving Charlie a powerful pat on the back.

Charlie laughed with relieved delight and clapped his hands. He pressed his fingers against his lips in a silent prayer—David had beaten Goliath. The accomplishment was not lost on him, but it became less important when he noticed sheer amusement on Kalvis' handsome face.

"No," said Charlie, finally deducing the villain's scheme. It did not matter if the kid won or lost, because either outcome was the same: Buck had taken Jimmy's place.

Charlie pushed his way through the crowd and snatched the kid's arm. He dragged him through the mob, forcing Bartholomew to drop his cue.

"I present our champion, gentlemen," he said. "The wager stands at the behest of Wiktor. He will be granted satisfaction and exact his revenge on those who attacked him as per the gang motto, an eye for an eye. Kalvis, can you adhere to these terms?" asked Charlie.

"Indubitably," said Kalvis. "Not to worry Charles, I will honor our deal. Wiktor, do you care to take your first pound of flesh?" Kalvis stepped aside to open space between Wiktor and Link, one of his attackers. Wiktor drew back his elbow and punched Link square in the nose.

"Bloody hell!" shouted Wiktor. He waved his hand violently as though he had burned it. He should have known it would be like punching a rack of beef, hard and unforgiving. He rested his hand at his side, his face trying to conceal his pain, but the instant swelling suggested a break.

"Argh!" groaned Link, covering his bleeding nose with his gargantuan hands.

Charlie caught Kalvis' quick smirk of satisfaction.

"Now that that is out of the way, you let me know when you wish to collect on the other two. Maybe when your hand is better?" Kalvis teased.

"Sure," said Wiktor, forcing the word through his teeth. "Another time."

"Marvelous," cheered Kalvis, checking his pocket watch. "A pleasure as always, Charles," he said, extending a hand to Charlie.

"Likewise," said Charlie, though he hoped this pleasure would be for the last time.

"And you, young Buck." Kalvis turned to Bartholomew. "I believe I owe you a grave apology."

"What for?" Bartholomew was unaware Kalvis owed him any such thing.

"I mistook you for a mangy Hoover," said Kalvis. "Had I known you were a lad of talent I would have done better to treat you as such."

"Well, ya didn't," gloated Wiktor, not pleased with the manipulative tone in Kalvis' voice.

"No, I didn't," admitted Kalvis, not taking his eyes off Bartholomew. He stared for a few more seconds waiting for the lad to reply, but to his displeasure Bartholomew did not. "Well boys, I believe Honest Harry has shown us enough hospitality for one day." Kalvis gestured a *good day* to the bald man before descending the steps.

"So, Charlie, we square?" asked Wiktor as the last of Kalvis' men disappeared. He cradled his hand close to his chest, his knuckles already turning blue and purple.

"Sure thing, Wiktor, we're square," said Charlie, swinging an arm around Bartholomew and as they walked toward the flight of stairs, they left behind the smell of melting cheese and the scratchy tune of Ethel Waters singing *Stormy Weather.*

Alley Cat

Charlie and Bartholomew stood on the corner outside Harry's Hall. They waited quietly for their chance to cross the busy intersection, both not having said a word since leaving the second-floor pool hall. Charlie's stomach growled for the third time as the pains of his long day began to catch up with him. He thought about making a brief stop at Grocer Pawlak's market, but after mulling it over, Charlie did not find the idea entirely appealing. The store was almost two miles south in the opposite direction and he did not have the energy to make the trip nor the patience to deal with Grocer Pawlak's prying personality. His empty stomach would just have to wait until morning.

Bartholomew, meanwhile, took an interest in a group of children on the corner. They huddled in a cluster, fixated on what was happening in the center. Bartholomew watched a short boy with stubby legs pace the outer rim of the circle, trying with all his might to catch a glimpse of the action. The short boy settled behind two taller kids and pushed up on his toes. Bartholomew found the whole scene oddly entertaining and was curious about what they were doing.

"AHHH!"

From the center of the circle a collective scream burst over the sound of the bustling street. Even a few of the adults walking by paused to see what all the ruckus was about. Several of the kids, the short boy included, broke away from the cluster in a fit of fright. The short boy fell onto the sidewalk as a reddish-brown tabby cat leaped over him and landed on the curb. It swooshed its tail and gnawed at a long piece of string tied to four silver cans. The cat's fur spiked high on its back and it made a swiping motion with one of its front paws as several of the kids crawled backwards to avoid the cat's anger.

"Reow," hissed the cat, scaring the children. It lifted its cunning pink eyes to survey the street and unintentionally they caught sight of Bartholomew. The cat turned on a dime and ran, the silver cans clanging behind it.

Charlie stepped off the curb, only to watch Buck already beating him to it, except he was running in the wrong direction.

"Buck!" yelled Charlie, standing in the way of oncoming traffic.

Bartholomew did not bother to answer and jumped over the short boy onto the pavement.

"Buck!" called Charlie again.

"HONK!"

Charlie hopped back onto the curb to make way for an approaching freight truck. He saw the driver shaking his fist at him as he went by, but paid him no heed. He was more interested in the truck moving out of his way—or was he? With everything that had happened, was he still up to the task of tending to his new tagalong? In the back of his mind, a voice tempted him to leave the kid and run, to where it did not matter, just as long as it was away from the gangs, the orphanage, and Chicago. He had only stayed this long because Jimmy was his home and to him the place did not matter, just as long as they were together; and without him, he did not belong anywhere. Charlie smiled, daydreaming of the prospect and imagining all the adventures he might have, like Huck Finn and Tom Sawyer. But alas, as soon as the truck passed the dream died. Charlie watched Buck round the block onto Union Avenue heading south into the heart of Kalvis' neighborhood.

Charlie fought the impulse to run after him and even pointed his feet north, but he did not move one step further. *Remember, Charlie—take care of those smaller than you.* The words of his mother could not have come at a more inconvenient moment. He felt the presence of her hand on his shoulder again, this time filling him with courage, further solidifying his connection to the stranger he saved, and knew he could not allow Buck to wander onto Kalvis' streets alone, not after his performance in the pool hall.

"Damn," he cursed under his breath and started after him.

* * *

The tabby cat crossed Union Avenue, dodging traffic despite the weight dragging behind it. Bartholomew pursued with ample speed, but halted in the middle to avoid a Model T. The driver pressed the brakes, screeching the wheels, the pitch gaining the cat's attention. It paused to take in the disturbance, its eyes on Bartholomew. It inspected its pursuer and once satisfied he was uninjured, the cat darted off further down the street until finally ducking into an alley another block and a half away.

Bartholomew ran in front of the idling automobile and followed the feline. He stood at the mouth of the alley, expecting to see the cat, but it was not visible. Several trash bins lined the brick-laden dead end, and shadows danced from the linen strung between the two buildings overhead. Bartholomew walked gingerly to avoid stepping on shards of glass, kicking newspaper, or making any sort of noise. He checked every nook and cranny, and listened for the sound of clanking cans.

A light jingle rang out, and in a valiant attempt, the cat tried to make a break for it, but Bartholomew was too quick. He stomped his foot on the string just before the cans could get by him. The cat hissed angrily, its front paws flying over its head, landing on its cream-colored belly. It gradually lifted its chin off the ground and rotated its small head, its pointed ears pressed back, annoyed. It glared at Bartholomew, its pink eyes gleaming with dissatisfaction, for rarely was the shape-shifting spy ever caught.

"Hello, Master Chameleon," greeted Bartholomew, in a pleasant and polite tone. He bowed out of respect and waited for the cat to return the Euxian gesture.

The cat rose and circled back to the end of the alley leading the small slack of string behind it. It stopped at Bartholomew's feet and with ears perked, it presented a bow.

"Greetings, Master Breedling," said the cat. "I see years of imprisonment have not deterred you from the formalities of your station. It has been far too long, Bartholomew."

A shiver crawled up Bartholomew's spine at the sound of his name, but he brushed off the chill. He had little time before Charlie discovered where he had gone and he needed to make sure the cat was not alone. He tugged at his patchwork trousers to protect his shoeless feet and sat on the ground.

The cat lowered onto its hind legs like a regal statue, though its pink eyes wandered about, as though searching for any means to escape.

"Are you alone?" asked Bartholomew, his eyes searching for signs of the Fates' bounty hunters, the Retrievers.

The cat ignored the Breedling.

Bartholomew reached into his pocket and pulled out the crumpled parchment. "Did the Apothecary send you?" he demanded.

The cat's eyes narrowed at the wadded ball in the Breedling's hand. "My sender sends his regards," it replied.

Bartholomew delayed his response, not expecting the Chameleon to answer honestly. Also, it had been one thing to send a message through the Herald, but to send the Fates' spy, now that was a risk that could prove ill for them all.

"Master Breedling, cat got your tongue?" teased the Chameleon.

"Why?" Bartholomew managed.

"Why what?" asked the cat.

"Why would the Apothecary send you, or more importantly, why would you risk coming here? If the Fates find out you left Euxinus on this errand…"

"I came because he asked me to," said the cat, standing on all fours.

"You mean ordered you." Bartholomew tilted his head skeptically.

"No, my sender did not force me, nor order me," said the cat. "My sender asked if I would make this journey to Eden."

"To what end?" asked Bartholomew.

The cat batted its paw at him. "If you need to ask, Bartholomew, I fear for the success of your mission."

"Do not call me that," said Bartholomew as a piercing ring filled his head.

The cat tolerated the pause, giving it a moment to observe the soulcatcher. It was peculiar the Breedling had such reservations about his name. The cat narrowed its eyes, scrutinizing the Breedling, and as it stared, its irises became full moons, discovering what lay beneath the surface of the former Euxian. Inside, it saw an extraordinary tug-of-war between a life once known and something yet unnamed.

"That is your name, is it not?" pressed the cat.

Bartholomew did not reply. Of course, the answer was *yes*, but for some reason he was unable to acknowledge it.

"Master Breedling," resumed the cat, refraining from calling him by his name. "My sender asked that I look after your progress. By evidence of the parchment, I see the Herald has already gone ahead of me, but that simply means you know my sender's wishes."

"Why should I trust you?" he challenged.

"Use your logic, Master Breedling. My sender would never lie to you."

"But you are not him."

"True, but you hold his words in your hand and he has given me his proxy," said the cat. It looked beyond Bartholomew at the mouth of the alley, watching two girls as they skipped by with glass bottles in their hands. Lost in their chatter, both of them were oblivious to what was happening in the alley.

"Then speak them," said Bartholomew, stuffing the parchment back in his pocket.

The cat flicked its paw and groomed a claw before bringing its focus back to the Breedling. "Why are you playing games?"

"Excuse me?" Bartholomew blinked.

"You were told to stick with the mortal in order to find the mortal Damek, not fraternize with mortals. You know the laws."

"I am not bound to such laws," said Bartholomew. "Or have you already forgotten I am no longer bound to the Laws of Euxinus?"

"I forget nothing, Master Breedling," said the cat. "But you cannot escape what you are. You are still a soulcatcher, despite your broken allegiance. Mortals can never be privy to the wonders about them. You know what happens when they see through the veil."

Bartholomew bit the inside of his cheek, unable to argue the cat's point. Certainly, he knew what would happen. If Charlie were to uncover his secret, it would lift the veil of ignorance that blinded him to the truth about the supernatural elements in Eden. And for enlightened mortals, it never ended well. Their souls earmarked in the afterlife by the Mistress of Heaven or the Master of Hell.

"Do not try to confuse me, Master Chameleon. I know I cannot tell Charlie the truth, but it is not as easy as it once was for me to pass like a shadow through Eden." Bartholomew paused and under his breath he spoke what he had felt since Charlie found him on the floor of the orphanage. "Something is not quite right." He debated whether or not to confide in the feline, but conventional wisdom told him to keep his insecurities to himself.

"As you say, Master Breedling," said the Chameleon intentionally, ignoring the off-the-cuff remark, "but be warned—if it was easy for me to find you, it will not be hard for others."

"There are others?" Bartholomew looked around again for the white-skinned Retrievers, half-expecting them to be perched behind him at the ready to use their paralyzing grasp to drag him back to Euxinus.

"Master Breedling," said the cat, regaining Bartholomew's attention. "Euxians are not the only creatures in the City in the Garden. The Spirit of Flame and his agents also roam the streets."

"But why? Hades," said Bartholomew, using the Master of Hell's current incarnation, "would only have cause to be flanked by agents if he…" Bartholomew stopped. He pressed a hand to his chest, shell-shocked as a dormant spark within him flickered for a split second. "The Eden Wanderer," he breathed aloud. "Stingy Jack is here, in the city."

"Master Breedling," said the cat, to reengage the Breedling's attention.

"How?" Bartholomew looked down at the tabby, as the crack of linen overhead flapped in the wind. "How did he know?" he added in reference to the Apothecary.

The cat stared blankly.

"Answer me!" said Bartholomew with a flutter of impatience.

"Your sender did not know for certain this is where you would be, Master Breedling, but of all the cities in Eden, it is not by mere coincidence you entered through the City in the Garden. You were drawn here, Master Breedling, and not just by the Eden Wanderer Stingy Jack, but by Damek, and in a way the mortal Charlie. This is where all paths converge, as though by design. Not by the Fates, mind you, but there are other great forces at play here and the council suspects Hades and his sister Everlyse finally have enough power to take this realm."

Bartholomew wrapped his fingers around the cat's soft fur and picked it up, holding it underneath its front legs, exposing its belly.

"That is not possible," he said.

"Then why else would dirt from so far away be stripped from the ground and carried with the wind? Why else would these winds produce a storm so terrifying and dark it blocks out the sun? Mortals may call it a Black Blizzard, Master Breedling, but it carries the fury of its creator."

"Hades," said Bartholomew, his arms growing tired from dangling the cat in front of him. If the Chameleon was right and the Master of Hell had managed to amass the power he needed to take Eden for his own, then saving the Shepherdess was paramount. Bartholomew felt an unsettling worry churn in his gut, a sense of helplessness mixing in with it. With no connection to the mythos of his previous life, it was truly in Charlie's hands to help him. He needed Damek in order to reaffirm his charge.

"Now you understand?" asked the cat. "With the continual absence of Earth and Sea, Hades will claim Eden as his dominion."

"But they are not absent," said Bartholomew absentmindedly. He gasped and bit his tongue. He could not afford to give his secret away, not to the Fates' spy.

"As you say," replied the Chameleon, again without flinching. "But from what I know, the two Lost Creators have not been seen for some time. The Spirit of Earth was barely in her ascended form of the Golden Faun before vanishing, while the Fates exiled the other Elements from Euxinus. As for the Spirit of Sea, well the Black Tortoise has been in hiding since Eden's Great Flood." The cat twitched its whiskers then continued. "However, I guess the notion is not so difficult to believe—them not being absent. For if an Euxian immortal, a mere soulcatcher no less, with no free-will can die and thus escape the will of the Fates, then I can believe the Lost Creators are not entirely lost."

Bartholomew readjusted his grip, upset he had said anything to prompt any sort of discussion on the Lost Creators. He needed to stay on his guard and not let the Chameleon trick him into telling it the truth—that after so many eons of searching, he knew where one of the Lost Creators was hiding and that with Stingy Jack's help, he would be able to find it again. But first, he needed to save the Eden Wanderer's love.

The cat swung its tail like the pendulum of a grandfather clock. "Master Breedling..."

"Please, Master Chameleon, amend me to my charge," said Bartholomew in a fit of desperation. "You have done it before."

"Master Breedling, you ask too much of me," said the cat.

"You yourself have already made it perfectly clear you are not bound by the same laws as me. I cannot help you. Only the mortal Damek has the power required to restore the tether of your broken compass."

* * *

Charlie rounded the corner to the sound of vociferous meows. He walked towards Bartholomew, almost certain the cat was talking to him, but knew that was ridiculous. Charlie shook his head, ready to have a laugh, but what happened next gave him pause. If he had not heard it firsthand, he might never have believed it. Charlie stopped dead in his tracks.

"Master Breedling, you left your prison cell for a reason," challenged the cat, trying not to beg, but unable to mask its discontent. "Do what you promised and find Stingy Jack."

"But the mortal…"

"Buck?" Charlie whispered, his thoughts reeling, uncertain if he trusted his own ears.

Bartholomew's body prickled. Not because of the name spoken; on the contrary, the name Charlie had given him seemed familiar and comfortable. His body prickled because he did not know how much Charlie had heard. Bartholomew turned his head, opening his shoulder for Charlie to see the furry animal in his hands.

Charlie stared dumbfounded. Was Buck actually carrying on a conversation with a tabby? He wanted to dismiss the thought, despite witnessing it, but it was hard for him to dispute since his mother had talked to animals all the time. And it was not so much the fact that Buck was talking to a cat, what really had him perplexed was what the boy had said, *but the mortal*—What did Buck mean? Was he saying he himself was not a mortal? Charlie met Buck's eyes, the old soul behind them prominently in the forefront. His head swirled with questions, but he could not amass the strength to bring himself to ask a single one. Instead, he glanced down at the silver cans tied to the string and understood the cat's dilemma.

"Here, let me help you with that," Charlie offered, untying the string from the cat's tail.

The cat gave a pleased meow and licked Charlie's hand.

"Huh, ain't you a nice kitty?" cooed Charlie. He petted the tabby as Buck cradled it in his arms.

The cat purred.

"Yes, you're quite welcome," said Charlie. He scratched the cat underneath its chin as its eyes squinted shut. "You know, it's kinda queer," he continued.

"What?" whimpered Bartholomew, wondering if Charlie was going to ask him something he could not answer. The Herald's warning rang in his ears.

"I've seen hundreds of cats, but I've never seen a cat with pink eyes, at least not one that wasn't albino."

"Really, it cannot be all that strange, can it?" Bartholomew pursed his lips.

"Well, come to think of it, I did see a two-headed cat at the World's Fair last year in the Odditorium. Jimmy didn't find it as fascinating as me, but it was the strangest thing I'd ever seen." Charlie paused, giving the cat another stroke. "So I guess it ain't all that queer if this tabby has pink eyes," he admitted. "All right Buck, I think it's time we were getting off. We've a few more blocks to make up and I want to get indoors before the early-evening drunkards come out because I'm completely done in."

"But the cat," objected Bartholomew.

"I'm sorry, Buck, but Father Van Lewen doesn't like cats, nor does he allow them in the church, which is where we'll be spending the night."

"But…" Bartholomew tried to think of a plausible objection. "The cat might starve."

Charlie laughed halfheartedly. "No, I'm sure the cat will fare much better than us in that regard. It'll be fine. There're plenty of rodents in this city it'll be able to feast on."

"But…"

"Buck, no more buts, the cat will be fine," insisted Charlie. "Now, I won't tell you again. Put the cat down."

Bartholomew placed the tabby cat on the ground before he changed his mind.

The cat ran up the alley, but paused before the sidewalk. It circled around to look at Bartholomew and gave him a final set of meows.

"Beware of the storm, Master Breedling," meowed the cat with one final bow. "Until next we meet."

Bartholomew tilted his head slightly in an attempt to keep his nod subtle, but he felt Charlie watching him. He swallowed hard as the cat disappeared out of sight, trying his hardest to ignore the unnerving pins in his stomach and the curiosity of Charlie's stare.

LAMENT

Charlie and Bartholomew made their way north towards St. John Nepomucene Church as the sun began to set. Along the way, Charlie described the church to Bartholomew, telling him it was not like most of the ornate churches in Chicago. It did not have any towers or flying buttresses, no gargoyles or lavish masonry work to decorate it. Simply put, it resembled a warehouse. A boxy rectangular building with five small street-level stained-glass windows and a second story of squared windows, which once housed a school, but was now a boarding house for the poor. They crossed Thirtieth Street and headed for the side door. It was locked, and Charlie wasted no time picking the lock. He could have just as easily told Father Van Lewen he was going to seek sanctuary for the night, but he was too tired to engage his friend and needed to let the reality of his cousin's death hit him first before talking about it.

The latch popped.

Charlie opened the door and went inside. He moved through the pews to the center aisle of the nave and headed towards the altar, leaving Bartholomew alone at the door. He paused at the crossing and bent his head low in reverence to the ornate sculptured fortress beyond the communion rail. Remaining silent, Charlie walked in front of the white marble of the pulpit and knelt on the second step before the shrine of the Virgin Mary.

Bartholomew lingered as the oak door closed with a gentle slam behind him. His eyes panned the interior of the church, finding it not as impressive as the ancient churches of Europe. It was quite small, intimate, and simple. The main entrance consisted of the door and a slight overhang from the tiny loft, which did not house a grand pipe organ. Instead, a wooden harmonium sat alone in the far corner of the tiny balcony. All the walls were painted off-white with no visible illustrations or paintings. In the center of the nave, six twelve-foot pillars rose up out of the pews in support of the flat ceiling. On the ceiling, two thick beams ran from the main entrance to the dome of the altar stage. The church smelled of burning wax, sweat, and dirt, mixed with scents of exhaust and stale air from the street.

Bartholomew shuffled through the pew to the center aisle as the cool floor soothed his sore feet. He paused for a moment to admire the front of the church, where three arches bent like rainbows, though the center one was bigger, outlining the dome. The fortress sculpture behind the marble altar was decorated with statues and crosses, elaborate details and columns, painted with brilliant colors all trimmed with gold. It glistened in the soft candlelight provided by the lanterns posted around the six pillars. Bartholomew made his way down the aisle to find Charlie kneeling on the steps beneath the statue of a woman with a crown of flowers on her head. He did not want to disturb him, so he tiptoed into the pew, sat down, and waited.

The church fell still, but soon a mournful sob pierced the silence.

Bartholomew lifted his head and found Charlie hunched over, his face kissing the floor.

Charlie let out another loud cry, unable to conceal his sorrow any longer, not caring if Buck or the people upstairs heard him. Worn out by the day's events, tired, angry, hungry, and confused, his guilt crushed him. His family was gone. His sweet, inquisitive cousin Jimmy; his hard-hearted Uncle Gert; his infant brother Niko; his sassy yet intelligent older twin sisters Ursula and Yanka; his outrageously comical older brother Wendell; his soft-spoken father Cletus; and his teacher, his best friend, his mother Adele. All of them now were ash and dust, taken away from him by the same fiery beast. He wanted to curse, to damn the world, to blame someone for his misfortune, but all he could do was cry and wish he were dead.

"Mama, what am I to do?" he pleaded through his sobs. "Please, tell me what to do."

Bartholomew shivered at the eeriness of Charlie's sorrow, finding it familiar. It reminded him of the Shepherdess. The image of the mortal girl's pleading tears haunted him, challenging him to keep his promise.

Charlie rolled onto his side and curled into a ball, pressing his legs in close to his chest to keep himself from falling apart. Pain coursed through every inch of his body and he felt weighted to the floor as though gravity had strengthened its hold on him.

"Jimmy, I'm so sorry," he breathed softly and squeezed his legs tighter as a sorrowful tremble shook him, piercing his heart and soul. Through his sobs, his breath became more sporadic, and his head throbbed. "It's all my fault. If I had done something sooner, if I didn't go back…"

Charlie hated himself, but he hated the slight sense of relief he felt buried beneath his sorrow even more. He was free to do as he pleased without the burden of someone else's life on his shoulders. No longer did he have to listen to his mother's voice telling him to look out for those smaller than him. He burrowed his forehead deeper into his knees. Charlie wailed, lost in conflict with the teachings of his old life and the selfish thoughts of his new one, his selfish inclinations winning. He did not want to shoulder the weight of responsibility any longer, nor did he want to take in any more strays. Someone else could do it. The only person he wanted to worry about was himself. Pressure built in his head, his torment draining what energy he had left, allowing fatigue to strike. As his sobs waned, he drifted off to sleep, his mind escaping to happier times in his dreams.

Charlie's five-year-old head lay in his mother's lap while they swung on the front porch of their farmhouse. His older brother, Wendell, sat on the white-painted rail, leaning against one of the support columns and grumbling about being too old for Sunday afternoon story time. A stern look from his father, Cletus, however, changed his tune. Charlie's twin sisters, Ursula and Yanka, sat cross-legged on the porch floor, their matching bluebell day dresses clean for once. Charlie and his siblings, and even his father and Uncle Gert who were rocking in their chairs and talking in low voices, listened to Adele as she read from her favorite book—the only possession she had from Czechoslovakia. She ran her fingers through his hair as she read.

Today's story was titled "The Trickster and the Shepherdess." Wendell called it a watered-down version of Shakespeare's Romeo and Juliet, *but Ursula and Yanka disagreed. An argument ensued between the siblings until Cletus settled the matter with yet another stern look, the kids knowing well it was their father's favorite story.*

Charlie's mother continued, her voice tranquil. "It was no secret the Shepherdess was in love with the Trickster. For under the pettiness and uncouth deeds beat the silent heart of a man more giving than even he knew possible. She did all she could to help him regain his gentle nature, but at times, the Devil's twisted hold on him could not be tamed, not even by her. One day the Shepherdess approached the Trickster and without warning, he turned on her, setting a cruel trick that would leave her forever exposed to his enemy. Grief-stricken by what he had done, the Trickster knew he could no longer put his faithful love in danger, and so he made his decision to leave—and yet he could not just slip away into the night. Oh, no. He owed it to his love to say goodbye. He told the Shepherdess of his intent, and, without giving her a chance to fight for him, the Trickster kissed her and vanished into the stormy night. Heartbroken, the Shepherdess ran out in search of her love's rival, the Devil himself, hoping against hope the Master of Hell would set him free."

Bartholomew rested his head on the pew as the remaining daylight disappeared on what had been a most tiring day. The hardwood bench beneath him was not comfortable, but it was a welcome change from the unforgiving stone of his former prison cell. He listened to Charlie's whimpers until they settled into sorrowful breaths. Bartholomew rolled onto his side and focused on the dancing shadows on the ceiling. They too did not hold his attention for long as a high-pitched whistle stung his ears and a chill washed over him. He lifted his head to discover the source, but could not seem to find it. He gained his feet and entered the crossing. He listened for the whistle to return and, when it did, it made his skin prickle. Bartholomew walked over to the other side of the church and discovered several fragments were missing from the stained-glass window. The cool air filtered through the cracks, reaching out to warn him.

"Beware the storm," he said under his breath...*Mortals may call it a Black Blizzard, Master Breedling, but it carries the fury of its creator...* Bartholomew leaned his back against the bench, folding his arms across his chest.

"Is it possible?" he mumbled.

Some say the Blizzards are the work of the Devil, he recalled Charlie saying.

"Hades," he whispered.

Confession

A loud bang rattled the silent church.

Bartholomew jumped, but was not as startled by the sound as he was by the sight of a tall, shadowy figure standing next to the door he and Charlie had used. He ducked into the sea of pews, making sure he was out of sight.

Please do not let it be Hades, not here, he silently pleaded.

Confident footsteps headed down the side aisle, each step drawing closer.

Bartholomew's heart beat loudly with each one, fear mounting in his chest. He pressed against the cool stone, trying to meld himself into the pillar. He was not ready for a confrontation with the Master of Hell.

The footsteps halted two pews ahead of him.

Bartholomew's stomach tightened as his heart sprang into his throat. He pressed a hand to his neck, holding his breath with anticipation.

Knock, knock, knock!

Bartholomew heard the pounding on the door, followed by a heavy sigh from the shadowy figure. "Thank the stars," he whispered, relieved it was not Hades. He listened as the footsteps moved away from him towards the door. He crawled out into the aisle and followed the shadowy figure in a low crouch, but was only able to get past six pews before hiding again.

A high-pitched whistle sliced through the church.

"Father Van Lewen!" shrieked a young female voice. "I know the lateness of the hour, but I seek your counsel and compassion."

"How did you know I was here?" asked the priest.

"I knocked on the rectory door and a little girl, Phyllis, told me you had gone inside the church," replied the young female voice. "Please, Father, please forgive me," she begged.

"Shhh, it will be all right," spoke the priest.

Bartholomew inched his head around the edge of the pillar. He saw the tall shadow of Father Van Lewen above the shorter shadow of the woman as they passed out of sight into the pew.

"Please, child, tell me what has happened," said the priest, his voice full and deep with a hint of gravel, yet gentle in nature. Bartholomew found it shared similarities with the Apothecary's tone and he felt comforted to hear it.

"Bless me, Father, for I have sinned," began the woman between sobs. "Though it wasn't my fault, at least, I don't remember. But I must have."

"What is it you think you have done?" asked the priest.

"I killed them," screeched the woman.

The priest did not answer. Instead, he took the poor girl's hand and spoke to her without a hint of judgment in his voice. "Who, my child, who is it you say you have killed?"

"I was weak, Father, seduced by a charlatan. He promised me everything and I fell for him." The young woman buried her puffy face in her hands and hid behind a curtain of red-tinted brunette hair.

"Please my child, tell me what happened," insisted the priest. "Surely you're not capable of such a travesty?"

"I work at the orphanage, you know, the one near the railroad tracks by Thirty-Seventh Street."

"I know of the place," said the priest with a hint of worry.

"A week ago, a smooth-talking swindler called on me and, at first, I ignored his calls, but soon he began to send me flowers and candies; he even sang to me one evening. I fell for his charm and agreed to see him. He made so many promises and said he could take me away from here, away from the stench of the Yards, the violence, the noise. He offered the world and it was too tempting and agreed to go with him."

"But there was a price."

"Yes, Father, there was, but I didn't know what it was until just last evening. I swear to you, I didn't know." She began to cry again.

"Please finish," advised the priest, dread apparent in his tone.

"Yesterday in the evening, he came to the orphanage—the boys were already in bed. The warden was out, so I told him he couldn't come in. I didn't want to get in trouble, but with just a flash of his brilliant smile I melted and without hesitation invited him in. He said he wanted to run away with me and, feeling ready, I accepted. I packed my things, but before we left there was something I wanted to do. I thought it would be fun, sneaking a little whiskey from Miss Schwarman's liquor cabinet, but I didn't think, I didn't know. One thing just led to another and..."

"What?" asked the priest, shifting his weight on the bench. "Did he hurt you?"

"No, maybe, I don't remember," squealed the young woman. Her hands covered her mouth as she tossed her head. "I drank so much, I don't even remember starting the fire."

"Fire?"

Fire—Bartholomew realized the young woman was talking about Charlie's orphanage.

The young woman dropped, her knees one solid thud on the

marble floor.

"Miss Schwarman had told me about you, how you cared for the Reese boys. Charlie was a brave young man," she said in past tense. The young woman resumed her sobs, her fingers gripping the priest's frock. "There is nothing for it," she continued, "such a life wasted."

"Are you certain?" asked the priest.

"The other boys were adamant," she said. "They said he stayed inside to find Jimmy and they never emerged. When the fire was finally put out, there was nothing left of the inside."

Bartholomew heard the priest sigh, wondering what the man could possibly say that might absolve her of her sin. Sure, Charlie was in fact still alive, but that did not save her from judgment. Jimmy was dead and despite her unintentional involvement, by proxy blame had to be laid at her feet. No one could forgive that, neither Charlie nor this priest. At least no one he knew of that would save her soul from Hell and Hades.

"You are forgiven, my child," said the priest in a somber voice.

Bartholomew could not believe his ears. In his lessons with the Apothecary, absolution was a divine right bestowed on those worthy of its grace, granted by the ancient rule of seven, the Fates, and the Elements. Surely, no mere mortal had such power, or was his knowledge of absolution false? Was it possible a mortal had the power to absolve?

"Oh, thank you, thank you, Father," wept the young woman between gasps. She lifted her head and kissed the priest's hand.

"Yes," remarked the priest. He took her by the arms and helped her onto the bench. "But you cannot just take me at my forgiveness. You must make amends, for, such that it is, your sin is great."

"I will do anything you ask of me."

"I know you will, but it is not my words you should heed or

listen to, rather your own."

"I don't understand," sniffled the young woman.

"You will," replied the priest with a soft smile in his voice. "Though for now, I believe a good night's rest is in order. I have room in the parsonage."

"Oh, no, I couldn't," refused the young woman.

"I insist," said the priest in a commanding tone. He was not willing to send the poor girl back out onto the streets, not after what she had been through.

The priest rose from the pew and assisted the young woman to her feet. She wiped her face with the sleeve of her peach dress and followed the priest out into the aisle. Bartholomew watched them pass and then crawled after them, taking special care to stay close to the pews just in case.

"All will be well, my child," reassured the priest. "I will have Phyllis' mother see to your needs, she…" The priest stopped, both in speech and in stride.

Bartholomew crouched behind the end of the first pew and peered around it to see Father Van Lewen's shadow leave the young woman's side, move past the pulpit, and kneel on the floor.

"Charlie," whispered the priest, his voice full of relief. He looked up at the young woman standing in the dim light, her body trembling. "Do you see another boy in the pews around you?" he added, with panic in his voice.

The young woman frantically searched the first seven rows on either side of the center aisle, her heeled feet scuffing the marble floor.

"No, Father, I see no boy," she said.

"You poor thing," the priest spoke under his breath. "You did not deserve such loss."

Father Van Lewen stretched out his hand, but let it hover just above Charlie's shoulder. He contemplated waking him, but the wave of heartache he felt rise into his palm was case enough to let Charlie sleep. He regained his feet, walked over to the first pew, and retrieved the altar cloth he had left there earlier in the day. He unfurled it and laid it over Charlie's curled body.

Charlie breathed out a soft moan as the woman joined the priest to stand over him.

"Rest easy, Charlie," whispered Father Van Lewen.

"Will he be all right?" asked the young woman, relief filling her tearful eyes.

"In time." Father Van Lewen placed an arm around her. "As will you, I have no doubt. For no matter how far gone we may think we are or others perceive us to be, there is always hope we will find our way back to the light we once stood in."

"Thank you, Father," whispered the young woman.

"You are most welcome," said the priest as he ushered her out of the church.

Bartholomew rose, his legs wobbling beneath him. He hobbled to the center aisle and took his original seat near Charlie. His mind raced with questions he wanted to ask his mortal companion, but he knew Charlie needed his rest. Bartholomew lay back on the bench and stared at the dark ceiling.

"Is it possible?" he whispered, pondering if his transgression could be absolved.

He did not expect an answer, but from the darkness in the church a melodious voice replied.

"If you keep your word, all will be forgiven."

Jack O' Lantern

Bartholomew remained in his hiding place until the church had fallen still again, and even then he waited a little longer just to be sure. He sat up and scanned the room, making sure he and Charlie were alone. He did not see it at first, whether it was simply because he missed it or because his reflexes to notice the otherworldly were in flux, but he did eventually spot it, the ghostly visage of the creature. The elegant white dress floated through the church, a haunting reminder of all this past. Bartholomew stood and moved out into the aisle, bowing low to greet the creature, his reverence a welcomed sight.

"It is pleasing to see you, Master Breedling," said the creature.

"And you as well, Madam Teller," said Bartholomew, his ears ringing from the tranquil chimes of her melodious voice. He arose and found a warm, sandy sun-beam radiating from her translucent skin. The smile on her face filled him with a security he had lacked since his escape, a reassurance that all would be well. At least, that was the brief air she presented, until a grey cloud blocked the sun. She floated past him, her footsteps mute.

"Madam Teller." Bartholomew turned towards the altar stage, the ghostly creature unresponsive to his address.

The Tales Teller paused between the two rows of pews, her eyes not on the Breedling, but on the bundle lying beneath the statue of the flower-crowned woman. She debated whether or not to entertain the Breedling's unspoken questions or to fulfill her given task.

"Madam Teller," repeated Bartholomew. "What word does the Apothecary send?"

This time, the Tales Teller rotated her posture to address the Breedling properly.

Bartholomew drew closer to the altar stage, bothered by her lack of response.

"Please, Madam Teller, did the Apothecary tell you of the mortal Damek?" said Bartholomew, pulling the crumpled piece of parchment from his pocket. "Please, I need to know more. So far, I have come across destitute mortals and rival gangs, none of which the Apothecary would have deemed worthy to endow with such magic. Is he certain Charlie will lead me to this mortal Damek?"

"Of that, he is," replied the Tales Teller.

"Then how will I know?" asked Bartholomew. "This could take days, weeks, the Fates forbid, maybe years. How will I know he has led me to the right mortal?"

"I know this is not what you want to hear, Master Breedling, but only you can answer that question."

"Why can you not just lead me to the mortal yourself?" asked Bartholomew, his unseasoned emotions growing anxious. "I could be with the Eden Wanderer by now on our way to saving the Shepherdess."

The Tales Teller curled her lips into a smile, amused by the Breedling's frustration, for she too had felt the same when presenting a similar question to the Apothecary, and now understood the Eldest Euxian's reasoning.

"Because, Master Breedling, one cannot forget that all parts of the journey are important. Even the ones that appear to be mundane at the time. This is a riddle you alone can solve."

"Then why are you here, if not to forward my direction?" asked Bartholomew, returning the wadded parchment into his pocket.

"I am, Master Breedling," said the Tales Teller, her skin flushing a pale red. "But I am not here to give words to you."

"If not me..." Bartholomew looked at Charlie. "I don't understand. What are you going to say to Charlie? Both the Herald and the Chameleon warned me to keep the mortal separate of my affairs."

"I am not here to speak to him, Master Breedling," said the Tales Teller, floating towards the sleeping bundle. "I am here to speak at him."

"Is that wise?" asked Bartholomew.

"Wisdom is not what is at play here, Master Breedling," said the Tales Teller, the flush of her skin deepening into a shade of midnight.

Bartholomew stopped, the echo of his footfalls lost in the poor acoustics of the church. He had only seen the Tales Teller show this color once before, during the conclusion of his trial. It had been right after the Apothecary read his sentence, banishing him to a prison cell. He had seen her as the Retrievers escorted him from the palace, her visage grave as though death had appeared. Bartholomew watched the white dress drift toward the marble floor, the Tales Teller positioning herself next to Charlie.

"What has happened?" asked Bartholomew, braving the question.

"Time is at its end, Master Breedling," said the Tales Teller, her feline ears flattening. "The trial of the Shepherdess will commence six Eden days hence, for I can no longer delay the proceedings."

"Does the Apothecary know?" asked Bartholomew, positioning himself against the first pillar.

"I have informed the Eldest many times during your imprisonment, and though there was no need to take the threat seriously, now it has come to fruition." The Tales Teller lifted her head, her glowing feline eyes somber. "Your escape, Master Breedling, has sent a tremor throughout the four realms, and though the Fates have not yet taken notice, your truth of escape will not last long nor will the secret you harbor about the Lost Creators."

"The Chameleon has already lectured me on my lack of skill to be as a shadow," said Bartholomew, crossing his arms in front of his chest.

"It is not solely your act, Bartholomew," said the Tales Teller, studying the Breedling as he cringed at the sound of his name, the Chameleon's previous report precise in its observation of Bartholomew's state.

"What then?" asked Bartholomew.

"It is not a matter of what you are or are not doing, Master Breedling, but what you no longer possess. The object of the Fates' grace has left you and yet, looking upon you with my own eyes, I see what the Chameleon meant about the shift in your aura." She paused to admire the tiny flecks of dust intertwining with dotted fireflies. The midnight shade of her skin changed, but remained within the house of grey, with an undertone of blue.

Bartholomew unwrapped his arms and tucked his chin, his eyes trying to see what the Tales Teller saw, but whatever it was he found no trace of it. He kept his head down, the words coming out of his mouth before he could prevent himself—he needed to confide in someone.

"While in my cell, I felt the Fates' grace slowly leave me. It is probably why it took me so long to come to the conclusion I find myself in now. But while I was in there, their charge that connected me to the Eden Wanderer remained steadfast. Granted, the longer my imprisonment lasted the intensity of the Fates' command faded, but I could still sense him." Bartholomew lifted his head. "Now, all I feel is a gaping emptiness, as though I am not fully present. Sure, I was able to harness enough focus during my escape to draw me to the City in the Garden, but now that I'm here, I can no longer sense Stingy Jack. The Eden Wanderer could be standing right next to me and I would be none the wiser."

The Tales Teller's skin shifted to a shade of navy blue, her voice reflecting her concern. "It is a point of concern the council has discussed, Master Breedling, and we fear that without a true tether to the realm of Eden, it is hard to know if your presence here is permanent. Might I suggest not sleeping until the mortal Damek has reaffirmed your charge?"

Bartholomew nodded reluctantly, the weight of fatigue already taunting him. "And what of Charlie?" he asked, his eyes falling on the restful mortal, tears still lingering on his copper tone skin.

"Not to worry," she said, placing a hand on Charlie's head. "The compulsion spell will not hurt him, nor will it affect the veil that protects his eyes; he will remain innocent. The spell will be masked within the tale I shall recite, which will dwell in his subconscious, so he will not even know it is there."

"And this spell will compel him to lead me to Damek?" said Bartholomew.

"That is the way of it," said the Tales Teller, admiring the story Charlie's spirit was allowing her to read. "Fortune smiles on us, Master Breedling." Her words referring to the mortal's purity—*the Apothecary chose well.*

Bartholomew took a seat on the floor. "If only that were the way of it for Charlie," he said.

The Tales Teller smiled, her skin returning to the shade of a sandy sun again. She stroked Charlie's hair, an act his mother Adele had performed many times over when he was younger.

"Your emerging empathy is commendable, Master Breedling," she said. "But you do not give his suffering enough credit. The tragedies that have befallen him have shaped who he is and allotted him a strength few mortals ever achieve."

"I do not understand," said Bartholomew.

"Of that, Master Breedling, only time can gift you the understanding," said the Tales Teller. "Now, if you kindly refrain from speech, I only have 'til the dawn to complete my task."

Bartholomew noted the request and leaned against the pew. The Tales Teller began, her words hypnotic, and he did everything he could to prevent the repetitive story from putting him to sleep, fearful that if he did, the Tales Teller's warning might come to pass.

The Tales Teller continually ran her silvery-shaded fingers through Charlie's hair, her spell penetrating his dreams, until images of his family were overpowered by the image of the Eden Wanderer, a trickster known as Stingy Jack.

Every mortal dreams of tricking the Devil, but few ever have and only one has done it twice.

Stingy Jack was such a lad, who invited the Devil out one night for drinks. The two tricksters, masters of their craft, talked into the witching hour, all the while knocking back rounds of aged whiskey. In his drunken state, the Devil confided in Stingy Jack his most well-kept secret—that he possessed the ability to transform into any object. Astonished, Stingy Jack nagged the Devil to turn himself into a coin so he could pay for their drinks. The Devil was hesitant, but after drinking his twelfth whiskey, he disappeared, leaving a gold coin in his place.

True to his name, Stingy Jack left the bar without paying and instead put the Devil into his pocket next to a silver cross, preventing him from retaking his form.

Eventually, Stingy Jack released the Devil, but only on the condition he leave him be for one year, and if he should die before then, he could not take his soul.

The Devil begrudgingly agreed to the terms.

One year later, the Devil found Stingy Jack in an apple orchard and sought again to take him for his own. As per his last request, Stingy Jack asked if the Devil would climb the tree and get him the prized fruit near the top. The Devil raised an eyebrow in suspicion, for he would not let Stingy Jack trick him again. Stingy Jack sensed as much and baited the Devil by telling him such a feat was impossible.

The Devil felt his skills were under attack and could not stand the disrespect Stingy Jack showed him. Furthermore, he permitted no mortal to speak to him in such a manner, let alone one who had tricked him once already. Therefore, in his vanity, the Devil climbed the tree out of spite and while he did, Stingy Jack carved a cross into the bark, preventing him from coming down. The Devil was furious and spouted threats of fire and brimstone.

Stingy Jack simply smiled at his mastery and proposed yet another deal. He would let the Devil go, if he promised not to bother him for ten more years and that if he should die, he could not claim his soul. The Devil once again reluctantly agreed.

Soon after, Stingy Jack died.

As the Irish legend goes, upon his death, God refused to allow such an unsavory soul into heaven, and making good on his word, the Devil did not claim Stingy Jack's soul. Instead, the Devil sent him off into the night with nothing but a wickless candle to light his way. Stingy Jack put the candle into a carved-out turnip and went out into the black as the Devil's laughter followed him.

He has wandered Eden ever since…

Rations Market

The portly man stood in front of the doorway to Rations Market, dressed in his white apron, wrinkled trousers he had slept in the night before, and his signature red hat that had a permanent sweat ring along his forehead. He swept the sidewalk on the Aberdeen corner, but knew his effort was a wasted one. He gave the occasional nod to folks as they passed by, muttering obscenities under his breath after them. He pounded the bristles of his broom on the concrete, irritated he could not coax them inside.

"Good morning, Grocer Pawlak," greeted a sophisticated woman's voice, her Polish accent as thick as her perm.

The man lifted his gaze from the sidewalk to return the greeting, his eyes sizing up the tall woman standing in front of him.

"Aw, Mrs. Hamerski," he greeted the affluent woman, refraining from using a patronizing voice with her. He tightened his grip on the broom straining a smile that was more grimace than sincere.

The wind chased around the corner, tousling Mrs. Hamerski's skirt. "Oooh," she squeaked, pressing her hand down on the rambunctious cloth. "Interesting bluster we're having," she added, in an attempt to divert from her embarrassment.

"Indeed," said Grocer Pawlak, as pleasantly as possible.

Mrs. Hamerski pursed her lips into a smile, already tired of making small talk with the portly man, his overbearing personality reeking of desperation.

"And what brings you out to the curb?" she asked in an accusatory tone. "I hope our Charlie is well?"

Grocer Pawlak's jaw tightened, stifling a growl. He was not the boy's keeper. If he were, he would show Charlie a thing or two and belt his hide raw for being late, especially on a day he could be capitalizing on the threat of the approaching storm. He grumbled to himself, forgetting Mrs. Hamerski's presence, detesting the tall woman's shine to the orphan.

"I beg your pardon?" chimed Mrs. Hamerski.

"Oh, nothing," said Grocer Pawlak, trying to save face. He did not want to alert Mrs. Hamerski that anything was amiss; after all, she was the most gossipy woman in the neighborhood. "Is there anything I can do for you, Mrs. Hamerski?"

"Oh yes," she replied. "Your brother, the butcher, said you were getting a new shipment of flour in this morning and I was wondering if it had arrived yet."

Grocer Pawlak rumpled his bulbous nose at the mention of his young brother. "No, I am afraid the freight truck has not yet arrived this morning; running a bit late it is," he lied with a grin, his eyes disappearing into the folds of his dimpled cheeks.

"Oh, all right then. I'll just stop by a little later. I'll give your brother your regards."

"Much obliged," replied Grocer Pawlak, through clenched teeth, his hatred for his brother stronger than his dislike of the tall woman in front of him.

"Well, good day to you then Mr. Pawlak," said Mrs. Hamerski, overly polite.

"And to you," grumbled Grocer Pawlak, unraveling his temper as the tall woman disappeared beyond the corner, angry another customer was walking away empty-handed. He looked down the street again.

"Where is that boy?" he griped.

Grocer Pawlak went back to sweeping the sidewalk, wondering if his good-for-nothing younger brother had anything to do with this, especially since their most recent argument had left them at odds with one other.

"Maybe the scallywag offered my boy double the wage, or meat perhaps," he mumbled. "Maybe the old coot is trying to teach me a lesson. Well, I'll show him a thing or two."

Grocer Pawlak lifted his head to the street again, this time managing to make eye contact with two toffee-colored eyes. He snatched up his broom.

"Excellent," he muttered greedily and entered his store, not bothering to wait for Charlie.

Charlie and Bartholomew reached the corner across from Rations Market. They looked across the street, the view of the store visible through the three large display windows on either side of the corner doorway. Charlie watched Grocer Pawlak waddle his way over to the window, the portly man switching out a few of the ads. He caught a glimpse of man's hot-headed demeanor with an evil glare. He pulled his eyes away to prolong the inevitable, for he knew he was in for a tongue-lashing. He glanced down at Buck, prepared to ask him if he was ready, but noticed he was admiring the window ads.

"Say, Buck," he said, putting forth his best poker face, despite being worn down.

"Hmm?" Bartholomew tilted his head to look at Charlie.

"What say you take a gander at the window ads for a tick while I go inside and square things with Grocer Pawlak?"

"What for?"

"Well, because I have to ask permission first if you can come into the store. It's the proper thing to do."

"Oh, of course," said Bartholomew, taking Charlie's fib as proper etiquette. "But, what if he says no?"

"Well, seeing how Kalvis and Wiktor took to you yesterday I don't see a problem," said Charlie, withholding his true feelings. After the events in the pool hall, he wanted nothing more than to keep Buck away from Grocer Pawlak, for the last thing he needed was another interested party charmed by the kid's mysterious allure. He could have easily left him with Father Van Lewen, but like Jimmy, he would not have felt right if Kalvis had sent men to find him there. The best he could do was to keep them moving. Plus, he was starving. Having gone without food for a whole day, Charlie did not want to waste time explaining himself and was unwilling to spend hours in a breadline that would only give him scraps. Grocer Pawlak was his best choice to get food without stealing it.

"Besides," he continued, "it's probably best I deliver the news about the outcome of the truce myself. It'll give me a chance to tell him about you. You know, before making the proper introductions. He'll be especially pleased to learn you helped Wiktor."

"Really?"

"Definitely," said Charlie, though the probability of him telling Grocer Pawlak the whole story was highly unlikely. After all, he was still unsure how Buck had actually pulled off his win, and he did not trust the portly man with details, especially not if it included Buck having a curious talent for overcoming impossible odds.

The boys walked across the street.

"Charlie, is Grocer Pawlak a good man?" inquired Bartholomew, curious if he was a man worth trusting, but more importantly, if he was a man worthy enough to be marked by the Apothecary.

Charlie thought hard for a moment. "I wouldn't say 'good' necessarily," he started to say, knowing Grocer Pawlak was a rather greedy man.

"What then?"

Charlie waited to respond as they stood in front of the doors. He had never been fond of Grocer Pawlak, but, like most of the people he had recently surrounded himself with, the portly man had never done anything harmful to him or to Jimmy. So did that make him an evil man? Manipulative certainly, especially with children, but evil? Charlie found the word a tad strong.

"I would say he's a man who always thinks he knows what's best."

"Is that a noble thing?" asked Bartholomew, trying to ascertain the man's worth.

"It can be," offered Charlie, catching a glimpse of the portly man's chubby face through the glass, giving him more credit than was necessary. He thought again about the breadline down the street, but his stomach growled in protest, urging him to see to his daily chore. "So—you think you can stay out of trouble for a few minutes?" he asked.

"I think I can manage to keep myself busy," said Bartholomew, turning away from the doors.

"Oh, and Buck," said Charlie, disturbing the bell as he opened the door. "If anyone gives you any guff, I mean, if anyone bothers you, just pound on the window."

Bartholomew agreed and began his examination of the window display while Charlie headed inside.

The ads in the window were unlike anything he had seen before. Some of them were vibrant with color and some were faded. Some contained pictures of animals and mortals of all ages, while others exhibited brilliant scenery. He stood in front of them one at a time, pondering them individually. The first one he liked was a faded picture of a man wearing a red hat upon his bald head with a white ball of fluff on the end. The man's cheeks were chubby and rosy, his nose stubby, and his smile merry. Below him was a box with red and white spirals wrapped around it. In the center of the box, red letters spelled the word CHESTERFIELD. Bartholomew was unsure why he trusted the cheerful man, but he thought if he could try a Chesterfield, whatever it was, he might enjoy it.

Bartholomew moved onto the next design as the small hairs at the nape of his neck prickled. He turned to the street, certain the Chameleon was watching him again, but he found no sign of the feline. Bartholomew returned to the image of a man and a young woman standing on the helm of a ship, but again, he sensed someone watching him. He took a deep breath to calm his nerves and watched the street behind him through the reflection. Over his shoulder, across the street, a tall man in black leaned against the lamppost and for a moment, Bartholomew thought the man was looking at him, but it was hard to tell. What his eyes missed, however, his instincts warned him about.

"Impossible," he whispered, thinking the man in black was none other than Hades. He quickly turned, but by the time he was able to look across the street, the man was gone.

Bartholomew kept his eyes on the street for a few more seconds until his uneasiness subsided, then examined other pictures, filling him with the urge to try Royal Crown Cola, Campbell's Tomato Soup, and a Hershey's Chocolate Bar. He lost himself amongst the fantasies on the window, ignoring everything else around him. It was not until the bell rang that he pulled away to find Charlie with a brown beret covering his messy hair, and trying to hide his swollen red eyes.

"Are we square?" asked Bartholomew.

"We're all set, Buck," confirmed Charlie, his energetic tone hardly matching his depressed demeanor. It was getting hard to mask, but he had been able to keep the truth of Jimmy's demise from the portly man, at least for now. "Grocer Pawlak said if we help him move some of the boxes into the alley and restock some things, he'll give us soup and a cola for lunch. How's that sound?"

"What is soup and cola?"

Charlie laughed, not fully realizing Buck was serious.

"Is something funny?" asked Bartholomew, oblivious to the humor in his question.

"Always one bizarre question after another with you."

"Is that bad?"

Charlie laughed again and for a brief moment felt more relaxed, just enough to indulge an explanation and not burden himself with further speculation about Buck's sanity or feed his outlandish theory about Buck's true identity. "No, Buck, it's not bad. You're just what my ma would have called inquisitive." He steadied his breath. "To answer your question, though; soup is a brothy liquid. Sometimes it's made with chunks of vegetables or meat. And cola," he paused, "well, the best way I can describe it is a cool, crisp, caramel, carbonated beverage, also known as the four cees. It's quite the substitute for liquor." Charlie removed his cap and scratched his head.

"Is it better than tea?" asked Bartholomew. It would be his choice of drink if given one.

"Ha ha, there you go again. Maybe to some upstate Ivy

Leaguers or hoity-toity Brits, but to me, there isn't anything greater."

"Fair enough," said Bartholomew, disappointed, lingering on the thought of a warm beaker with honey and rosehips.

"Hey you kids, I ain't paying you to jaw in the street!" shouted a garbled voice through the glass.

"To work?" said Charlie, worried that if he idled too long, he would collapse from the crushing weight of his grief.

"To work," agreed Bartholomew.

The sound of music welcomed the boys as they entered the store. Twelve rows of white shelves, housing a plethora of cans, sacks, boxes, and bags of strange candies, were situated neatly behind the island counter directly in front of them. The small counter was clean and glossy, and trapped within its center, the portly man stood with his sleeves rolled back to his inflamed elbows. The man's round, chubby face was ruddy, much like the face of the man in the Chesterfield picture. If it were not for the darkened circles under his squinting eyes, Bartholomew might have mistaken them for twins.

Grocer Pawlak gave Bartholomew a once over and squinted even harder. He knew his eyes were bad, but he had a feeling they were playing a trick on him again. After a moment, he grabbed a pair of round spectacles from the counter and set them on the thick bridge of his nose.

"This ain't Jimmy," he deduced, disgusted by the boy's unfashionable attire.

"No, this is..." started Charlie.

"Buck Hormel, sir, pleased, er, to make your acquaintance." Bartholomew held out his hand for the man to shake.

Grocer Pawlak glanced at Charlie then back to Bartholomew. He looked down at the small ivory hand and hesitated.

Bartholomew snuck a peek at Charlie from the corner of his eye to see if he had done something wrong. Was there something Charlie had forgotten to tell him? Bartholomew returned his attention to the grocer and saw a shrewd grin on his face. The dimples on his cheeks pinched his skin, which twitched before he gave way to a chuckle.

"Pawlak, you'll have to excuse my friend," said Charlie with a chuckle in his throat, playing off Buck's blunder. He should have told him not to speak.

"Just off the boat, ay," the grocer said with a snicker. He slammed his hand into Bartholomew's hand and shook it forcefully, almost pulling his arm out of the socket.

"Something like that," mumbled Bartholomew through his teeth. He wondered if it would be better to keep his mouth shut in the future.

"Ha, ha, ha, Charlie, where do you get such unusual strays? First, it was that little blonde-headed German girl, and there was that mute Lithuanian boy, and the Negro boy who was nearly as tall as the doorway. Hell, you sure know how to pick 'em."

"I guess you could say I have a gift," shrugged Charlie, "though I prefer to think they fall into my lap." He forced a tired smile, not at all pleased with the grocer's train of thought or with himself for upholding his friendly pretense with the portly man. Charlie shared another laugh as the grocer recounted the three strays, telling Buck tall tales about them, because the way he remembered things was completely different.

He had meet the little blonde-headed German girl one day sitting in an alley, half frozen in the December cold. He had not known what else to do, other than to bring her to Grocer Pawlak, he being the closest. Once she felt better, it became apparent the young girl had an uncanny talent for dance. Seeing the potential,

Grocer Pawlak had sold her off to some traveling circus and Charlie never saw her again. As for the mute Lithuanian boy, who, despite his lack of voice, had an exceptional ability for creating music and not just on the piano, but with every instrument he touched. Grocer Pawlak had the kid playing in his store for a few weeks, until a mobster from uptown took him, paying Grocer Pawlak a small fortune for him. Then there was the dark-skinned boy, who was as strong as an anvil and could lift the front end of a Model T clean off the ground. Grocer Pawlak had used the boy for a publicity stunt during harvest season, at which point some men in the coal-mining business approached him. After that Charlie never saw him again either.

Charlie eyed Buck, aware that his pool hall feat would soon become local legend, but with any luck, Grocer Pawlak would not find out for a few days. Of course, that was merely wishful thinking, for he knew one of Wiktor's snitches kept the portly man in the loop on all the gossip going on in the neighborhood. It was more realistic to think Grocer Pawlak would know by day's end, but for now, he had time to use the man one last time. Charlie watched Buck pull his arm back, cradling it. He elbowed him in the side and glared at him to make his discomfort less obvious.

"All right, you scallywags, let me show ya what I need." Grocer Pawlak waved the boys to follow.

They walked down the center row, its shelves bare. At the end of the aisle, five boxes sat against the wall, each labeled Campbell Soup Company.

"You boys can stock the soup," said Grocer Pawlak, as they continued to the back room, "and then there are fifteen sacks of flour here in the pantry that need to be stocked. Charlie, I think you should handle them, your friend doesn't look much up to it."

"We'll take care of it," said Charlie, tipping his cap. He was eager to get started.

Grocer Pawlak widened his cheesy smile and headed back to the front of the store, pleased he would be able to open, but even more pleased that Charlie had brought along a new friend.

"Buck, I'll get you set up."

Charlie grabbed one of the boxes, carried it a fourth of the way down the row, and set it on the tile floor. He then took out a small knife from his back pocket and cut into the box.

"Now, remember, Buck," he tilted his head to look at the kid, and was caught off guard by his surprised expression. "Rule number six," he said, "always have a knife handy."

"You just made that up," said Bartholomew.

"Maybe," shrugged Charlie, "but really, a knife in any situation may well be your only friend." He went on explaining what they had to accomplish and when Buck seemed to get the hang of it, he hauled the other boxes down the row, cracked them open, and headed back to the pantry.

Bartholomew started stacking the Cream of Mushroom cans and soon fell into a sort of hypnotic rhythm. The work was monotonous and dull, certainly not something suited for a creature of his status, but the tedium kept his mind from racing and every so often he glanced over his shoulder at the portly man. From their handshake, he sensed a mysterious shroud hiding the man's true nature. There was an odd familiarity about the portly man, his charm too much like Kalvis, and yet, none of his instincts warned him of any danger.

"Buck, you need to pick up the pace a little," Charlie teased as he finished the fourth and fifth box before Bartholomew was even half done with the third. Charlie helped him empty the box, and then grabbed it, leaving Bartholomew sitting on the floor.

Bartholomew leaned up against the fully stocked shelves as Charlie disappeared with the boxes. He rested his head on the edge of the shelf and vacantly stared, not quite seeing the rows of Malt-O-Meal in front of him. He heard the steady pace of footsteps crossing the floor, the ding of the bell on the front door, the low chatter of voices, and scratchy music. The sounds were not soothing, but his eyes, for the first time since emerging from the fire, grew disturbingly heavy. He tried to fight an onslaught of sleep by shaking his head and slapping his cheeks, but nothing worked. In a matter of seconds he closed his eyes and sank into a deep abyss. It was comfortable at first, but then familiar darkness settled around him as though it were pulling him back to his Euxian prison cell. The smell of sulfur ravaged his nose and he sensed his chains of obedience latch onto his wrists. The abyss tugged Bartholomew even further into its embrace, the sounds of the store fading into an eerie silence.

"Buck," called Charlie's voice.

Bartholomew heard him and tried to break free of the abyss, but he felt it barricading his escape.

"Buck, Buck," called Charlie's voice just beyond the rim of his consciousness.

Bartholomew shouted Charlie's name, but his voice lingered in the void of his cell, and conscious of his surroundings, he did not know whether he was trapped in his own mind or if he was no longer in Eden.

Nourishment

Charlie shook Buck gently, doing all he could to prevent rattling the entire row of shelves, but he already felt the curious eyes of two women standing at the end of the aisle. He darned not shake him again, but aside from slapping the kid, nothing was working. Charlie touched Buck's forehead, surprised by how clammy it felt. Something was wrong, he could feel it, as though the kid were slipping further away than sleep would allow one to travel. It did not matter to him how he knew, his grief-stricken and starved mind temporarily useless, but he understood the kid needed to wake up from whatever hell he had fallen into. He dug his fingers into Buck's shoulders, anxiously waiting for the two vultures to move on. And to his relief, they relinquished their judgmental stares and drifted out of sight. Charlie leaned in close to Buck keeping his voice low.

"Buck, awake up," he demanded.

There was no change for a brief moment, but slowly Bartholomew fluttered his eyes.

Charlie searched Buck's face, as his ivory skin turned an awful shade of green and the fear in his eyes became magnified by his empty stare. *What are you hiding?* Charlie knew better than to ask his question, especially not in the middle of Grocer Pawlak's store, but his trust in the kid was faltering and soon he would have to confront him or suffer the consequences.

The numbness of Bartholomew's body had not yet worn off and though in a way he sensed Charlie's touch, he could not feel it. His head began to pound and his eyes stung. He tightened his eyelids, hoping to make it stop as well as the burning sensation building in the back of his throat. A knot punched him in the gut and like the thump of a heartbeat he sensed the energy of not one but two otherworldly creatures in close proximity. He was uncertain who they were, his instincts briefly strong enough to sense them, although he was certain it was not the Chameleon or the Tales Teller.

"Buck?" said Charlie, his voice eager to get through to him. He lifted his hands to Buck's cheeks and searched his blank expression further. The warmth of his fingers burned against the eerie chill of his skin. Buck's reaction this time was instant as he shot to his feet in a fit of terror. Charlie scrambled to his feet.

"Buck, it's all right," he said, holding his hands out in front of himself to show the boy he meant him no harm.

Bartholomew's eyes danced around the store. Several pairs of questioning eyes glowered at him, but the only one that brought any sort of comfort came from Charlie. His head pulsed and he pressed a hand to his angry forehead. He blinked a few times until the throbbing subsided. He wanted to say something, but he felt so weak.

"Buck," whispered Charlie, aware that everyone in the store was watching them, including Grocer Pawlak. "Buck, it's all right, you just fell asleep."

"Charlie!" said Grocer Pawlak from behind the front counter, his roar causing several of his customers to jump. One even popped open a box of cornflakes, which erupted all over the floor.

Charlie glanced over his shoulder at the portly man, whose insidious nature temporarily overtook his false glamor.

"Take it out back!" said Grocer Pawlak in a lower tone, trying not to further alarm his customers. "Your payment is there."

Charlie did not bother acknowledging Grocer Pawlak as he inched toward Buck and carefully took his arm. He hoped his touch would not cause another outburst and luckily, Buck did not flinch.

"Charlie?" mumbled Bartholomew, his ribcage simmering with panic. He had a sudden urge to unburden himself, to tell Charlie everything.

"It's all right Buck, it's just me." Charlie pulled Buck closer to his side and wrapped an arm around him.

"Can we leave now?" muttered Bartholomew, not particularly fond of the exposure.

"Sure Buck, we can go," said Charlie, as he escorted him to the back of the store.

Charlie opened the back door to the alley and helped Buck down the weathered stairs. The screen door creaked then slammed shut behind them. Charlie propped Buck against a trash bin near the steps and gave him his space to collect himself. Maybe some time to think might loosen his tongue.

Bartholomew curled into a ball, unable to think or speak. He just stared blankly at the wall in front of him and noticed the bricks were different shades of red, cemented together in a stretcher-bond pattern. Bartholomew broadened his gaze then blinked. He refused to fall back to sleep—he could not risk reawakening in his prison cell again. If it were not for Charlie, he might have been permanently stuck there. Bartholomew turned his head to look at the mortal and watched him put a spoonful of red broth in his mouth.

"Soup's on, Buck," said Charlie.

Bartholomew was not interested in the soup Charlie offered. He was too distracted by the lingering of the other two otherworldly entities in the city. Plus, he was concerned with what Charlie was thinking. The mortal was smart and possessed an uncanny knack for reading others. Bartholomew wondered if he, too, was transparent to him. Either way, he would not be able to hide from his outburst.

Charlie poured the liquid into a tin cup and tried handing it to Buck.

Bartholomew refused with a shake of his head.

"Come on, Buck. Don't be like that, you need to eat something. Rule number eight."

"Charlie, I do not wish to hear any more of your rules," said Bartholomew, his stomach protesting with an uncharacteristic grumble. He pressed a hand against his side.

Charlie sighed, telling himself to keep a level head. Whatever had happened during Buck's forty winks, it had rattled him, and he had not yet recovered from the ordeal. It reminded him of a moment a few months back when Jimmy had fallen asleep during the bottom of the third inning at a Sox game. He had slept through most of game until the top of eighth when Luke Appling hit a home run. Jimmy awoke with a start just as the fans began to cheer and threw a fit. Charlie had tried to calm him down, but he was a complete wreck; whatever he had been dreaming about tortured his awakened eyes. Before the top of the ninth could start, Charlie managed to get Jimmy out of the stadium and went straight to Father Van Lewen. At the church, Charlie and the priest tried to get Jimmy to eat or talk about what had spooked him, but he would not and his tantrum only worsened until he was so exhausted he fell asleep.

Charlie had made the mistake of not being stern with Jimmy

at the time, partly because of his age, but also because he did not want Jimmy to hate him. With Buck, he had no qualms with giving the kid some breathing room, but he would not let him starve himself and took no issues being firm.

"Fine," Charlie countered, "get this through that thick noggin of yours. You don't eat, you die, simple as that."

Bartholomew huffed. "If you insist," he surrendered and took the tin cup. He looked inside at the thick red broth with vibrant chunks of orange, white, green, and yellow. He breathed in the smells—tomato and, if he was not mistaken, parsley. He had never found the sight or smell of mortal food appealing, but the steam from the soup was winning him over. He tried not to show his approval and waited until Charlie was not looking to have a taste.

Charlie, however, kept a watchful eye on Buck, letting him think he was ignoring him, a trick he had used on Jimmy hundreds of times. Charlie cracked a smile as he let the familiar taste tantalize his own taste buds. Minestrone, his favorite, though it was not as good as his mother's plentiful soup.

Bartholomew pressed the warm tin to his lips and let the broth run down his throat. The warmth of it seared the top of his dry esophagus, but it mellowed after the next sip and the next. Oddly enough, it quenched his thirst and was quite unlike anything he had ever tasted. Upon the last sip, he took his finger and lapped up the remaining broth, making sure to capture every bit of flavor. He let out a sigh, sad there was no more left, but also upset he had made such a fuss.

"Charlie," Bartholomew said sheepishly.

"Buck, there's no need," said Charlie, glad he had won Buck over. "I know how I can get sometimes when I haven't eaten for awhile. Sometimes, I can be a downright rascal—it's not very pretty." He smiled, hoping his enthusiasm might lighten Buck's spirits.

Bartholomew returned the gesture and joined Charlie on the steps as he opened a tall glass bottle.

Charlie took a sip. "Would it be too much to ask for you to try some cola?"

"Is it Royal Crown Cola?" asked Bartholomew with interest.

"Indeed it is," said Charlie. "It's not as good as Coca-Cola, but it has a crisp-enough bite to it."

Bartholomew examined the brown liquid inside the clear bottle, watching the bubbles float to the surface as condensation ran down the glass over the yellow-and-red label. On the bottle neck, he read the capital letters spelling ROYAL CROWN. Bartholomew pressed the bottle to his lips and took a swig of the strange drink. The carbonated bubbles tickled his warm throat and he giggled. It was an enjoyable sensation and so he took another sip to experience it again. Bartholomew caught sight of Charlie's large grin as he lowered the bottle and asked him for the meaning of its origin.

"Nothing is amiss, Buck—it's just best to try new things at least once, wouldn't you agree?"

"I suppose you are right," said Bartholomew, giving Charlie the satisfaction of victory.

The two boys laughed together and, for a brief moment, they did not care about anything else but the pleasure of the other's company, both consciously storing the memory for safe-keeping.

Bartholomew gave Charlie the bottle and let him polish it off.

"Ah," sighed Charlie and rose from the steps. He set the bottle in the nearest wooden crate. He turned to retrieve his cup, but he stopped short, for Buck had nicked it and was using his finger to lap up the abandoned broth.

Bartholomew looked at Charlie and pulled his finger from his lips. .

Charlie shook his head.

"What?" asked Bartholomew, feeling foolish. He set the tin cup back on the step and moved away from it, realizing maybe Charlie might have wanted the last of his soup. "Sorry," he said, lowering his chin.

"No harm, Buck," said Charlie, remembering the gesture to be a trademark of Jimmy's. "It's like my cousin would always say, 'waste not a drop.'" He picked up the cups and went inside.

Bartholomew lifted his head when the screen door bounced and he leaned against the brick wall in wait for Charlie. The mention of Jimmy made him feel guilty again. He looked at the red streak of soup caught between his knuckles and wondered why he had not left the last bit alone. He felt wrong about it, as though Jimmy's trait had become his own. Bartholomew curled his fingers into his palm and wiped the streak away on his pant leg. He had no desire to replace Charlie's cousin, and yet, a strange part of him did. There was a longing within him to be loved as Charlie loved his cousin and as the Shepherdess loved the Eden Wanderer. He had never experienced love before, nor had he the mortal trait to mind the lack of the emotion, but ever since that fateful night the Shepherdess died, he secretly harbored a craving to experience the mortal passion. Bartholomew sighed as Charlie entered the alley. For now he would have to stifle such thoughts, knowing he could not open himself to Charlie and must remain as he saw him, a mortal runaway.

"Well, shall we go?" asked Charlie after the screen slammed behind him. He was ready to do anything to keep his mind off the previous day's events.

"What do you have in mind?" asked Bartholomew.

"First, I can show you around Bridgeport some more if you like, and along the way we'll see what we can find to do. There is plenty of the day left, at least half from the looks of it." He double-checked the sky. The sun was directly overhead.

"Sounds splendid to me," said Bartholomew with more cheer, excited to learn more about the city and welcoming the distraction. "Where to first?"

"I thought a walk down Thirty-Fifth through the Central Manufacturing District would be keen. I can show you all the factories there and then we can go by McKinley Park and maybe stop by Herdina's Barbershop for a spell—the usual. And you never know, maybe we'll get into all sorts of trouble along the way." An air of mischief bloomed on Charlie's face. The thought of doing something reckless was a pleasant thought indeed.

Boys Will Be Boys

Charlie showed Bartholomew around the western streets of Bridgeport, taking him as far south as Pershing Avenue and west to McKinley Park. Most of the buildings there were large factories constructed with heavy milled brick and were home to the productions of steel, iron, lumber, crackers, paper products, gum, and various others, but tucked in between the spectacle of modern industry, the boys stumbled across the occasional residential cottage or bungalow. As they traveled down Racine, they stopped to admire the White Eagle Brewing Company, where the smell of hops dominated the air. The left side of the building, mainly one large brick wall with a few small windows near the roof, had an iron staircase that snaked down from the roof to the tops of the curbside windows and a base of limestone. The main section of the building had a more castle-like appeal to it with circular towers on top. At least that was how Bartholomew observed it.

Throughout their walk, Charlie answered an arsenal of Bartholomew's questions, welcoming each one as it progressively numbed his grief.

They walked along the cement sidewalks and through the macadam roadways, passing well-placed fire hydrants, beds of tulips, ornamental lampposts, and finally the wading lagoon in

McKinley Park. Bartholomew did not appreciate the dark water of the lagoon, but he did enjoy watching the ducks and Canadian geese land on the surface. When the boys' feet grew tired, they sat down on a wooden bench beneath the helix-striped barber pole in front of Herdina's Barbershop. They conversed for a time about nothing in particular, until Charlie explained the rules of people watching, a game he and Jimmy often played.

"And what about that one?" Charlie pointed at a man dressed in a brown suit with a green tie around his neck.

"A banker or a lawyer," replied Bartholomew, not sure either answer was correct, but he was not so much playing the game as he was scouting for anyone who could be the Apothecary's breadcrumb.

"Very good, Buck," praised Charlie, impressed at how fast he was catching on. "I'd venture to say a banker only because he's not carrying a briefcase," he added. "Lawyers always carry a briefcase, or so I'm told."

"Oh," said Bartholomew, disappointed more so because the brown-suited man was not it. He had had a strong sense of his character.

"No worries, Buck, you're right to think both. It could have gone either way," encouraged Charlie. "What about the old woman across the street?"

Bartholomew followed Charlie's gaze to a woman wearing a multicolored tweed sweater with burgundy trim on the shoulders. She was also clothed in a lengthy burgundy skirt and brown boots. He studied her mannerisms for a moment, trying to remember all of the descriptions Charlie had rambled through earlier when he was explaining the rules of the game.

"I would say a schoolteacher?"

"Nailed it on the head," said Charlie, as she disappeared into a two-story flat. "What about the one walking out of the drug store?"

Bartholomew studied the lad as he crossed Damen Avenue and headed toward them.

"Um, what did you call those kids that run around?"

"Street urchins," assisted Charlie as the lad caught his eye, recognizing him.

"Yes, a street urchin," said Bartholomew, wondering if this lad could be the mortal Damek.

Charlie shifted on the bench. He knew the lad was anything but a street urchin. "Well, it was a good guess, but…"

"Charlie, ole boy," greeted the lad. He stopped in front of them, stepping underneath the overhang to get out of the sun.

"Afternoon, Felix," acknowledged Charlie, not bothering to stand.

The lad's blotchy face distorted. "And this must be?"

"Buck," blurted Charlie, before the kid could open his mouth. The last thing he needed was for him to come up with a different last name. "You know, you met him yesterday."

"Very good," said Felix, as he fidgeted with the paper bag in his hands.

"What do you want, Felix?" grumbled Charlie. He fixed his beret so he could see the boy's face better.

"Right," the lad pulled his eyes away from Buck to look at Charlie. "Wiktor wishes to see you."

"When?" asked Charlie.

"Now," said Felix, stealing another peek at Buck.

Charlie noticed and snapped his fingers. "What is this about?" he asked.

"Nothing of any real concern," shrugged Felix.

"Then I guess it will have to wait."

"But…" insisted Felix, realizing his blunder. His curiosity made the request less urgent. Wiktor would not be pleased.

"Like you said, Felix, the matter is of no great concern and if he wishes to meet with me, I will do so in my own good time. Now, as you can see I am occupied at the moment."

"But, Charlie, I insist," said Felix, already able to hear Wiktor's voice shouting at him for his failure.

In days past, Charlie would have gone straight away, but he was at no one's beck and call. Not anymore. He was not stupid. He knew what Wiktor wished to see him about and he was not willing to let the brute get his hooks into Buck just to get to him.

"Charlie, Wiktor won't be happy about this." Felix tried to sound threatening, but his nerves got the better of him.

"Felix, as I said, I'll meet with him later," said Charlie, rising from the bench. "Just not today."

Felix eyed Charlie, and then Buck, and then Charlie again. He gave a passive nod and without another word proceeded to the park.

Charlie kept an eye on Wiktor's errand boy for a few blocks until he was far enough away. He sat back on the bench and picked up right where he and Buck left off.

"The answer is no, Buck."

"But I did not say anything."

"I know, but the answer is still no," said Charlie. His eyes inspected the street further for anymore of Wiktor's guys. His instincts told him they were being watched, but he could not find another familiar face.

"No to what?" asked Bartholomew.

"Felix."

"What about him?" Bartholomew looked after the lad, a little despondent about another failed guess.

"He's not a street urchin," replied Charlie, double-checking the street for any of Kalvis' goons as well.

"Then what is he?"

"One of Wiktor's runners, a messenger, if you will," said Charlie. He looked up the street towards the river.

"Charlie?" said Bartholomew, rethinking his question.

"Hmm…"

"Has Wiktor always been like he is?"

Charlie turned back to Buck, shifting his weight on the bench, and raised his eyebrows. "Why do you ask?"

"Oh, no reason," said Bartholomew. "Call it mild curiosity, I guess."

Charlie prepared to answer, but waited to prevent eavesdropping as an elderly man departed from the barbershop. "Well, as you know," he began, "I have not known Wiktor that long, but from what I've gathered, even before the deaths of his father and older brother, he was always a little terror. According to his mother, Wiktor has always relied on his physical strength, which I'm sure is partly due to his lack of smarts. You know, brawn over brains."

"Then he has always been a brute," said Bartholomew.

Charlie confirmed with a nod and glanced up the street, his eyes ever intent.

"What about Kalvis?" inquired Bartholomew.

"Kalvis, though the youngest of five sons, was not involved in the family business for years. Rumor has it his mother didn't want him in the gang and tried to prepare him for university instead. Kalvis' attractive features and proper etiquette made him a sure fit for such a life, but his downfall was that he couldn't turn a blind eye." Charlie paused to watch a young woman walk north towards the river, her peach day dress with hibiscus print flouncing in the wind. From the back, it was hard to tell, but

Charlie had a suspicion he knew her, the woman's physique similar to Hanna, the assistant caretaker of the orphanage.

"Charlie?" said Bartholomew.

"As I was saying," Charlie resumed, giving Buck his attention again. "On his way home from studies one day, Kalvis spotted the former leader of the Morgan Street Lithuanians roughing up some dame. Being a gentleman, Kalvis intervened and beat the bloke within an inch of his life. After that Kalvis was looked at as a champion of the neighborhood and, much to his mother's dismay, was given the reins as acting leader."

"But that does not account for his sheep's clothing routine," said Bartholomew, catching sight of the girl in the peach dress as well.

"No, it doesn't," said Charlie, continuing. "But tricksters are made, Buck. Sure, you can make a brute as well, but a trickster has craft, a calculating mind, and a ruthless spirit far more sadistic than a brute. For such a talent to exist it takes time and tutelage. The gang life corrupted what might have been a great man."

Bartholomew agreed, but did not say it out loud, his mind distracted by thoughts about the Eden Wanderer, Stingy Jack, and he wondered what man he might have become had Hades not twisted him. His mind failed miserably to conjure a plausible answer, and concluded that without his twistedness, Stingy Jack would never have crossed paths with the Shepherdess.

By mid-afternoon, Charlie and Buck grew tired of playing their game and moved onto listening to the chatter inside the barbershop. Mr. Herdina had propped the door open and had offered the boys each a glass of water. Charlie chugged the cool liquid down without a second thought. Mr. Herdina chuckled at Charlie's thirst and offered him another. Bartholomew, though thirsty, had merely taken a few sips, his eyes too busy judging the old barber. He took the opportunity to test the man, shaking his hand when Charlie introduced him, but like all the others, Mr. Herdina did not fit the bill.

The smell of shaving cream and shoe polish mingled with the warm air on the street. The men's voices inside carried on about the news of a pending strike in Minneapolis. Several of the men disapproved, while others took the opposite side. Charlie sensed a fight coming on, but Mr. Herdina craftily steered the conversation to talk about the eerie weather, a topic the men were more than willing to discuss.

"Okay, Buck," said Charlie, breaking the silence between them. "Now, I want you to listen to the men inside. Listen to the words they use, how they talk. It'll be a good way for you to try to break some of those proper habits of yours."

Bartholomew did as Charlie instructed, despite the ridiculousness of the idea, partly because he knew it would not work. Then again, maybe his adaptation skill could be useful; it would not hurt to try. Bartholomew listened as the men changed topics again, discussing the approach of the Black Blizzard. Their tones were filled with worry that the ash would strangle the city and last as long as it had over the Great Plains.

Mr. Herdina's baritone voice put the men at ease. "The serpent will have his day, gentlemen, by Jove he'll have his day—but if we are to lose hope now, then the Devil wins."

The men mumbled in agreement before moving onto lighter conversation, their jubilant chatter about baseball. At one point, an argument broke out about which team was better, the Cubs or the Sox. Mr. Herdina settled the matter by asking the men how good the pitching looked this season. Everyone was in agreement that Luke Appling was by far the best.

"So, Buck, what do you think about baseball?" asked Charlie after a while.

"Um, it's a great game," said Bartholomew, repeating the exact words one of the men had said earlier in the discussion.

"The greatest," said Charlie, pleased to hear Buck's tone was not so proper. "Are you a Cubs fan or a Sox fan?"

"Cubs," Bartholomew answered, simply because he liked the sound of the word better.

"Really? I'm a Sox fan myself, so was my pa and Uncle Gert. I mean, when your old man tells you stories about his idol, how can you not fall in love?" A glimmer of pride sparked in Charlie's eyes as he recalled the stories his father had told him before bed when he was younger.

"Who was your father's idol?"

"Shoeless Joe Jackson—he was one of the greatest players that ever lived and don't let no one tell you otherwise. It's not fair what happened to him. Even after the trial, my pa wouldn't believe the accusations against him."

"Trial?" asked Bartholomew, his stomach churning, the Tales Teller's melodious voice whispering a warning. *The trial of the Shepherdess will commence six Eden days hence.*

"Yeah, the Black Sox trial," said Charlie, noticing the kid's discontent, apparent he had struck a nerve. "So, what's your favorite position?"

"What's yours?" asked Bartholomew, wishing he knew everything there was to know about baseball.

"I'm a pitcher myself," gloated Charlie, his voice cocky. He jumped off the bench and got into his signature-pitching stance. "I've been known to throw a mean curve ball. My older brother, Wendell, hated me for it, on account of the fact I always struck him out."

Charlie wound up and threw an imaginary ball down the block, his arm almost hitting one of Mr. Herdina's customers in the face. "Sorry, sir," he said, standing straight.

The man sniffed, not accepting Charlie's apology, and walked on.

Charlie wiped the back of his hand across his forehead and looked back at Buck. "You ever pitch?"

Bartholomew began to fidget with his fingers, a tick Charlie was finding irksome.

Charlie's enthusiasm faded, realizing Buck had simply been playing along. "You've never played the game before, have you?"

"No," said Bartholomew in a low voice.

"Don't fret, Buck," said Charlie, trying not to sound disheartened. He should have been more careful not to get himself wrapped up in their easy rapport. In some ways Buck was just like any other kid, but then he was reminded of all the questions that still had no answers. Buck had not said it, but he knew something terrible had happened to him. The kid was broken, and though he tried to hide it, it was clear he could not piece himself together, not entirely. None of that mattered though, because with each passing minute, Buck became more familiar to him, as though they had known each other for years. The thought of their expedient bond alarmed Charlie and he was hesitant to get any closer, but nothing could be done about it now.

Charlie put a hand on his hip as his stomach growled, his biological clock telling him it was time for dinner. Typically, he and Jimmy would return to Rations Market for a box of Cracker Jacks or some pretzels before returning to the orphanage for a meal of watered down soup and stale bread. With no orphanage to return to, Charlie wondered if he would be able to work for a proper meal. Again, he was not keen on the idea of taking Buck back to the grocer's store, but hunger in his belly trumped his reservations.

"Well then, are you ready to go?" asked Charlie.

"Where?" asked Bartholomew.

"Back to Grocer Pawlak's."

"But is he not upset with us? I mean, I did make a scene in his store and he did not seem at all pleased."

"Oh, it'll be all right, Buck. There won't be any customers in the store by the time we get there. Besides, we can help restock the shelves and earn ourselves some dinner. And then we can get a good night's sleep," said Charlie, uncertain exactly where they would be holing up for the night.

"I suppose," Bartholomew shrugged, hoisting himself off the bench. "But are you sure Grocer Pawlak will let me come back?"

Charlie waved at Mr. Herdina and thanked him for his generosity before addressing Buck. "Like I said," he replied, taking the kid under his wing again, "just let me do all the talkin'."

Scarlet Phœnix

The air was already thick by the time Charlie and Bartholomew crossed the Thirty-Fifth Street Bridge, leaving the steady hum of the factories behind them. The wind's gusts became more malicious, creating a spine-chilling feel about the city. The street was unusually quiet for the early evening. No vehicles moved along the road and every stretch of concrete was absent of life. Everyone was already indoors in preparation for the coming storm.

Bartholomew ignored the seeding instinct to run and hide with the rest of the mortals, and remained vigilant for any sign of Hades or one of his many agents. The breeze nipped at his face while a phantom voice penetrated deep into his ears, the sound tickling his eardrums. At first he thought it was a whistle, but found it to be a low registering hiss, the unfamiliar sound piggybacking on the wind. Bartholomew stopped just across the bridge in front of the entrance to the Albert Pick and Company building. Bartholomew's stomach fluttered nervously as he tried to discover the originating direction of the sound. He suspected Hades was close, too close, and that at any moment, the Scarlet Phoenix would spring forth from some unforeseen hiding place. His fear rose, but not for himself, more for Charlie. He knew he had to stay with the mortal, as the Apothecary, the Chameleon and the Tales Teller had told him, but he could not help the feeling that he was putting Charlie in danger.

The wind tossed the reverberating sound and created a disorienting tornado, spinning Bartholomew in every direction.

"Buck, what's the matter?" asked Charlie, retracing his steps.

"Charlie, do you hear that?" Bartholomew asked.

"What?" asked Charlie, looking about as though to discover something specific. "I hear the grinding factories, the freight trucks, trains on the switch tracks, not to mention the…"

"Shh, just listen," said Bartholomew, giving Charlie another moment. "Can you hear it?"

"Buck, if you're hearing things, I swear…" said Charlie, unwilling to add "crazy" to the list of unusual traits.

"No, just listen," said Bartholomew. "I promise I am not hearing things. It is very faint. I think we may be too far from it."

Charlie stilled, ignoring the protest in his gut, and closed his eyes. He drowned out all the distractions around him, having taken little notice to the vacancy of their surroundings. The distinct city sounds faded and he released a breath of concentration. The breeze picked up again and blew past the strands of his hair peeking out from underneath his beret, and with it came Buck's phantom sound.

"A reed," said Charlie, familiar with the instrument.

"A reed? I do not think a plant can make that sound," said Bartholomew.

"No, not a *reed*, Buck, a reed. It's one of many chambers on a harmonica," said Charlie. He tried to catch the sound again, but the wind lulled. Charlie headed back towards the street corner, meeting a fresh breeze from the north and with it the sound beckoned him to follow. At first, his feet hesitated, but his mind forced them to move.

"Charlie, wait!" shouted Bartholomew and ran up Racine Street after him, but could not keep up with his gait. "Charlie!"

Charlie paused midway up the fourth block and rotated in a circle in search of the sound. He caught sight of Buck running towards him, but paid him no heed. Another blast spiraled around him, forcing his balance to shift. The harmonica was only a little further, and though he wanted to go on ahead, he fought the impulse and waited for Buck to catch up.

Bartholomew doubled over in front of Charlie and gripped his knees.

"Are you square?" asked Charlie.

"No," panted Bartholomew. He stood up and placed his hands on his hips. He waited a second to get his bearings before speaking, his ears catching the sound of distinct notes, "Music?"

"Of course it's music. What did you think it was?"

Bartholomew shrugged. He had not thought of anything in particular, just that it was unfamiliar.

"Don't you know what a harmonica is?" asked Charlie.

"I have never seen one before," admitted Bartholomew, his attention diverted to a woman closing her windows and drawing thick curtains.

Charlie sighed. He was growing tired of explaining everyday things.

"A harmonica, or blues harp as I've heard some people call it, is an instrument, Buck. You know what that is, right?"

"Of course," said Bartholomew, oblivious to Charlie's sarcasm.

They stood and listened for a while, the melody growing more baleful in tone. Each note plucked away at Charlie's subconscious, bringing forth a desire to face the harmonica's master. Charlie knew that meant the musician, and yet, he somehow understood there was more to it. A soft voice spoke in the recesses of his mind, reciting the same words over and over and over again. He could not make sense of the words, but its cadence matched the haunting melody in the air. In his heart, he felt a compulsion to go into battle, though what kind and who with were unclear to him. All he knew was that he needed to find the music's point of origin.

"Come on Buck," said Charlie. He threw his arm around the kid.

"But—" protested Bartholomew, unable to object to the tug of Charlie's stride.

Bartholomew tried to exude confidence, but every fiber of his being was warning him that danger was near. He wanted to be as strong as he knew he could be, as he used to be, but seeing the hefty crowd of mortals standing across the street as they approached brought out the coward in him. He selfishly did not want to discover what he feared might be waiting for them. That the player Charlie was eager to face was yet another reminder of his old life, one he had no defense against.

Charlie let go of Buck and crossed the street alone. Every inch of his skin was captivated by the minor notes and malicious cadence therein, creating goosebumps—the spell of the Tales Teller, causing an unknown and unexpected side effect. Without being fully aware, he had no concerns about the true character of the musician even though what laid beyond the sea of onlookers was an archetype of trickery. He waited on the outer edge of the massive crowd, their empty expressions giving him pause. If it were not for the slow rise of their chests, Charlie might have thought them statues. The haunting notes floated about the street, their Piped Piper melody charming each mind in the crowd into a vapid shell. A shiver caressed Charlie's skin as the air became weighted by an invisible fog. He felt the allure trying to win him over, to control him, but the hypnotic notes had no effect on him.

Charlie forced a gulp, the impulse to continue something he could not fight. He rolled back his shoulders and shook out his arms as if preparing for a physical altercation, and stepped into the crowd.

Bartholomew made his way through the crowd shortly after Charlie, and struggled as he maneuvered around the practically cemented mortals. "Charlie!" he shouted, having lost sight of him. He dropped to the ground for an alternative line of sight and saw Charlie standing in the inner circle, watching a man sitting beneath the curved branch of the lamppost. Bartholomew studied the musician, his body hunched over, dressed in an unhemmed black suit. His bony elbows rested on his knees, his hands lost underneath the curtain of his long jet-black hair. Bartholomew closed his eyes. He did not want to believe them, wishing his intuition was wrong, but he felt a rapture of terror blast against the eerie spell of the harmonica, as though every mortal transfixed in the circle was screaming, trying to make it stop. Bartholomew scrambled to his feet. He pushed with all his might and when he had the ability to grab Charlie, he pulled him back into the confines of the crowd.

"Charlie, we should not be here," said Bartholomew.

"What? Nonsense," said Charlie.

Bartholomew searched Charlie's eyes, half-expecting them to be glazed, taken over by the musician's influence. To his surprise, however, Charlie was attentive—*impossible.*

"Buck, I'll be fine," said Charlie. "Trust me. I know what I'm doing. I'll deal with this trickster."

"How?" said Bartholomew, astounded by Charlie's acuteness. "How do you know he's a trickster?"

"I..." Charlie paused and scrutinized the man sitting underneath the lamppost, before panning to the mob surrounding them.

"Buck, what's going on?"

"All will be well," said Bartholomew. He took Charlie by the wrist with half a mind to drag him away kicking and screaming if needed. "Charlie, you do not have to do this. You have nothing to prove here."

The ridge of Charlie's nose crinkled, his subconscious resurging his drive to face the trickster. "Buck, sometimes it's not about being brave or having something to prove, but rather taking the risk because you have nothing to lose."

"But—"

"Buck, let go of my arm," ordered Charlie. The authority in his voice was sharp.

Bartholomew felt Charlie's words emanate a shred of magic, and his fingers loosened their grip. Something was horribly wrong. Mortals did not have the power to command any supernatural creature, and yet, as commanded, he released Charlie. Bartholomew stood baffled. Clearly, Charlie was not bewitched like the other mortals surrounding them, but there was something off about him. He judged his demeanor, discovering the speck of silver streak deep in his eyes. Bartholomew held in a gasp, realizing it was the Tales Teller's spell.

"All right then," said Charlie. "I won't be long, just wait here."

Bartholomew attempted to grab Charlie again, but he could not muster the strength to do so. Panic set in, his mind trying to reconcile his dilemma—*this should not be happening.* Bartholomew shifted his body and stood on his tiptoes. He would just have to trust in Charlie and that whatever was happening to him was strong enough to keep him safe.

The mysterious man finished playing his tune to the welcome sound of stark applause, lacking any fervor. He lifted his head, his hair falling away from his face, revealing pallid skin. He lowered his bony fingers from his mouth, a smirk replacing the object in his hands.

Bartholomew saw the red glow in the man's eyes as he stared curiously at Charlie. He fell back on his heels and tried again to move. His body, however, would not respond. Bartholomew sprang to the balls of his feet, then his tiptoes and watched the musician stalk over to Charlie like a predator to prey, his eyes flickering with a hint of mischief.

"Good day," saluted the musician with a hint of charm.

"Good day, sir," said Charlie, concentrating on the musician's face and not his skeletal physique. "If I may be so bold," he added.

"By all means, please," invited the showman before giving a courteous bow.

The hiss in the musician's voice irritated Charlie, sending a warning tremor down his spine. The man's demeanor reminded him a great deal of Old Hob, a devilish character in one of his mother's stories. Inside he was terrified, and he could feel every muscle in his body tremble. He was concerned he appeared to be having a fit, however, his feet remained stationary. His outward appearance was composed and unmoved by the musician's intimidation.

"Please," said Charlie, his impulse molding to his character. He held out his hand to sway the musician from his formal display. "I am no gentleman, sir. There is no need for such pleasantries."

"Ah, but young master, to be party to such pleasantries is the nature of my business and, as such, I stand by them." The musician bowed again, his long black hair cloaking his shoulders.

"I'm sorry if I've offended you," said Charlie, returning the gesture in kind. His intuition was encumbered with instructions on how to play the game, although, what game he was playing was vague.

"Not at all," said the showman, straightening his black tie. "Now, your question, young master?"

Charlie glanced down at his fingers, making it appear he had suddenly lost confidence, and began to fidget. "Please sir," he said, his voice muffled, "can you tell me how you can make those sounds with your harmonica? I have never heard the like before." Charlie brought his head back up and saw the crooked grin below sharp cheekbones on the showman's face. He wanted to smile himself, however, he would lose his innocent appeal if he did.

"Ah, a lad of music," sang the showman. "Do you play, young master?"

"Me, a dabbler mostly," said Charlie, keeping his answer modest.

"Marvelous," said the showman. "Then you must play for me and my audience."

"What? Oh no, not I, sir, I couldn't," said Charlie.

Bartholomew felt as though he was about to go mad. He had to do something before Charlie found himself caught in a wager he could not avoid.

"Please, I insist," said the showman.

Charlie heard the light persuasive tone in the musician's voice, but did not give in to it.

"Ladies and gentlemen, give the lad some encouragement," said the showman. He raised his lengthy arms into the air to rouse his audience.

The crowd came to life, bursting into a roar of cheers and claps, but their faces remained vacant.

"Sure, why not?" said Charlie with a nonchalant shrug.

No—Bartholomew strained every muscle, pushing all his energy into his feet.

"You see, my fine audience, now here is a lad who is not afraid to rise to a challenge. What is your name, young master, so that all may know you?"

"Charlie."

"Charlie, well then." The showman lifted his arms again to showcase his latest volunteer. "My fine audience, I give you Charlie!"

The crowd responded with great applause, although it was empty of any true excitement.

"Stop!" shouted Bartholomew, finding his voice. The mortals parted around him to reveal his hiding place.

"Buck, what's wrong?" asked Charlie, suspending a subdued version of a reckless Mr. Hyde.

"Charlie, we…" Bartholomew glanced over at the showman, meeting his red eyes. His heart skipped a beat as an unpleasant sense of fear suffocated him. His body began to shake and, unlike Charlie, his was outwardly visible. How was Charlie able to stay so composed?

"Greetings, young squire," mocked the showman, changing his demeanor.

"I am no squire," said Bartholomew, taking the greeting as an insult.

"We shall see," hissed the showman, a wide crescent forming with his pale lips.

Bartholomew turned away and forced a pleading expression upon his face. "Charlie, please do not do this."

"Not now, Buck," said Charlie under his breath.

"Charlie, please."

"Buck, be still," ordered Charlie.

Bartholomew tried to object, but his mouth would not open. He tried to move his arms, but again they refused his command. He was frozen. Bartholomew glanced at the showman, whose eyes danced with curiosity. Bartholomew knew that look. The villain wanted to study his new opponent.

"Now, as I was saying, young master Charlie, before I was so rudely interrupted…" The musician pulled out a rectangular object from his pocket and placed it in his hands. "This here is no ordinary harmonica; in fact, it is one of a kind." The musician displayed the harmonica to the audience and then handed it to Charlie.

Charlie examined the beautiful instrument in his palm, the weight of it uncharacteristically heavy. It was made of glossy cherry wood with a polished silver mouthpiece. A winged creature was engraved on the side, its wings engulfed in flame.

Bartholomew did his best to catch a glimpse of the small instrument as Charlie handled it and was not surprised to see the crest of the Scarlet Phoenix.

"What say you, Charlie?" said the showman. "Will you play for us?"

Without a single conscious thought, Charlie pressed the harmonica to his lips. The polished silver was warmer than he anticipated. He pushed air through the mouthpiece, expecting seamless music. Instead, the notes came out muffled and pitchy, nothing even close to the genius the musician had played. Charlie breathed again, but the same screechy notes came from the harmonica.

Charlie's cheeks flushed as the crowd's taunts irritated him and frustration clouded his reason. He turned over the harmonica as though it might reveal its secret—no such luck.

"You win, Buck, let's go," he said, maintaining a low voice in order to verbalize his humiliation, setting the stage for another round.

Bartholomew felt his body relax. He gave Charlie a small, sympathetic smile and turned to make his way out of the circle. The mortals, however, scrunched together in protest.

"Wait, young master!" said the showman, subduing the laughter.

Bartholomew's heart sank. They were trapped and the only way out was to play the Devil's game. He moved closer to Charlie's side.

"One more try," tempted the showman. "One more try, and this time if you can play my harmonica, I shall give it to you."

"What's the catch?" asked Charlie, his voice weighted by an uncharacteristic timbre.

"A clever lad," said the showman, tapping a finger along the point of his nose. "I require only one thing if you should lose." The showman paused for dramatic affect and placed his bony hand on Charlie's shoulder. "Your soul."

Charlie felt a burning sensation sear his skin, penetrating the marrow of his bone as though the showman had placed a hot iron on his shoulder. It paralyzed him for a moment, but he managed to roll his shoulder back, unable to stem a grimace from distorting his face.

"Charlie." Bartholomew put a hand on Charlie's arm, examining his shoulder, and felt the heat radiate through the fabric of his shirt.

"So, young master, do we have an accord?" asked the showman.

Charlie's stomach curdled, his ribcage radiating like an oven. Every ounce of him was telling him to walk away. He heard his own voice shouting at him in his head, but no matter how much he tried to convince himself of the danger, his heart failed to see reason.

"Very well," he agreed, "let the wager stand."

The crowd exploded as the showman moseyed around the circle, coaxing them to cheer even louder. With the villain distracted, Bartholomew turned to Charlie and took the opportunity to whisper into his ear, hoping his assistance might make the difference.

"The only way to win is to surrender," he said.

Charlie stared down at the harmonica, his thoughts mulling over Buck's words. On the surface it was not good advice. Surrendering to the trickster would not help him solve this puzzle. On the other hand, maybe it was not the trickster he needed to surrender to; maybe it was the instrument. Charlie ran his thumb across the crest of the fiery bird, recalling something his mother had once told him about playing the piano. *Anyone can play the piano, Charlie, and play it well, but to be great, to truly be a master, one must understand the partnership. Together a musician and the piano make music. Together they bind their souls of mortal breath and resonating tone. To feel is to master release, to cage one's emotion is to restrain—never restrain, for the piano will never trust you. Be honest, surrender, and above all hold nothing back.*

Charlie placed the warm silver to his lips and blew ever so lightly. The first few notes came out low and soft, but they were not screechy or pitched. They were rich and pleasant. Charlie built his confidence, much like the melody he was playing, the notes growing louder and stronger. The tune became more somber and personal as Charlie pushed every ounce of self into the music, stealing the audience away from the showman's power.

Bartholomew observed the showman's face as it grew livid, a fury rising from deep within him. His eyes ignited, his face tightened and his teeth clenched. Bartholomew left Charlie's side and took his place once again in front of him in order to confront his greatest adversary.

"He has tricked the trickster, Hades, now leave him be."

The showman brought down his pointed chin, the song

of the harmonica fading and time itself came to a pause. "Ah, Bartholomew," he said, assessing the Breedling.

Bartholomew's heartbeat pulsed in his neck, causing him to twitch, the sound of his name paralyzing him.

"My demons have been reporting whispers of your escape," said Hades. "I, of course, punished them for such blasphemy, but I guess I owe them praise, for here you are—the coincidence of meeting like this is uncanny, no? Still searching for the Eden Wanderer?"

"Do not concern yourself with my affairs," said Bartholomew.

"Oh, but I do, Master Breedling, your affairs concern me greatly," said Hades. "After all, you know where my siblings are hiding."

"And hidden they shall remain. I will never tell you the whereabouts of the Golden Faun or the Black Tortoise," said Bartholomew. He pursed his lips. He had given away too much. He did his best to conceal his blunder, for he could not afford to have Hades trick him into sharing his secret. He knew better than to manipulate his expression, so he diverted the conversation. "The mortal has beaten you, Hades. Now, let us go. We will not interfere further in your dealings."

"I think not, Master Breedling," said the showman. "Pity too, since he has no means to protect himself. The mortal veil can be such a tricky burden. And yet, he did manage to best me, without an ounce of knowledge of who I am. One might call it dumb luck, but this mortal reminds me a great deal of my rival Stingy Jack. Yes, I have decided, Master Breedling, your mortal friend intrigues me and I would delight in the pleasure of possessing his soul."

"Leave him alone," said Bartholomew.

"Then tell me what I wish to know," said Hades. He bent at the waist to meet the Breedling's face.

"No."

"Then you leave me no choice, Bartholomew."

"Do not call me that! My name is Buck," said Bartholomew, embracing the name Charlie had given him. The sound of it floated off his tongue with a new spark of life, one much stronger than the weight of his given name.

"How quaint, the squire has been given a new name," said Hades, waving off the emotional fanfare. "Do not speak to me of names, Bartholomew, I know who you are."

"You know nothing about me," said Buck, losing ground in the argument. "Now, you leave Charlie out of this!"

"Ah," said Hades, raising a bony finger. "I am afraid it is too late for that, Master Breedling, the mortal now bears my mark, and a spark of my flame resides in him. Why with a snap of my fingers I could ignite his whole body with a fury that would bring him to his knees screaming. So you see, you have involved him more than I am sure you intended." Hades stood tall, his height dwarfing Buck. "Heed my words, Breedling," he threatened, "the veil that protects young Charlie will thin, in fact it already has, and soon, very soon, he will see you for what you truly are and his soul will conveniently be mine."

A foreboding quiver traversed along Buck's spine. *No more*, he breathed and presented a slight bow before retrieving Charlie, forcing him to stop his melody.

"See how easy it was for the young lad," said the showman, bringing time back to life. "Now, who else would like to give it a whirl?"

The hypnotized mortals shouted with eagerness as Buck crossed the street, Charlie stumbling behind.

"Poor fools," said Bartholomew, ignoring Charlie's attempts to break free of his hold. He knew they were not to blame for falling victim to the charm of Hades. After all, the Master of Hell had played a significant role in the creation of mortals. In fact, Buck could only think of two mortals in the history of Eden capable of resisting the full extent of Hades' magic: Stingy Jack and Charles Reese.

Qualms

"Buck, Buck."

Nearing the corner of Thirty-Fifth and Racine, Buck still ignored Charlie's attempts at conversation. He continued to drag Charlie along until at last he could no longer hear the hypnotic sound of Hades' harmonica, the minor notes giving way to the droning and bustling sounds of the city. Buck kept his eyes vigilant for any sign Hades was having them followed, his thoughts plagued by the Master of Hell's taunts.

Charlie squirmed again, this time ripping his arm away from Buck's unusually strong grasp.

Buck stopped, less ready for this confrontation than the one he had just had.

"Buck, what's your deal?" asked Charlie, rubbing his arm as a truck pulled out of the Albert Pick and Company parking lot.

"My deal?" said Buck, turning to Charlie.

"Yes, your deal," said Charlie, his true demeanor returning, the impulse of the Tales Teller's spell subsiding. He was tired of playing this game and he unbridled his peeved disposition. He wanted answers and would not stop until he got them.

Buck turned away.

"Buck, don't you turn away from me," said Charlie. "You owe me an explanation."

Buck hesitated as an uncomfortable level of apprehension rushed through him. He could not tell if it was from the fire in Charlie's tongue or if it was from the sheer probability that he would have to tell him the truth. Buck exhaled to build up his nerve then looked back at Charlie, whose expression radiated ferocity, although, much to his credit, he was trying to hold it back.

"This should not have happened," said Buck, realizing after the fact it was the wrong way to start the conversation.

"What do you mean this shouldn't have happen?" asked Charlie, his mind unraveling into a state of madness.

Buck bit his lower lip. "I tried telling you," he redirected, "but you would not listen."

Charlie crossed his arms. "So, what, you're telling me you know that performer?"

"The man is no showman, Charlie, and I think you know that," said Buck.

"Tell me," said Charlie, unable to admit it to himself. "I want you to say it."

Buck opened his mouth, but the words would not come out. He turned and ran across the street.

"Buck!"

Buck ignored Charlie. He needed a moment to think, to come up with some sort of plan. He had been able to dodge most of Charlie's questions thus far. This time, however, he would not be able to change the subject or talk his way out. Buck dug his fingernails into his palms. He should have known better. He should never have let Charlie set foot inside Hades' trap. Why did the Tales Teller have to do that spell? But more importantly, what went wrong? She had said no harm would come to him, and now, things would never be the same for Charlie. Hades would see to it and use him the same way Kalvis used Jimmy, in order to force his hand and reveal the whereabouts of his siblings.

"By the powers," he swore, frustrated by his predicament. Everything was becoming progressively more complicated and he felt overwhelmed by it all. What was he to do?

Charlie caught up to Buck, just as he disappeared into a nook on the other side of the refinery, the John Magnus clock tower counting the eight o'clock hour. He rolled his sleeves to his elbows, ready to beat the words out of the kid if necessary, his temper demanding nothing less than a match of fisticuffs or at the very least a verbal outburst.

"Charlie," said Buck, unwilling to look him square in the face. "I know you are displeased."

"Angry would be the word I'd use," said Charlie. He balled his fists and hid them in his elbows.

"As you say," said Buck. "I know you are angry with me, and maybe you have every right to be."

"You're damn right," said Charlie with venom in his tone, dropping his fists at his sides.

"Charlie, believe me, sometimes things are better left unsaid—better not knowing."

Charlie burst into laughter as every preconception of not wanting to get involved in Buck's affairs melted away. "If you think that will satisfy my temper or my curiosity, you're sorely mistaken."

"Charlie, trust me," said Buck. "Trust that by not telling you anything, I am protecting you."

"Protecting me from what? And trust you?" Charlie unclenched his fists. "What in all of creation have you done that would make you believe I can trust you? There has been nothing, and I repeat nothing, but half-truths coming out of that mouth of yours since we met. And sure, I let it slide because we went through hell, but I'm not going to let you bury this one. Not this time."

"Charlie, please, I do not want to fight you," said Buck. He needed Charlie to let this go.

"Whoa, now you want to be the bigger man? Protect me from the big bad truth, ay," mocked Charlie, Buck's stalling fueling his determination to know every detail. "Well, let me tell you something, buddy," he added, poking Buck in the chest. "I don't need you to protect me."

"Well, someone has to!" shouted Buck and pushed Charlie away from him.

Charlie stumbled back, shell-shocked. He clasped his hands behind his back in an attempt to keep his uncharacteristic desire to punch Buck under control. He tried counting to three, like his mother had taught him, but everything inside of him was on fire, all fueled by the searing pulse in his shoulder. It was hard for him to articulate to himself how he felt, only that what he was experiencing was not like him. It was as though someone had hijacked his body, the wordless voice returning, a surge of hatred coursing through him. Charlie locked his fingers together to channel his attention on reason. He took a reluctant step back in order to clear his head, his instincts still trying to convince him Buck was untrustworthy.

"Maybe you're right, Buck," said Charlie, lowering his voice. "Maybe it is best not to know. Maybe grief has driven me mad—the thing is, Buck, a lad's got to know who has his back. And frankly, you haven't been so forthcoming."

"Charlie…"

"No, no, let me finish." Charlie held out a hand to silence Buck. "You see Buck, I know nothing about you," he continued, his tone smoothing to the point of imitating Hades. "Well, save for a few queer things here and there, and I think I've been keen on giving you some time to process what has happened. But now, after this, I can't. I can't just let this one be square. I need to know. I need to know who's got my back."

"Charlie, please do not ask this of me," said Buck.

Charlie softly ground his teeth and linked his hands behind his back again.

"Charlie, try to understand," Buck continued. "To tell you the truth about me, about what happened, about him—I just cannot bring myself to put you in that sort of danger."

"Danger? I'm already in danger!" yelled Charlie, losing his head. He advanced toward Buck again and grabbed him by the arms. "I nearly lost my soul over a harmonica. And instead of dragging me away kicking and screaming, you told me to surrender, to that, that charlatan. Just saying that aloud sounds crazy."

"You are not crazy," said Buck, too cavalier. He tightened his lips.

"Fine," said Charlie in low spirits. He threw, his hands in the air when it was clear yelling was not going to help him get his way. He needed something more drastic. "If that is the way you feel. If you can't trust me, then I suppose this is where I will say my farewell."

"Charlie, wait," objected Buck.

"No Buck, if I can't rely on you to be straight with me, it's just as bad as you not being able to keep your word. Goodbye, Buck."

Charlie headed towards the street, counting his steps, each one stripping away mountains of responsibility from his shoulders. The sensation was more liberating than he thought possible, but as he drew closer to freedom, his steps became bittersweet. A gray cloud of guilt descended upon him and he hated himself for backing Buck against the ropes. This was not him and he finally started to realize just how fractured he was inside.

Buck's heart leapt into his throat. He stood at a crossroads and though he had been warned about keeping Charlie in the dark, the young mortal's enlightenment was unfolding just by pure association. Buck clawed at his pants, his thoughts indecisive. He did not want to be responsible for awakening Charlie, for to do so would seal his fate. Enlightened souls were a rare commodity, hunted not just by Hades, but also by the agents of Heaven and Euxinus. And Hades already had a head start branding Charlie's soul with his mark. On the other hand, to deny Charlie the knowledge to understand his vastly expanding world would leave him defenseless. Still, a part of him wanted Charlie to walk away and disappear.

"Charlie, stop!" Buck shouted.

Charlie rocked back on his heel and turned into the alley. "Are you going to tell me the truth?" he asked, giving Buck one last chance.

"Just so we are clear, Charlie, as I want no misgivings, I did warn you," said Buck.

"Yes, yes, you warned me. Now, stop stalling and out with it," said Charlie.

"The Devil," said Buck. "You would call the showman the Devil, though he goes by many names. Where I come from he is known as Flame, the Scarlet Phoenix, Hades."

"Hades," said Charlie, unfazed by the name. "You mean the Grecian Lord of the Underworld?"

"If that is what you need to equivocate the Master of Hell's existence, then yes," said Buck.

Charlie felt the blood drain from his face, his heart beating erratically against his ribs. "What are you?" he asked, braving the question.

"What I am is not something you can yet comprehend," said Buck, "but I will try my best to explain." He paused, prepared to ignore his standing orders to maintain Charlie's ignorance. "When I told you I did not have parents, I was not lying. I came from a world ruled by an impartial, heartless trio. This trinity, my former masters, referred to those of my race as Breedlings, mortal-like creatures, as you see; soulcatchers, created for the sole purpose to ferry mortal souls to what you would call the afterlife."

Buck paused again, to allow Charlie the opportunity to process what he was saying. It felt strange telling the mortal about himself, although in a way it was equal parts cathartic. It did not mean he was ready to tell his whole story, but it was a start. He watched Charlie, the mortal's thoughts forming in the creases of his brow. There was a question he wanted to ask, and though Buck was prepared to answer, Charlie was not ready for the question.

"Can you bring Jimmy back?" asked Charlie.

Buck felt as though Charlie had punched him in the gut. The plea was so innocent and sincere, a question he had never been asked before. Of course he could not bring his cousin back, no soulcatcher could, not really, unless…Buck sabotaged his thoughts. This was not the time to give Charlie false hope. For it was one thing to admit what he was, who Hades was, but it was another to explain the intricacies of how a mortal soul could be granted a reprieve from death. The mere thought of saving Jimmy brought about a mixture of emotions he did not know how to handle and he became horrified by the notion of what would happen if Hades knew about Jimmy, and to what lengths the villain would go in order to claim Charlie's cousin for himself.

"No, Charlie," he said finally, unwilling to give the prospect of Jimmy's return another thought. "That is not within my power."

"Then what good are you!" said Charlie. Tears pooled in his

eyes as his body began to shake. He felt betrayed, as though he were Shakespeare's Julius Caesar. He turned away, unable to withstand the sight of his quisling. He hardened his heart and forced the fire within him to retreat. He would not be ruled by false emotions or mystery anymore. He took a breath and drifted out of the alley.

This time, Buck did not stop Charlie and resigned himself to an unwelcomed chase, his feet moving him forward.

"Let him go, Master Breedling," said a familiar melodious voice.

Buck halted and turned back into the alley, where the Tales Teller and Chameleon both stood behind him.

"Best to give the mortal a moment," continued the Tales Teller, her translucent skin a somber shade of gray.

A lengthy pause followed, allowing Buck the chance to switch his focus.

"You said your spell would not harm him," he said. "You said it was supposed to assist in finding the mortal Damek. It did neither of those things, and I am no closer to the Eden Wanderer. In fact, I have lost any and all sense of him. What happened?"

"Nothing that was intentional," said the Tales Teller, her skin glowing an embarrassed blue.

"We are at a loss, Master Breedling," added the Chameleon. "We were assured the spell would simply compel the young mortal to fulfill his purpose. Charlie is still your best source at finding the mortal you seek."

"We never thought…" said the Tales Teller.

"What, that Charlie would be compelled to seek out Hades?" said Buck, his voice a sufficient roar.

"There was nothing wrong with my spell, Master Breedling," said the Tales Teller, her voice grievous.

"So, it is Charlie's fault, is that it?" asked Buck. "He consciously made the decision to let himself be lured by the Scarlet Phoenix."

"In a manner," said the Chameleon. "Fault can always be found in free will, you especially can attest to such a claim."

"But Charlie, he did not ask for this, he did not chose this path," said Buck. "He is not some pawn to be manipulated."

"No," said the Tales Teller, her skin warming to a soft orange. "He is not, but it appears the path has chosen the young mortal."

"What are you saying?" asked Bartholomew.

"Only time knows the answer to that, Master Breedling," said the Tales Teller.

"Stop speaking in riddles!" said Buck, frustrated, able to sympathize with Charlie.

"Master Breedling, you will know your place," said the Chameleon, stamping a paw onto the ground.

"I do know my place, Master Chameleon, and it is not with the likes of you." Buck did not give either of the Euxian creatures a chance to refute him and stormed out of the alley before breaking into a run in order to catch Charlie. His mind raced with his feet, his thoughts questioning loyalty, duty, and free will. He began to doubt himself, wondering if he was only doing what was expected of him or if he was in control. The realization infuriated him and he made a silent pact with himself. He was not going to let the council force this charge upon him and for a moment, he did not care about the plight of the Shepherdess, finding the Eden Wanderer, or restoring the Golden Faun and the Black Tortoise as rulers of Eden. All he cared about was right in front of him— Charlie.

Lullaby

The freakish giant entered Rations Market, his two ogres flanking him, unsettling Grocer Pawlak's customers. The portly man addressed Wiktor with a natural greeting, not hiding the fact he was on good terms with the Polish gang leader. Grocer Pawlak saw to the rest of his clientele as the hooligans wandered around the room picking what they wanted off the shelves and tossing it into a basket. Wiktor picked up an apple and took an immediate bite, not even bothering to pay for it. The doorbell jingled in frantic succession until the last of the shoppers departed, leaving an ominous air about the store.

"I think congratulations are in order," said Grocer Pawlak, closing the cash register, not that he was concerned Wiktor would rob him, just merely out of habit.

"Then Felix has kept you well informed," said Wiktor, returning back to the front of the store, his eyes unfocused on the portly man.

"Per our arrangement," said Grocer Pawlak, referring to the pact the two men had made years ago when Kalvis had taken over for the Lithuanians, their mutual understanding a twisted concept of respect. "So, I have to ask," he added. "Did you make Link bleed?"

Wiktor held up his bandaged hand, not at all ashamed of his

battle wound, though still bitter he only managed to get in one punch.

"Broke your hand, did you. Not surprised. I've always said that boy's got a metal plate in his head," said Grocer Pawlak. "Charlie played his part well, then."

"It wasn't Charlie," said Wiktor. He took another bite of his apple, squirting the juice on the counter.

"Then it was the boy," said Grocer Pawlak, his squinty eyes gleaming with dollar signs.

"Yes, well," said Wiktor, determined not to indulge his ally's greed, at least not yet. "That is why I'm here, Pawlak. I'm looking for Charlie. Have you seen him?"

Grocer Pawlak's natural demeanor soured. He grabbed a cloth and wiped the stickiness off the counter. "He came by this morning," he grumbled. "Felix told me he was down by McKinley Park, last he saw him."

"Any chances he might be coming back?" asked Wiktor.

"I ain't the boy's keeper," shouted Grocer Pawlak and huffed his ruddy cheeks.

The portly man's outburst gained the attention of Wiktor's two ogres, who were fighting over strands of black licorice twists. They suspended their quarrel and as though on cue, they started to knock boxes and bags off the shelves.

Grocer Pawlak rumpled his bulbous nose, his specs sliding to the rounded point of his beak. "That's not necessary, Wiktor," he groused.

"Boys," shouted Wiktor, his command stopping the ogres for vandalizing the store. "I know you're a reasonable man, Pawlak," he said, returning his attention to the grocer. "And I'm prepared to make it worth your while."

Grocer Pawlak's eyes gleamed again, the Polish gang leader

piquing his interest. "What'd you have in mind?"

"Charlie, if he comes back, I want you to keep him here. The boy too. All night if you have to. I've got some business with Trusty Pat down in the Back of the Yards," said Wiktor, pausing. "You shouldn't have any problem keeping them here all night. Charlie's vulnerable, just lost his cousin, if you hadn't heard. So, make 'em feel at home, dazzle 'em with generosity, the whole nine yards." Wiktor took a final bite of his apple. "I know Kalvis is already looking for them and I ain't about to give that Lugan the opportunity to steal the best weapon this side of Morgan Street."

"And what's in it for me?" questioned the portly man, pushing his specs back into place.

"The boy, Buck, you can have him when I'm finished with him. Just need him a bit, you know, to motivate Charlie," said Wiktor, setting his apple core on the counter. "So, old friend, do we have a deal?" He extended his good hand.

"We have a deal," said Grocer Pawlak with a cruel grin.

* * *

Charlie stared blankly at the empty store beyond the panes of glass, his thoughts weighing heavy. He felt numb inside, his heart cracked to the point of shattering at any moment. Everything about the buildings around him, the people running to and from their automobiles, even the air seemed different, insignificant somehow, as though he were no longer a part of the everyday mundaneness. He looked down at the harmonica in his hand. It was not the brilliant cherry wood he had played, but rather a tarnished silver. The showman must have used a sleight of hand to steal it back when Buck pulled him away. He wanted to curse for being cheated out of his prize and had half a mind to go back and demand his spoil. Charlie curled his fingers around the instrument. He did not want the vile thing in his possession. He wanted no reminders of his entanglement with Old Hob.

His thoughts turned dark after that, slipping into a state of disillusion, his mind sorting options on how to be rid of Buck and leave Chicago. He entertained some of the most diabolical thoughts he had ever had, but in his gut, he knew he did not have the stomach to be so cold. His mother's nurturing goodness would prevent the unnatural impulses from forcing his conscious self to commit such unadulterated abandonment. Furthermore, his fragmented sense of reason was still strong enough to know he would rather die than act in the same vein as Kalvis, Wiktor, or even Grocer Pawlak. Charlie pushed the ill ideas out of his head and settled on a generous solution, one that would see Buck cared for and allow him the freedom to flee. All he needed was an opportune moment.

"Charlie…" he heard Buck say, his tone sorrowful.

"You were right, Buck," he said, keeping his eyes on the harmonica, allowing it to remind him of how he was feeling. "I should never have forced you to tell me. I never should've set foot in that circle."

"Charlie, it is not your fault, you…" said Buck.

"Don't," said Charlie. He rotated his head, just enough to look at Buck, the Breedling's emerald eyes housing his deepest regrets. Charlie sighed, refusing to allow himself to trust the creature. "Here," he said finally in an attempt to falsely patch things over. "Take it. I don't want it."

"But I do not play," said Buck, taking the instrument. His eyes shifted from Charlie to the harmonica, unsurprised to see silver instead of the cherry wood.

"That's all right. I'll teach you a few things," said Charlie, relieved to be rid of the poisonous object, his spirits instantly lifting. "Besides, you told me how to beat—the showman," he added, refraining from calling Hades out by name. He was still unsure how Buck had known the secret to beating Old Hob at his own game, and though a part of him was eager to know, he managed to stifle his curiosity. He had learned his lesson. "You're the true winner."

Buck looked at Charlie closely, judging his earnest expression. He did not feel right about taking the instrument, unfamiliar with the mortal custom of gift giving. After all, Charlie was the one who bested Hades, not him, and so to the victor went the spoils.

"Thank you," he said finally.

"You're welcome," said Charlie, feebly.

"But next time," said Buck. "If you feel compelled…"

"Don't worry, Buck," said Charlie, cutting him to the quick. All he wanted to do was put this moment behind him. "I don't plan on a rematch."

Buck nodded and placed the harmonica in his pocket.

"Good," said Charlie. He clapped his hands together, flipping a switch to being the first stage of his escape plan, and the first thing he needed was a little assistant from a greedy grocer. "Now that that is settled, why don't you head to the back door and wait for me to square things away with Grocer Pawlak?"

"Are you sure?" asked Buck.

"Don't worry, I'm sure he's forgotten all about this morning," Charlie lied. "And hey, maybe I can talk old Pawlak into giving us each a bottle of cola this time."

"That would be delightful," said Buck, thankful their quarrel was over, at least for now.

"That it would," said Charlie, putting on his best smile, while at the same time his brain continued to concoct his plan to separate himself from his tagalong and the ghosts of the city.

* * *

Buck sat on the steps, his fingers twirling the harmonica, his mind in conflict, his thoughts debating when to reveal more to Charlie or if he even should. It was one thing to answer the mortal's questions, but it was another to outright share. He wanted to tell Charlie more, every ounce of him up for the task, and yet there was a part of him that wanted Charlie to ask because it would mean more if he did, as though by asking, Charlie was accepting him. Buck sighed and caught the beam of silver out of the corner of his eye. He stopped moving the harmonica and laid it flat in his palm. He contemplated the song Charlie performed, the notes he had used, and the skill it took. He closed his eyes, listening for the somber tune and, without a conscious thought, he lifted the cool instrument to his lips and visualized every note. He blew hard into the harmonica, forcing his breath upon the chambers. He withdrew the instrument and rethought Charlie's first few measures. How low and timid they were, the sacrifice he had used to play them. Buck positioned the harmonica once more on his lips. At first, the notes were too soft, but as he recalled the crescendo, the melody progressed into a haunting lullaby. With every breath, the notes flowed with ease and he felt captivated by them. Buck smiled, delighted his ability to adapt could be of some use to him. He continued playing, falling deep into the intricate emotion of the melody, blocking out everything around him, even Charlie.

Charlie entered the alley, awestruck by the voice of the harmonica, and listened while Buck played the spoils of his victory. He watched how gently Buck's ivory hands cradled the instrument, a mirror image of his style, maybe even better. Buck's breath intertwined with the melody and became a part of the song, true surrender. The somber notes plucked at his heartstrings, tugging at the emotions he was trying to avoid, temporarily suspending ill plans. A swell of water washed across his eyes and he did his best to hold back tears—but even the most callous man would have broken under the circumstances. The teardrops fell down his cheeks, his fatigue weakening his resolve. A sorrowful gasp escaped his mouth and he placed a hand over his heart.

Buck stopped, waiting a moment, before he heard Charlie's sobs. He opened his eyes just as Charlie fell to his knees and instinctively he sprang from the steps, dropping the harmonica on the ground. He reached out and caught Charlie in a weak embrace, the dead weight of his body pressing against him. Buck maneuvered to allow Charlie the support he needed and shuffled his feet towards the stairs in order to lower Charlie to them. Buck crouched down, taken off guard by the amount of distress emanating from the mortal. It came off him in waves and Buck bore witness to the mounting grief consuming Charlie. Buck reached over to place a hand on Charlie's shoulder, hoping it would have the same effect as it had the day before, offering what little comfort he could.

"Charlie," whispered Buck.

Charlie's eyes rose from the ground to look at Buck. He sensed the touch of the Breedling's hand resting on his shoulder, pulsating with a cool calming presence. It was opposite what he had experienced with Hades, the ambers of the Devil's touch still within him became all but extinguished.

"Charlie," repeated Buck, watching the sadness melt from Charlie's face.

"Buck," Charlie whispered, realizing for the first time why the loss of Jimmy had not yet torn him a part the way he knew it should. It was Buck. After they had left the breadline, when he had broken down while speaking about his family, about Jimmy, it was Buck who had placed his hand on him, numbing the pain he had felt. When he had awoken in the church, Buck had been sitting next to him and oddly he had felt refreshed. Charlie caught his breath, mortified he might never be able to mourn his cousin.

"Charlie, are you square?" asked Buck, oblivious to the effect he was having on Charlie. "Did Grocer Pawlak throw you out?"

"What?" said Charlie, his voice pinched. "No, it was your playing," he admitted, doing what he could to gain control of this numbing emotions. "The beauty of it overwhelmed me, is all—I thought you said you couldn't play?" He wiped his eyes on the wristband of his navy blue shirt.

Buck removed his hand from Charlie's shoulder and rose. "Well, I can, sort of," he said.

"Wait, did you just admit a lie?" asked Charlie with a half-smile.

"No, I, um, well, when I told you I did not know how to play, I was telling you the truth. I did not know how," said Buck.

"And now you do?"

"Well, I just have a talent for picking things up," Buck shrugged.

"Kinda like having the knack for winning a virgin game of pool," said Charlie, digressing from his deal to keep his questions to himself. "Is that something all—Breedlings can do? Become pool sharks and musicians on a whim."

"Not all Breedlings were created equal, Charlie," said Buck, not attempting to deny Charlie an answer. The last thing he wanted was another fight. "So no, not all have the knack as you say to pick up on things."

"Do you have any other abilities or powers?" asked Charlie as though he were a five-year-old asking a magician to reveal his secret.

"There are only a few dozen Breedlings endowed with such gifts, I was one of those few, but it appears my ability to adapt is the only skill I have retained since running away."

Charlie chuckled. "You spin a good yarn, Buck," he said, not taking the answer to heart, rejecting the truth of it. "Well, however you do it, you're quite the natural, maybe even better than me."

"Is that why you are upset? Because I played it better?" Buck looked down at the harmonica lying at Charlie's feet.

Charlie's gaze followed and he picked up the instrument. "Of course not, Buck, it's just…" He paused, distracted by the warmth of the silver, the harmonica heavy in his hands. "The song means a great deal to me, that's all."

"May I ask why?" inquired Buck.

"It was a lullaby my Uncle Gert used to play for his dear wife when she was pregnant with Jimmy. After she died in childbirth, Uncle Gert played it for Jimmy. I think it made him feel close to her somehow. Anyway, on the eve of the house fire, I just happened to have my uncle's harmonica in my overalls, partly because I had been playing it out in the barn for my sick horse, Taurus." Charlie paused, clenching his fingers around the instrument, determined to fight back the magic it possessed. "After that, I played it for Jimmy every night, at least until Miss Schwarman stole it from me." Charlie's throat tightened, but Buck's calming demeanor kept a fluster of anger in check.

"Charlie, I…" Buck did not know what to say.

Charlie held up his hand in polite protest. "There's no need, Buck. You had no idea. And to be honest, I'm quite thrilled you can play it. After all, it was by your request." A weak smile lifted

Charlie's weary cheeks as he handed the harmonica back to Buck. His soul was relieved to be free from the weight of the cursed prize.

Buck accepted the gift and returned it to his pocket, none the wiser about its effect on Charlie.

Charlie stood up, releasing a deep breath, again feeling refreshed.

"Are you square, Charlie?" asked Buck.

"Yeah, I'm square." Charlie straightened his shirt and fixed his beret. "Now what say you and I go work up some grub? Grocer Pawlak has agreed to fix us dinner if we clean up a mess in aisle six. Apparently, there was a frenzy at the end of the day and there is sugar and flour all over the floor, plus, it practically cleaned him out of his entire canned stock and oh, what was left of the cereal. And boy," said Charlie, still suspicious of the portly man's agenda, "was Pawlak ever glad to see me walk in the door."

"You do not say," said Buck, lowering his chin.

"You know Buck, it sounds queer when you say it like that," said Charlie, as he opened the screen door.

"Like what?" asked Buck.

"Never mind," Charlie sighed, understanding why Buck lacked ordinary speech and liked it better when it was just a quirk, rather than a supernatural thing. "Anyway," he continued, "Pawlak's closing the store right now, so I'm sure it's safe for us to go in—after you, young squire." Charlie extended his arm for Buck to enter.

Buck felt the sting of the insult and he did not find Charlie's attempt at humor tasteful. He did, however, walk up the stairs and enter the market, his mind unable to reconcile what Hades had meant by the demeaning title.

Two Coins

"Ah, Charlie my boy, you brought your friend with you—Buck, was it?" said Grocer Pawlak, his greeting as fake as his cheery disposition, though Buck was none the wiser.

"That's right," offered Charlie, finding the grocer's absentminded question cause for alarm, leading him to further believe the portly man was up to something.

"Splendid!" said Grocer Pawlak, as he placed green stacks of paper in a black bag. He looked at Charlie with a contrite expression. "Apologies, Charlie, for my shortness earlier. It seems that despite your young friend's outburst this morning, this has proven to be a most profitable day. And what have the two of you been up to?"

Charlie did not like the way Grocer Pawlak posed the question. The portly man, never inquired about his day, not unless he was after something. "Oh, you know," he said, keeping to the easy facts. "We walked the district, checked in with Mr. Herdina, the usual. Nothing special."

"Well," said Grocer Pawlak, "as we discussed, Charlie, you boys can clean up that mess and stock a few things for me and I'll see to your supper. Just come on upstairs when you're done."

"Upstairs?" said Charlie, his sensitive intuition forewarning him. "That's not necessary, Pawlak."

"Nonsense," objected Grocer Pawlak. "It's the least I can do."

Charlie contemplated declining, but his stomach urged him to take the deal. "We have an accord, Pawlak," he said. He spit into his palm and shook the portly man's hand.

Grocer Pawlak locked the doors before exiting the room, his heavy footsteps audible on the stairs. Charlie went to work right away, heading to the back room and carrying out large boxes of cereal. He and Buck stocked the shelves, their voices for the most part silent. At one point, Buck asked Charlie why he had spit in his hand, but he gave a short reply and left it at that. When they were finished, Charlie took the rest of the boxes to the alley, and left Buck near the cans of SPAM.

Buck took out the piece of parchment and reread the Apothecary's note, beginning to wonder when the Eldest Euxian had put thought to ink. How much time had passed between the writing and the delivering? And how old was Damek now?

"Hey, Buck," called Charlie from across the room.

Buck scrambled to return the page to his pocket and followed Charlie through the hall and up the stairs.

"Ah, come in, lads," said Grocer Pawlak, luring them into his apartment. "Please make yourselves at home, dinner'll be ready in a moment."

The boys found themselves immediately in the small living room. It smelled of mold, cabbage and dirt. The walls were light brown, decorated with a faded border of hounds hunting ducks on a pond. The textured ceiling was plagued with water stains and a spider web connected the corner with the pan of the window, which overlooked the street. On the floor, several tattered rugs covered the cracking tile. Buck and Charlie sat down on the leather couch, sinking deep into the broken cushions. Grocer Pawlak joined them carrying two bowls. He placed them both on the coffee table then took a seat in his newly upholstered armchair. He invited the boys to dig in. Buck was sad to see creamy liquid instead of the red tomato, but once the smells of onion, garlic, and bay leaves reached his nose, his mouth watered. He lapped up the creaminess, pausing every so often to chew the earthy flavor of what Charlie told him was a mushroom.

"Damn boy, you slop that soup up any faster and you'll be wearin' it," said Grocer Pawlak with a hearty chuckle from his gut.

Buck stopped, somewhat embarrassed by his ravenous behavior, and picked up his spoon.

"Are you boys thirsty?" asked Grocer Pawlak.

"Parched," said Charlie. He blew on his soup before putting it into his mouth.

Grocer Pawlak went back to the kitchen and retrieved two clear bottles full of brown liquid. He popped the tops off with his church key and handed them one each. Buck slowly sipped the carbonated beverage, savoring the tickle of the bubbles, and giggled.

Grocer Pawlak pinched his right cheek into a smirk, pleased he was winning the boy over. He then glanced at Charlie, noticing how tired he appeared, and knew he would be able to broach the invitation.

"Oh, Charlie, I almost forgot," he began, setting up his lie. "Father Van Lewen called on you today, sometime after lunch if I remember right—anyhow, he told me about the fire and Jimmy."

Charlie grimaced. He had hoped to finish the day without having to talk about Jimmy and he kept his eyes on the floor to avoid looking at the portly man. He hated feeling small around Grocer Pawlak, knowing with every facial expression, gesture, or word that the grocer was judging him. Charlie slammed his bottle onto the coffee table. The fizz shot up and foam exploded like a geyser.

"My sympathy Charlie, Jimmy was a good kid." Grocer Pawlak cleared his throat, swallowing bile, disgusted by his own nicety. He spooned a swig of his soup to combat the foul taste.

"Thank you," mumbled Charlie, sensing no sincerity from the man.

"Yes, yes, tricky thing, fires. Anyway, Father Van Lewen wanted me to tell you he can find a place for you in the morning, but for now, you can spend the night. In the morning you can help me unload the truck and then be on your way."

Charlie lifted his head, trying to find the attached strings to the proposition. However, for once he could not tell if the portly man was playing him or telling the truth. He set his bowl on the coffee table, prepared to decline the offer, but a wave of fatigue burned through his achy body in protest. Instead, he welcomed the idea of having a comfortable place to sleep and negating sound judgement, he agreed.

"Very good. You boys can take the couch and the armchair if you like," said Grocer Pawlak, praising himself for his cleverness—*that boy is as good as mine.* "Well then," he added. "I best be saying goodnight." He rose from the armchair, not even bothering to clean up the bowls or bottles sitting on the coffee table. He yawned and patted his belly. He walked to the hallway by the front door and paused. "Oh, I almost forgot," he turned back to the couch, ready to make his final attempt to curry favor with the boys. "A little birdy told me, you are quite the accomplished musician, young Buck."

"A bird?" said Buck, his thoughts immediately refuting any possibility that Grocer Pawlak might be in league with a winged agent of Heaven.

Grocer Pawlak chuckled, his prominent belly bouncing. "You seem surprised," he said, although truth be told, his little bird was himself. He had followed Charlie to the back door of the store and overheard Buck playing the harmonica. "Tell him, Charlie," he added.

Charlie blinked his drooping eyes and said, "Wiktor keeps Pawlak up to date on all the comings and goings in the neighborhood. You'd be surprised by what he knows, probably even knows we had a spat."

Grocer Pawlak did not respond, completely unaware of the exchange. "Yes, well, Frankenstein and I have an understanding," he said, removing two silver coins from his apron pocket. "Now, I'm sure Charlie has explained to you the rules."

"The rules?" asked Buck. "Oh yes, the rules, he has told me several."

"Wonderful," said Grocer Pawlak, "then I would like to give you one of my own. Now listen carefully, as I will only say it once. All service is rewarded, young Buck, whether by coin or favor, for nothing comes without its price. Here is fifty cents." He placed the coins in Buck's hand. "If Charlie permits, I was wondering if you wouldn't mind playing for a bit."

"I would like that," said Charlie too far gone to notice Pawlak's true intent for Buck's audition.

"Then by your request," said Buck, "I shall play."

Grocer Pawlak clapped his hands at a masterful job. He stretched another yawn before taking his leave.

When Grocer Pawlak was out of sight, Buck moved off the couch into the armchair, his intention to give Charlie enough room to sleep, for he would not need any. Charlie stretched out his legs and sprawled across the whole couch. Every inch of his body pulsed with vengeful pain as he curled his arm underneath his head. He tilted his chin so he could see Buck and noticed how the light from below illuminated his ivory skin. It was not glowing, per se, but it did catch his attention, like the glow of a silvery moon. The fatigue within him made its final charge and this time he would have to give in—sleep was imminent.

Buck settled in the armchair and took out the harmonica. He looked at it for a moment and without having to ponder how to play, he began *Jimmy's Song*.

In the music, Charlie heard the innocent voice of his cousin whisper to him, telling him everything would be well. He felt his presence in the room and tried to hold on to it as long as possible. His mind had just been playing a cruel trick on him, and Charlie was hoping he would awaken from the nightmare. That maybe, come daybreak, Jimmy would be shaking him to wake up just as he always did. The melody began to grow distant even as the notes became stronger and louder. Charlie drifted into slumber as Jimmy slipped from his grasp, his presence fading.

"Jimmy," he whispered, trying to hold on—until at last he was fast asleep.

Buck concluded the melody with a decrescendo and set the harmonica in his lap. He watched Charlie for a while. In the light, he saw the sparkle of a fresh tear roll down his cheek. He turned away to gaze out the window toward the sky. Pitch clouds trudged forward as the wind strengthened. Buck looked down into the street and at the base of the nearest lamppost he saw the tabby cat, its pink eyes glowing. The cat stared at him for a moment, its tail flicking gingerly, and then wandered off, heading towards the approaching storm.

Buck rubbed his eyes, his lids heavy. "Sleep," he murmured. "How long will it be before my eyelids are too heavy?" Buck shivered. Just the mere thought of sleep reminded him of the smell of sulfur and the scream of the Shepherdess. *Without a true tether to the realm of Eden, it is hard to know if your presence here is permanent. Might I suggest not sleeping until the mortal Damek has reaffirmed your charge?* Buck took a deep breath. He needed to relax, but the Tales Teller's warning worried him. He would have to find Damek, regardless of his doubts, for without the mortal's ordained magic there was no telling how much longer he would have. He looked back at Charlie, the sleeping mortal talking in his sleep.

"In the morning," he said aloud. "I'll tell him in the morning."

Pieces of Eight

The Apothecary stood over his stove, stirring the boiling water in his cast-iron cauldron. He wished the bubbling would drown out the sound of his abettors, their frazzled voices digging daggers into his temples. It would have been easier to soothe their concerns with the truth, but he needed to be careful how he delivered snippets of his plan, for if he said too much to the Tales Teller or the Chameleon, no amount of trust would stop either one of them from going to the Fates and revealing his strategy. The Apothecary sighed, his ancient frame weary from the collective glares on the back of his neck. He set the ladle on the counter among the petals of an orange hibiscus and turned to face his guests. The Tales Teller appeared a sunburned bride and the fur on the tail of the Chameleon's feline form puffed with discontent.

"I am relieved you have both returned without incident," he said to calm his guests. "I understand what I have asked has caused some concerns, but I assure you…"

"My Eldest," said the Tales Teller, her whiskers twitching. "Have you not been listening to a word we have said? What you have asked is not our quandary. It is what you have allowed to happen."

"And what has happened?" asked the Apothecary. He had

been listening, but he did not want to patronize his fellow council members.

"The mortal, Charles Reese," said the Chameleon. "The one you chose to be Bartholomew's guide."

"What of him?" asked the Apothecary.

"He has not performed as you promised. You said he would lead Master Breedling to the mortal Damek," replied the Chameleon.

"By your previous accounts he already has," said the Apothecary with a sensible tone.

The feline eyes of the Chameleon and the Tales Teller drew away from the eldest Euxian to gaze in puzzlement at one another. Both had made frequent returns to the Apothecary's tea kitchen to give accounts on Bartholomew's progress, so it was hard to know where along the way the Breedling had crossed paths with the mortal in question. If the Apothecary was correct and Bartholomew had already met the mortal, why did the Breedling remain untethered to his mission?

"By your expressions, may I venture a guess this too has gone wrong?" said the Apothecary.

"There has been a complication," said the Chameleon. The cat sat on its hind legs and tamed its spiked fur.

"I see," said the Apothecary, reaching for a bundle of dried lavender.

"My Eldest," said the Tales Teller in objection. "I do not think you realize the severity of the situation. The spell did not compel Charles to seek out Damek, it delivered him straight to Hades."

The Apothecary did not respond. Instead, he began to pluck the stems free of their tiny leaves. He pondered the Tales Teller's news, not entirely surprised the mortal had thwarted his plan. It had been an unavoidable risk, but he was still certain, no matter what magic Charles Reese had acquired during his act to save Bartholomew, the mortal would fulfill his role and lead the Breedling to Damek.

"Master Apothecary," said the Tales Teller. "I do not understand, you have always been so careful and calculating."

"Yes, and in my haste…" said the Apothecary.

"You have allowed the creation of an enigma," said the Chameleon. "You promised the council you would only create seven powers of Eden, not eight."

"A power, you say," said the Apothecary without regard to the accusation.

"As we say?" said the Chameleon, standing on all fours. "My Eldest, please, confide in us. What is it we do not see? How can you stand there so calmly? Your plan has failed."

The Apothecary raised his head. Strands of his silver hair draped in front of his gray almond-shaped eyes. He brushed them aside, the fragrance of lavender keeping him calm.

"My plan has not failed, Master Chameleon," he said. "What you and Madam Teller have not yet ascertained is that my plan is no longer mine. It is all on Master Breedling now to fulfill the council's vision to see the Fates topple from their thrones. And as you know, it starts with the Eden Wanderer."

"But Charles Reese?" said the Tales Teller. "The compulsion spell should never have…"

"What has happened to the mortal is out of our control," said the Apothecary, his voice firm, though in his mind he made a contingency plan to learn more about Charles Reese. "Now, return to your posts. We cannot arouse suspicion."

The Apothecary watched the concern drain from his abettors' expressions. The Tales Teller's skin burst into a kaleidoscope of reds and she glided toward the front door in a tempered huff. She left without giving the Eldest security of her intentions and went across the square to return to her library where she would prepare for the trial of the Shepherdess. The Chameleon lingered, however, its fur a bristled mess. The black irises eclipsed the glowing pink, its tail swooshing back and forth, sweeping herbs off the counter. The cat crouched, readying to pounce. Its intended target, the ancient man standing before it.

"Your fury is ill-placed, my friend," said the Apothecary, returning to his herbs. He was confident the feline would stand down on its own, but the cutting of sharp claws proved him wrong. The cat tried to retreat, but the Apothecary's reflexes were too skillful for the feline. His skeletal fingers hoisted it by the scruff.

"Your senses on this matter are too cavalier, my Eldest," said the cat, its belly exposed. "I know you. I know your mind. You have left nothing to the chance of Eden or the influence of Heaven or Hell. But this Charles Reese may be a threat."

The Apothecary narrowed his eyes, prepared to reprimand the creature for second-guessing his strategy, but the scent of lavender struck him again. He placed the feline on the counter and removed himself from the tea kitchen. He ambled towards the open door, and waited.

The cat shook its fur and leapt off the counter. It prowled across the room, its eyes avoiding the ancient Euxian's gaze, its ears pulled back as it turned to the doorway.

"I value your council, Master Chameleon," said the Apothecary.

The cat's ears perked and its paws circled back. "You honor me, Master Apothecary," said the Chameleon.

The Apothecary grinned then looked about the square for eavesdroppers. He crouched to the floor and leaned forward, whispering in the feline's ear.

"If it is in you, Master Chameleon, that all may be lost, steal yourself away and learn all you can about this Piece of Eight."

"By your word, my Eldest," said the Chameleon. The cat bowed, its nose touching the igneous black stone of the street.

"Be well, my friend," said the Apothecary and rose as the cat darted into the darkness of Euxinus.

Devilish Trait

The storm arrived in the early hours of the morning, covering Chicago in an unnatural darkness. The howling wind rattled the windowpanes of Grocer Pawlak's apartment while ashen snow blew fiercely. The large black flakes fell from the sky in a whirlwind, but several escaped the dizzying dance and blanketed the barren street. Buck witnessed the developing storm, half-expecting Hades to appear in the street below, but the Master of Hell was nowhere to be found. He eventually turned away from the dismal scene to steal a glance at Charlie. The mortal was still asleep, sprawled out on the length of the couch. It had been a fitful night for him, what with the sudden outbursts of screams, sobs, and mumbled words. It was surprising Charlie had managed to sleep at all. Buck batted his eyes to convince them they were not tired, though the effort had become useless at this point, his eyes yearning for sleep. He contemplated whether he could make it another day without rest.

CREAK!

Buck looked toward the door and found the short, portly silhouette of Grocer Pawlak standing near the door to his apartment. It was hard to make him out in the faint light, but he saw the white cloth of his apron draped across his round belly, the brim of his soiled hat pronounced on his head.

"Did I wake you?" asked Grocer Pawlak in a gruff voice.

"No," said Buck, as he got up from the armchair. He crossed to the door. "Grocer Pawlak, if it is not too much trouble, is it all right if we let Charlie sleep a little longer? He has had a most trying couple of days."

Grocer Pawlak glanced over at the couch and saw Charlie's head resting underneath his dangled arm. Letting the lad sleep would give him time to manipulate the young boy without judgment from Charlie's pesky moral compass.

"If it be a matter of assistance, I can help you with whatever you require," offered Buck, pulling at his waistcoat to make himself look as capable as possible despite his unfortunate attire and shoeless feet. He ran a hand through his brown hair to flatten it.

"Very well," said Grocer Pawlak. He reached for the doorknob. "Come along, Buck. I believe I heard the truck pull up before I got out of bed."

At the bottom of the stairs, Grocer Pawlak unlocked the double bolt and opened the alley door, which nearly pulled his arm out of its socket as it swung open with a bang. There was a large green truck idling in the alley with two figures behind the windshield. The passenger side door opened with a bit of effort, and from behind it, a man ran to the back door. Grocer Pawlak opened the screen to let the young man inside.

"Weez can't stay long!" shouted the young man as he loosened ash from his hair. "Weez gots to hit every store before noon!"

"Fine," yelled Grocer Pawlak, his voice battling the volume of the storm. "I just need ten bags of flour, some oats, sugar, and five boxes of the Campbell's!"

"Okay, have the kid hold the door," said the deliveryman as he went back outside. "Earl, give me a hand!" he shouted, letting the screen door slam behind him.

"Buck, you think you can man the door?"

"Certainly," said Buck, pushing open the screen.

Grocer Pawlak let out a pleased chuckle at the boy's eager pliability. "Good lad," he remarked and stepped outside.

It took Grocer Pawlak and the deliverymen a few trips to bring in all the supplies, though it was long enough for Buck to feel a thin layer of black snow in his hair. Grocer Pawlak brought in the last bag of flour, and bid the deliverymen good day. He closed the door and locked the double bolt.

"Just in case," the portly man said with a shrug. "Well then, are you sure you can handle getting these things settled in the pantry?" Grocer Pawlak gave Buck a curious inspection.

"I think I can manage," said Buck, up for the task. Besides, he needed something to distract him from falling asleep.

Grocer Pawlak scratched at the stubble on his chin. In the light of the hallway, Buck's face was a poor shade of green and his eyes were puffy and red. The boy appeared quite sick to him and he had a fleeting thought to send him back to bed, but thought better of it. Letting Buck work himself to the brink of exhaustion would make him more cooperative when Wiktor came to collect him.

"Then I will leave you to it, young Buck," said Grocer Pawlak, and he disappeared into the store to begin his daily routine.

Buck smacked his hands on his cheeks to keep his eyes alert then lifted a bag of flour and nearly fell over from its weight. He slammed up against the wall to help regain his balance and readjusted his hands. With a better grip, he hauled the bag to the pantry, which he did successfully six times before Charlie came down the stairs.

***

Charlie lingered at the top of the stairs in a drowsy haze, peering at the light from the hallway below. His body tingled, the sensation of pins and needles pricking every one of his muscles. There was an irritating warm ache in his left shoulder, and he shook his arm to encourage blood flow. He rubbed his eyes and gave them a few blinks as Buck came into view. He watched him pick up a sack of oats and lose his balance in the process. Charlie flew down the staircase, skipping the last three steps and caught Buck before he fell over.

"Thanks," said Buck, the sack slipping from his fingers. "Charlie?"

Charlie's expression soured. "Buck, why didn't you wake me?" he asked.

"I wanted to let you get some extra rest." Buck struggled to hang onto the sack, his momentum coming to a crashing halt.

"Me? What about you?" argued Charlie, Buck's lack of sleep not lost on him. "You didn't sleep a wink, did you?"

"Charlie, I just could not let Grocer Pawlak wake you."

"You're missing the point, Buck," said Charlie, his mind not alert enough to make a proper argument. "Oh, never mind," he said. "Just hand over the oats and I'll finish up. You go get some rest." He tried to take the sack from Buck.

"No, Charlie," said Buck, not alarmed by the fact that his sleep deprivation was taking its toll on his manners. "I shall finish here. You go ask Grocer Pawlak if he has anything else." Buck readjusted his fingers around the sack and traipsed off through the swinging doors of the pantry.

Charlie sighed and rubbed his left shoulder, the warmth beneath his skin increasing. He shook his arm again, but it merely dulled the sensation to a mild irritation. Charlie furrowed his brow and sauntered through the hall into the store, preparing his thoughts to give Grocer Pawlak a piece of his mind. The lights were on, doing their best to ward off the darkness from outside. He scanned the room, not at all surprised Grocer Pawlak was the only one visible, standing in his normal spot at the front counter. Charlie made his way down the soda aisle and paused to take notice of the newly shaped Coca-Cola tower.

"Ah, Charlie my boy, you're awake," greeted Grocer Pawlak as he closed the register.

"Why didn't you wake me?" asked Charlie, not bothering to return the hollow salutation.

"Come now Charlie, we couldn't wake you after the day you'd had," said Grocer Pawlak, playing on the lad's vulnerable state of mind. "It wouldn't be right. Besides, Buck has proven to be an able-bodied young lad."

"Able? The poor kid…" Charlie paused, being sure to remind himself Buck was no ordinary boy.

"Charlie, I'm disappointed in you," said Grocer Pawlak, spraying the counter and wiped it off with a rag. "The lad is just trying to help."

"Help? He looks like death."

"Not to worry," said Grocer Pawlak with a crooked grin, his right eye squinting. "It won't come to that. I'm sure he'll pass out after some strenuous work."

Charlie opened his mouth to argue, but the grocer's statement gave him pause. There was something more in the portly man's voice. "Sylvester, what have you done?" he asked, the morning aches of his body briefly numbed by a tidal wave of panic.

"Nothing to worry about, Charlie," said Grocer Pawlak.

"I don't believe you," said Charlie, taking a step back from the counter.

Grocer Pawlak's expression twisted, his seedy disposition

showing itself. Charlie took another step back, prepared to make a dash for the back door, but made it no further than the Coca-Cola display. His eyes fell to the revolver, cradled in the portly man's fat fingers. Charlie's breath hitched, his flight instincts paralyzed by a sudden desire to die.

"I can't let you leave, Charlie," said Grocer Pawlak.

"You son of a..." started Charlie.

Grocer Pawlak cocked the revolver.

"Wiktor told me he needs you alive, Charlie. He didn't say unharmed," said Grocer Pawlak, rotating his wrist to point the barrel at Charlie. He pinched the corners of his lips, fixing a devilish grin.

Charlie balled his fists, his death wish prepared to goad the portly man on to shoot him, but the warmth in his shoulder stirred again, spreading into his chest, harboring a sense of self-preservation. He tried to shake the swelling sensation, but it became unprecedentedly all-consuming.

"And what did the brutish monster promise this time?" asked Charlie.

"A shiny new puppet," said Grocer Pawlak, referring to Buck as though he were a wooden marionette.

"Buck is not some Pinocchio you can make dance, Sylvester," said Charlie.

"Of course not, Charlie," said Grocer Pawlak, pulling a small purse of coins from his apron and plopping it on the counter. "I won't have to make the boy do anything. It is you whom Wiktor will make dance, or suffer for it."

Charlie built the connection in his head, realizing Wiktor's plan was to use Buck as leverage to get him to do what the monster wanted. A knot of anger unraveled in Charlie, consuming all civil reason. He felt like a pawn and refused to be manipulated in that way again. Only thing was, he would have to suspend his moral compass in order to play the grocer against himself. Charlie inhaled, embracing the gnarled surge in his gut and took a few paces until his stomach was flush with the counter, the revolver in point-blank range.

"You leave me no choice, Sylvester," said Charlie, his cheeks reddening. "If you allow Wiktor to take me, I will tell him about your deal with Kalvis. How you sold him out for your thirty pieces of silver."

Grocer Pawlak's ruddy cheeks drained of color, his squinty eyes dotting with fear. He was slow to react, but as the realization penetrated his thoughts, he lifted his arm and aimed the barrel at Charlie's forehead.

"Do it," said Charlie, part of him wishing to be released from his mortal coil. To be with his mother, his father, his uncle, his siblings, his cousin Jimmy. "Do it!" he shouted.

Grocer Pawlak's hand began to shake, his body becoming rigid.

"Come on, what are you waiting for, Sylvester! Take your best shot."

Grocer Pawlak roared and slammed the revolver on the counter, his breath heavy. Beads of sweat blotted the rim of his hat and he removed it, revealing wisps of gray hair. When he managed to calm himself, hatred touched every dot of his expression, his eyes glaring.

"What do you want, Charlie?"

"When are you expecting Wiktor?" asked Charlie, stealing a quick glance out into the stormy street.

"Any moment," said Grocer Pawlak, reluctantly.

Charlie grinned, twistedly amused by the portly man's discomfort. "Doesn't feel so good having to dance, does it?"

"Name your price, Charlie," said Grocer Pawlak.

"Tell me, is the alley entrance to Ziemba's Speakeasy still in use?"

Grocer Pawlak lifted a curious eyebrow, caught slightly off guard. "You plan to get that boy good and drunk, don't ya," he accused, still holding out hope he might best Charlie yet. "Charlie," he added, morphing his expression to one of concern, "if you're planning to abandon the boy, why not leave him with me. I'll see he is well taken care of and you can be on your way. No one will be the wiser."

Charlie placed his palms on the counter, his pinky finger brushing the dull metal of the revolver. A fleeting temptation rushed through him, as though the Devil on his shoulder were coaxing him to take the weapon.

"Save your false concern, Sylvester," he said. "You care only about yourself and I will not let you turn Buck into another one of your freak shows. I won't let him end up like the little German girl who you sold to that traveling circus or the Lithuanian boy you convinced Kalvis to pawn off to his brothers uptown or the colored-boy you had shackled and taken off to some coal mine in Virginia." Charlie pressed his hands on the counter, his palms burning. "I know your secret, old man," he said with an unnatural hiss. "Buck is my charge, Sylvester. Now, is Ziemba's still open or not?"

Grocer Pawlak huffed and opened the cash register. "You'll need the password, but yeah, the door's still open," he said, pulling a strip of paper then slammed it on the counter next to the revolver. "Here's a Lincoln," he added, "take it and go. I'll tell Wiktor I ain't seen ya."

Charlie did not even bother to thank the portly man and put the five-dollar bill in his pocket. He gave Grocer Pawlak a nod and headed for the back.

"Oh, and Charlie," said Grocer Pawlak, grinding the revolver's handle in his hand, "don't you come back here."

Charlie did not respond, but deep within the retreating warmth in his body, he felt satisfied he would never have to look upon the likes of the portly man ever again.

* * *

Charlie took a deep breath as he entered the hallway, the heat that pulsed through him finally subsiding to the dull irritation in his shoulder. He felt relieved, knowing that in a few hours, his waking nightmare would be over and he would not have to worry about anyone but himself. Soon he could run away from Chicago and never look back. *Soon*, he reflected. Charlie lowered his gaze, meeting Buck's puzzled expression.

"I am done, Charlie," said Buck, in a low voice. "Charlie?"

"Yes, Buck, I heard you," said Charlie, his tongue still sharp.

Buck stepped back.

Charlie noticed and relaxed his stance, dropping his hands at his sides.

"Is everything square?" asked Buck.

"It is now," said Charlie, and he headed toward the door.

"Charlie, wait."

Charlie unbolted the locks but kept his hand on the doorknob. He turned around and noticed the flour streaks on the sleeves of Buck's mangy shirt. "Leave it alone, Buck. Sylvester and I have concluded our arrangement. It's time to go."

"Sylvester?"

"That's his name, Buck," said Charlie. "Sylvester Pawlak."

Hearing the grocer's full name fractured Buck's hope that Grocer Pawlak was Damek. After receiving the coins last night, his perception of the portly man had changed, but it appeared he was a poor judge of character. Buck frowned unable to hide his disappointment, and wished the Tales Teller's spell had worked its magic properly on Charlie.

"Cheer up, Buck," said Charlie, punching him in the shoulder. "Your sorry face won't do where we're going."

"We are going somewhere? But the storm…" Buck looked into the alley at the accumulating ash, while rubbing the sting from his shoulder.

"We're not going far, just down the alley a tick."

"Where?" asked Buck.

Charlie cracked a smile, glad he would not have to convince Buck any further. "To Ziemba's Speakeasy, they have the best poker tables in the city. You do know what poker is, right?"

"I have never played the game," said Buck, but he had watched a group of thieves play it in a Bulgarian tavern nearly three hundred years ago. "I did see it played once, but it has been quite some time."

"Then it's settled," said Charlie with a spark of enthusiasm, the heat in his shoulder nothing more than a few meager pin pricks. He smacked his hand lightly across his thigh. "We'll fancy ourselves with a game." He pushed open the screen door before Buck could object and scooted him into the darkened alley. He pulled the door shut tightly behind him and let the screen door slam—*hopefully this won't take long.*

<h1 style="text-align:center">Ziemba's Speakeasy</h1>

"**P**assword," said a nettled baritone voice.

"Liquor is quicker," said Charlie to the invisible bouncer.

In reply, the door opened ajar, the dim light from below faintly spotlighting the alley with a soft glow.

Charlie went ahead first, the familiar smells of musty wood, smoke, and liquor welcoming him. He passed the bouncer, a large bearlike man, cautiously remembering from his previous visit that the man did not like it when people stared at his scarred face. Charlie kept his eyes forward and descended the narrow flight of stairs. He felt a tug on his shirt and heard a baritone growl. He stifled a chuckle, almost certain Buck had stolen a glance at the bear's face. Midway down the stairs, the right-side wall opened into a large room with smoke drifting along the ceiling. Buck coughed as they passed through it, the place buzzing with voices and the keys of a piano.

Charlie took the last step and headed for the bar. Not one section of it was visible with all the men gathered around it. Many of them were dressed in cheap suits, carrying on conversations of no consequence, although off to his left, Charlie overheard talk about an Irish fellow named Stingy Jack, who survived being kicked in the chest by a bull in the Stockyards. Charlie looked out onto the floor at the twenty round tables, each occupied by various characters and judged which one would be best to join.

"What be your poison, sir?" asked the bartender, swiping the brim of his bowler hat.

"I'll have two pints on tap!" said Charlie, the bartender having interrupted his inspection of the room.

The bartender removed two glasses from the bottom shelf and drafted Charlie's request. He had no qualms with serving the underage man, the speakeasy's mantra clear in his head. *All those able to enter will never be denied their worth in liquor.* And since Prohibition was over, there was no threat of a raid.

"Say," Charlie continued, "what do the poker games start at?"

"That right depends," said the bartender. "If yous lookin' for high stakes, then the fellas at the other end of the bar in the corner are the ones you be lookin' for. Bets start at a sawbuck."

Charlie glanced over to where the bartender was pointing and saw a bunch of men with fedoras and expensive cigars between their lips. "Too rich for my blood," he murmured. He was good, but not that good.

The bartender set the two pints in front of Charlie. "If yous be lookin' for small action," he continued, "the fellas in front here," he pointed over to where Buck was standing, "they've got the bets starting at two bits."

Charlie placed his Lincoln on the counter.

The bartender looked down at the crisp bill and eyed Charlie, puzzled—*he don't look like a high roller. Maybe he's one of Wiktor's boys.* The bartender swiped the bill from the counter and returned to Charlie four dollars and ninety cents.

Charlie eyed the change and attempted to address the bartender, but the man tipped his hat quickly with a hint of uneasiness on his face and went about his business. Charlie pocketed the change before someone else snatched it and grabbed the glasses. He made his way over to Buck, wondering how much liquor it would take for the supernatural kid to pass out. Maybe a pint or two while they played some poker.

Buck stood next to the closest table, watching curiously as the dealer shuffled the cards and passed them out to the other men at his table. Once the table was set, his eyes perused the speakeasy. He judged every table, his intuition scrutinizing each man, but none of them were worthy of a second glance. The room was full of cheats and vagabonds, scallywags and deviants, a cesspool of characters that would make the Master of Hell grin with prideful delight. He continued warily, when his attentiveness was distracted by a pudgy man at one of the tables closest to him.

The pudgy man kicked his chair to the floor in outrageous disgust and gathering his remaining coins he grumbled a borage of colorful swears. He then stormed his way towards the stairs, knocking into Buck.

"Watch it, kid," warned the pudgy man, his droopy face contorting a scowl.

"My…" started Buck, but Charlie cut him off, shoving the pint glasses into his hands.

Charlie picked up the chair and brought it back to the table. "You gents mind a late comer? I was lookin' to teach my cousin the finer points of the game." Charlie stood behind the chair glancing around the circular table.

"You got any dough, kid?" asked a man wearing a cowboy hat.

Charlie pulled out his money and slapped it on the table. The cowboy's eyes widened, as did the rest of the men. Charlie grinned. If he played his cards right, he could wheedle them into thinking he had more.

The dealer narrowed his eyes while shuffling. "By all means, lad, join the fray," he invited. He placed the deck on the table.

"Is he with you?" asked the cowboy, pointing beyond Charlie.

Charlie brought his chin to his shoulder. "Yeah, he's my cousin."

"Buck, Buck Hershey," said Buck, his eyes giving the five men a brief once over.

Charlie gripped the back of the chair as the men at the table laughed. He looked around the room to make sure no one else overheard Buck's blunder. He found nothing out of the ordinary, except for the staring eyes of a strawberry-blond fellow at the bar whose pale face gleamed with dark curiosity.

"Oh really, and what might your name be?" swooned the cowboy. "Dillinger?"

"Or maybe it's Capone," joshed a man wearing overalls to Charlie's left.

The men roared with laughter.

Nervous prickles panged in Charlie's stomach, his mind second-guessing himself, but his heart was determined to see his plan through, right or wrong. He stood and weaved through a few tables to the back wall, where he grabbed a broken chair lying on its side. He made his way back to the table carrying the chair over his head, and placed it next to the other. He took the pints from Buck and set them on the table.

"Buck, sit down," whispered Charlie, noticing a few more eyes taking notice of the fanfare, particularly a trio of men leaning up against the banister. They were whispering to each other, while the middle one picked at his nails with a knife. Charlie recognized the broad-shouldered man as one of Kalvis' enforcers. Charlie's throat warmed with saliva and he tore his eyes away, his thoughts in retreat mode. He needed to get Buck out of here straight away. Without thinking, he quickly snatched up his money and rose from the table, signaling to the men he planned to take his game elsewhere.

The men grew still, but the commotion around them continued.

"Oh, come on now lad, it was only in jest," said the cowboy.

"Yeah, we're square, kid," added a bearded man to Charlie's right.

Charlie held his stance for a few more seconds, watching Kalvis' men from his peripheral, and noticed they had removed their backs from the banister, no doubt at the ready to nab him and Buck on their way out. Charlie did not want to give them the satisfaction of another glance, but he tilted his head. The man with the knife was staring at him. Charlie did not notice it right away, but the longer he held his gaze, he saw a red flicker in the man's eyes. If he was even a man at all.

"What a mess," he mumbled. He should have thought this out better. It was not like him to go into a situation half-assed, but this time he had let his fears drive him. Charlie sat down, feeling trapped. He would have to come up with an exit strategy. Cheers erupted at the table, startling him from his thoughts.

"Hey bartender!" shouted the dealer. "Bring me a pint, wills ya?!"

"Charlie, is everything all right?" whispered Buck, leaning over to him.

"Don't worry about it," assured Charlie, taking a sip of liquid courage to suppress a sudden upsurge of adrenaline. "We came here to play poker, didn't we?"

"I suppose so." Buck shrugged, a little indifferent about the prospect.

"Well, I just got us in a game," said Charlie. "So, for now, keep your nose down and watch. And here—drink this." He slid the other glass in front of Buck.

"What is it?" asked Buck.

"It's an adult cola." Charlie took a third swig from his drink to combat his rising nerves.

Buck studied the glass. Inside, a yellowish ring of foam floated on top of a thick, dark liquid, which reminded him of Royal Crown Cola. He picked up the pint and took a sniff. It smelled nothing like cola. He gave Charlie an incredulous look, but it diminished at the sight of Charlie's scowl. Buck put the glass to his lips and took a sip. The vile taste filled his mouth and stung his throat. Buck made a face in response to the dreadful drink.

"Charlie, I do not like my drink." Buck placed the glass back on the table.

"Buck, don't be such a dame. If you want to learn how to play poker, you have to learn everything else too. And while you play poker, you drink liquor."

Buck reluctantly took the pint glass back and drank from it. He nearly choked on the bitter taste, but hid his disgust.

"Okay, kid, we're playing five-card draw," said the dealer, making his final pass around the table. "The pot starts at two bits. Cowboy, it's your call."

"I'll start at," the cowboy eyeballed his cards, "five bits."

Charlie leaned over to Buck and whispered. "Now you see that, the cowboy started the bidding at a modest level for a game based on mere coins. But did you notice his hesitation, the last-second look at his cards?"

Buck nodded as the next man with a scruffy ginger beard raised the bet two bits before rubbing his cards against his chin. Charlie called as well, followed by the well-dressed man who was nervously scratching his widow's peak.

"Your cards, gentlemen," announced the dealer, as he adjusted the garter on the sleeve of his red-and-white-striped shirt.

The cowboy opened the second round of bidding, raising the hand two coins. The bearded man saw the bid and raised the betting to a dime, forcing the others to withdraw, except for Charlie.

"Just you and me, boy," said the bearded man as the cowboy threw down his cards. "I gots me two pairs of eights."

"Hot dang," hooted the cowboy.

"Well, lucky for me I've got me two pairs of nines then," grinned Charlie.

The bearded man pounded his fist on the table. The tremor forced the coins to jump and the liquor to slosh against glass. The men at the table laughed. Charlie pulled the coins towards him and they prepared for the next round.

By the fifth hand, Buck had finished his first pint of liquor, much to his disdain. The horrid taste was stuck in his mouth and his throat felt raw. He asked again, what the dreadful liquid was and after a few persistent nags, Charlie finally caved and told him it was White Eagle Beer. Buck returned the glass to the table, his thoughts fuzzy. He diverted his eyes from the game to survey the rest of the room as an outburst of whistles erupted throughout the speakeasy. Even the men at the table stopped their current hand to join the fray in welcoming the Canary. Buck craned his head high in order to see over everyone. From behind the bar, a busty woman strolled over to the piano. Her long, coral silk dress clung to her figure, the studded rhinestones fashioning the thin straps as well as the V-neck. She had a cheerful expression on her face as she waved at the hooting men. The piano player struck a few chords, quieting the catcalls and after a few measures of a bluesy melody, the woman's rich voice filled the speakeasy with a strong presence.

Buck found himself captivated by her, her singing the call of an ancient siren.

"Yee haw, sing it Canary!" whistled the cowboy, waving his hat in a circle over his head.

"What's a Canary?" muttered Buck, turning to Charlie.

"You're lookin' at her," said Charlie. "It's just a name for a woman who can sing." He set his unfinished pint in front of Buck.

"Charlie, I really—"

"Buck, until you've played a few rounds you're gonna have to keep this up."

"But you have not finished yours," objected Buck.

"That's because I've been playing the whole time, it takes a lot of concentration to play poker." Charlie made his words convincing enough so that Buck would not know the difference. He knew he should have felt guilty for the fib, but a part of him was enjoying the thrill of his trickery. Besides, he needed to speed things along.

"Then let me play for a while and you can finish your drink," said Buck and slid the glass back to Charlie.

"Finish mine first and then I'll let you play," said Charlie as the song ended and the speakeasy exploded with catcalls again. Some of the men even gave the Canary a standing ovation.

Buck felt the urge to argue, but instead, he reached for the glass and chugged it as fast as possible in order to spare his taste buds. He slammed the glass onto the table.

"There, I am finished, now may I play?" asked Buck, as an unpleasant tingle streaked across his forehead.

"Well, gents," said Charlie, as the men returned their focus to the table. "I believe my cousin will take a crack at a few hands if none of you object to the switch?"

"He plays with your money," grumbled the bearded man, still sore Charlie had bested him two more times since he sat down.

"Sure," said Charlie and handed Buck his cards.

Buck studied the men at the table. The cowboy wiped a hand across his brow, and the bearded man twirled a finger in his whiskers. The dealer cleared his throat, the farmer tapped his fingers on the table, and the well-dressed man fiddled with his buttoned cufflinks. Each man around the table was showing his tell and Buck felt safe enough to call.

Charlie shot him a look. "Buck, what are you doing? Let me see your cards," he whispered, as the remaining three men called.

"I am playing poker," snapped Buck. "Is that not why we are here?"

Charlie swallowed his temper. He had never been one to take sarcasm well, but for the sake of not creating a scene, he allowed Buck to play his own hand.

The dealer asked for cards and the cowboy started the second round of bidding, placing a large silver coin on the pile.

"That be a right fifty cents," said the cowboy.

"Rotten hell!" said the bearded man. He threw his cards on the table, as did the rest.

"Hot damn, I got one!" swooned the cowboy.

"Wait." Buck tossed a dollar on the pile of coins.

The cowboy's jaw dropped.

"I call and raise you fifty cents," said Buck.

The cowboy's eyes glistened. He did not have that much left, but he greedily wanted the pot, and he was not about to let some doll-faced kid snake it out from under him. The cowboy looked at his silver wristwatch. He removed it and tossed it on the pile.

"Buck Hershey, the man has answered your raise," said the dealer. He pulled at his shirt collar and unfastened the top button.

The cowboy flipped over his cards—four aces.

Buck laid his cards revealing five hearts—a straight flush.

The cowboy jumped out of his chair. "I demand a re-deal!" he bellowed, his face burning with a flare of drunken rage.

The chatter in the speakeasy grew still, all eyes on the table.

Charlie grabbed his knees nervously. This was not how he wanted Buck to play poker. He did not need the whole speakeasy thinking he was some charmed beginner, least of all not the mysterious Irish bloke or Kalvis' men. Charlie flashed a glance at the stairs and saw the three men inching away from the banister. The man with the knife's mischievous grin accentuated his red eyes.

"The boy got lucky," said the dealer, trying to calm the cowboy.

"Aye, beginner's luck," agreed the well-dressed man.

"Buck, do something," whispered Charlie.

Buck was not sure what to do, except to give the cowboy his winnings. On the other hand, it was not his money to give away. It was Charlie's money. Buck reached for the center of the table and picked up the crumpled dollar.

The cowboy eyed Buck and then his watch. He was hesitant about the gesture, but took it as an invitation to the rest. The cowboy swiped his watch from the table and placed it back on his wrist, his fingers fumbling with the latch. He lowered himself somewhat shamefully back into his seat as the curiosity of the speakeasy reverted to jubilant chatter. The men at the table, however, sat in quiet disbelief.

"Well, I'll be a son of a bitch," said the bearded man. He paused and then lifted his glass. "To beginner's luck!" he saluted.

The rest of the men followed suit, even the cowboy.

"Buck, pick up your glass," said Charlie.

"But I do not have any more."

"Bartender!" shouted the cowboy, "another pint!"

Buck pursed his lips. He did not want any more. His head was still buzzing from the first two glasses. The bartender came to the table and handed off the pint to the cowboy in exchange for five coins. The cowboy then slid the glass across the table to Buck, whose hand stopped it from falling off the table, but not in time for the foam to spill over and soil his pants. Buck clasped the cool glass, but did not raise it.

"Buck, don't insult your toasters," whispered Charlie.

Buck sighed and lifted the glass.

"Here, here!" shouted the men and chucked back their drinks.

Buck chugged the whole glass as well, hoping it might stem the burn, but the cool liquid ravaged his throat. He felt a sudden queasiness warm his chest as he banged the glass onto the table. His gut cramped and his head swirled even more.

"Psst, Charlie," whispered Buck. "The powder room?"

Charlie burst into laughter. "There ain't one down here, Buck; you'll have to go out in the alley. I can take you out, if you have to go."

"I can go by myself." Buck stood from his chair.

Charlie grabbed Buck by the arm, pulling him down, his laughter ceasing. "Like hell I'm gonna let you walk out of here by yourself." He glanced over at the stairs and to his relief saw Kalvis' men were no longer there. He panned the room for any sign of them. He stole a quick glance at the bar for the Irish fellow who also seemed to have made himself scarce. Charlie grinned and knew it was time to take their leave. With Buck still coherent, he would not have to carry him all the way to St. John's. He collected his money and stuffed it into his pockets.

"You ain't leaving?" said the well-dressed man.

"No, just need a break, the liquor seems to be going right through my cousin," said Charlie.

"But he only had one," said the farmer.

"I've had three, thanks," stuttered Buck, unable to notice the sluggishness of his speech. He stood up and practically fell over from the pulsing rush that attacked his head. Charlie grabbed him by the arm and pulled him away from the table, just as the bartender brought yet another full round of drinks.

Vices

Charlie helped Buck up the stairs, reminding him not to look at the bearlike man, and reentered the ash-laden alley as the blustering wind welcomed them out into the storm. The alley was dark, the pitch-black clouds preventing Charlie from knowing what time of day it was. With the light behind him, Charlie made out three tall figures standing up against the opposite wall, their backs turned. He guided Buck around the corner a few steps away from the speakeasy door and stood close. He stuffed his hand in his pocket just in case he needed to pull out his knife. His stomach twisted, his thoughts scolding him for being so foolish. He felt his body stiffen as the center figure turned to face him.

The man's red eyes glowed in the dark alley, the dim light from the speakeasy spotlighting the man with the knife's devious expression. He took a provoking step forward and Charlie knew he had no choice but to retreat. He would never make it out of the alley before they nabbed him or Buck, and he was not about to find out if he was meant for Kalvis or Old Hob.

"Charlie..." began Buck, as he turned away from the wall, re-tucking his ruffled shirt.

Charlie did not even let Buck finish speaking. He reached for his hand and tugged him back through the door, the bearlike bouncer growling as he passed. *Charlie, what the hell are you doing? You're leading yourself right back into a trap.* He flew down the stairs, his feet missing every other step. Buck struggled behind him to keep up, but they managed to make it safely to the bottom. Charlie glanced up at the top of the stairs, the man with the knife barred in the doorway by the bouncer.

"Let's go back to the table," he said, before the three goons descended the stairs.

"Welcome back lads," greeted the dealer, the others welcoming them with a cheerful toast.

Charlie smirked and reached for the full pint glass sitting in front of his chair. He raised it in gratitude, though he did not take a sip nor did he take a seat. His senses were on fire again, his eyes suspicious of everyone around him. Out of the corner of his eye he watched Buck raise his glass and quaff half the liquor before going back to playing poker. Charlie ignored the table completely, his attention stolen by the jazz tune playing in the corner of the room, the Canary finishing a haunting rendition of *Undertaker's Blues*. At the piano, a thin man, dressed in a black suit, grinned over the height of the instrument at him. Charlie's skin crawled and his breath for a split second failed him.

"Hades," he mouthed, his voice unavailable to speak.

The piano player nodded. His red eyes, panning away to the staircase.

Charlie dared not look and sat in his chair, forcing himself to ignore the impending danger, as though it might disappear. His nerves responded by bouncing his leg, the tick a minor inconvenience. The dealer set up for the next hand while Buck was engaged in conversation with the cowboy, who had removed a small rectangular box with red-spiraled stripes from inside his jacket.

"Is that a Chesterfield?" asked Buck.

"Sure is," said the cowboy, lighting the tip of a white stick and letting out a puff of smoke.

"I'll give you two bits for one," offered Buck.

"Buck, I don't think you'll like them," said Charlie, realizing his master plan was starting to spin out of control, his anxiety present in his voice.

"Charlie, don't be a worry wart," said Buck as the cowboy lit his cigarette.

"No, no, that ain't hows yaw do it," said the cowboy, slurring his words. "Here, Iz show yaw." The cowboy took two big puffs and blew out three donut rings.

Buck placed the cigarette between his lips and took a puff. The smoke caught in his throat and he coughed violently.

The men at the table roared with laughter.

"Looks like we got ourselves some virgin lungs," teased the Canary, as she approached the table and pulled up a chair next to Buck.

Charlie watched the Canary, her sudden appearance disconcerting. He looked across the room at the piano, Hades no longer sitting at the bench in front of the instrument. He slowly rose from his chair and on his periphery caught sight of the man with the knife, inching his way towards the table, flanking the other two men.

"Hot damn!" shouted the bearded man, startling Charlie.

"Royal flush, the kid's on fire," said the well-dressed man in disbelief.

"Bartender, this calls for some shots of your best hooch!" said the dealer.

Charlie's stomach somersaulted. The atmosphere in the room suddenly turned stale and the heat in his shoulder smoldered. Everything around him slowed down, the bartender placing the shots on the table as though wading through a vat of molasses.

The poker players and the Canary raised the tiny glasses in salute and shot them back. Buck slammed his glass on the table with the rest of them, his eyes batting rapidly—and without warning, the three men advanced on the table and snatched Buck out of his chair.

"Buck!" shouted Charlie. He picked up his chair and slammed it into the man closest to him. The chair broke across the man's back, knocking him to the floor. The Canary shrieked and retreated to the confines of the bar. The outburst roused the attention of everyone in the speakeasy. Charlie grabbed his money and thrust it into his pocket. The men at the table rose from their chairs and tackled the man holding Buck.

"Leave the lad alone!" shouted the well-dressed man as he punched Kalvis' man in the face.

The punch did not faze the bulky giant and he pushed the well-dressed man into another table, igniting an all-out brawl. Charlie dropped to the floor and seized Buck's arm, hoisting him to his feet.

Buck stood for a moment, but the dizzying swirl in his head made him wobble. He leaned backward, ready to fall, but Charlie propped him around his shoulder and headed for the stairs. They dodged a few flying fists, but were unable to make it around the banister.

Charlie felt a tug on his collar and, without warning, he flew backwards, dropping Buck at the bottom of the staircase. He hit the floor hard, the wind knocked right out of him. His ears buzzed with a deafening ring and his vision blurred the man with the knife. The man's evil grin beamed down at him.

"The Master of Hell sends his regards," said the man with the knife. He clamped a hand around Charlie's throat and squeezed in a manner not to suffocate, but warn. "Hades looks forward to your next encounter, Master Charles, at which time he will claim what is his, but for now, his quarrel is not with you."

The man with the knife released Charlie and stepped over his flattened body.

"Charlie," groaned Buck, as the man with the knife advanced.

Charlie scrambled to his feet. He taunted the man with the knife, using an insult only a lackey of the Devil would find demeaning. The man with the knife torpedoed a fist at him in response and Charlie ducked. With all his strength, he jabbed the man with the knife square in the gut, forcing him to double over. In an instinctive reflex, the man closed his eyes as Charlie's fist rammed into his nose. The man with the knife collapsed to the floor, blood spreading across his face, his voice cursing in pain. Charlie punched him in the ribs for good measure and resisted the urge to gloat over his defeated opponent, to take his own pocketknife and run him through. He stepped over him and collected Buck, lifting him off the floor and rushed up the stairs as the bouncer flew by them. Charlie reached for the door as the sound of footsteps raced after them. He pulled it open and entered the alley to the sound of howling wind. He placed Buck on the ash-laden ground and propped him against the wall, keeping himself in the spotlight of the door. Charlie raised his fists, preparing to fight off his approaching attacker.

The footsteps drew closer until a shadow stood in the doorway.

It was hard for Charlie to tell who it was, but he knew it could not be one of Kalvis' men, the figure was not large enough. The shadow set foot into the alley and Charlie recognized the young man. It was the strawberry-blond Irish fellow, and to Charlie's surprise, he spoke.

"Word to the wise, mate," said the Irish fellow. "Run. Run as fast and as far as ye can. Hades won't stop until he has yer soul."

Charlie lowered his guard, taken aback by the stranger's advice. The Irish fellow did not have a hint of red in his eyes, yet he named the Master of Hell with a personal familiarity. Charlie could not explain it, but he felt an odd kinship with the stranger, as though their fates were intertwined.

The Irish fellow took a step forward, and instinctively Charlie reaffirmed his stance, raising his fists directly in front of his face, not willing to take any chances.

"Be on your way, friend," said Charlie. "I don't want any trouble."

The Irish fellow chuckled at Charlie's candor. "Best of luck, mate," he said, then darted off down the alley towards Grocer Pawlak's store.

Charlie dropped his hands at his sides and breathed. He looked at the opposite end of the alley, unable to see much of anything, but knew he needed to put some distance between him and the three men, whether they were Hades' lackeys or Kalvis' muscle. It did not matter. All he knew was he needed to move. Charlie snatched Buck's limp body from the ground and headed for the street.

The street was quiet and dark, but he could make out the red taillights of an idling freight truck outside of the local bakery.

"Charlie!" roared an angered voice.

Charlie did not even bother to turn around and darted for the truck. He heard the bell on the bakery door chime, followed by the slam of the driver-side door. He hoisted Buck onto the back and hopped up just as the man with the knife limped around the corner of the alley, his shadow eerily statuesque in the dark.

The truck let out a *pop* and a *thud* as it drove up Racine Avenue.

Charlie heard the man with the knife cuss as he fell farther and farther behind, until at last he could not hear or see him. He pulled Buck into his lap, securing him tightly.

"Buck, are you square?" he asked. "Nothing broke?"

Buck rolled over and tried to sit up, but his brain spun in circles, his equilibrium shot. Charlie helped to lift him.

"Buck?"

"I'm fine." Buck hiccupped and an unsettling warmth built in the back of his throat. His body jerked and in a flash, he threw himself to the edge of the truck and vomited into the street.

"Feel better?" asked Charlie.

"No," groaned Buck. His head felt like it was about to burst. He threw up again. "Charlie, make it stop."

"The only medicine that can cure you now, my friend, is a good night's rest."

Buck tried to protest Charlie's remedy, but he jumped off the truck before he could say anything. The freight truck idled at an unknown intersection.

"Time to get off, Buck," said Charlie. "Don't worry, I'll catch you."

Buck rolled off the back of the truck and into Charlie's burly arms.

They hobbled the rest of the way to St. John's Church, neither of them saying a word. For Charlie, the Irish fellow's warning spurred him, his plan to run more urgent than before. Just one more stop and his destiny would be his own and he would only have to be responsible for himself.

Bittersweet

Buck's eyes drooped as Charlie carried him to the second pew and lowered him onto the wooden bench. He could not afford to fall asleep, not without being reaffirmed to his charge, not without a true tether to Eden. He began to worry, his thoughts becoming irrational. He squirmed and tried to sit up, but his head weighed him down. No matter how hard he tried, his eyelids refused to stay open for long. He reached out for Charlie's shirt and clenched it, his grip weak.

"Charlie," he blinked, "please don't make me fall asleep."

"Shhh, it's all right Buck," said Charlie and placed a hand on Buck's shoulder.

"Charlie, you don't understand," stuttered Buck. "I…please, I need to find Damek."

"Damek?" said Charlie, puzzled. All this time, Buck had never mentioned he was looking for someone, let alone someone he knew. What could the soulcatcher want with him? Or better yet, did Damek know this creature? Charlie shook his head. He could not worry himself with questions, not now. His plan was in motion and he needed to make sure it stayed on point.

"Buck, it's all right, you're just tired. Nothing a good night's sleep can't fix," he said in his best consoling voice.

"No, please, I'm afraid," said Buck. He scrunched into a fetal position, shrugging off Charlie's touch. Every inch of his body trembled and it hurt too much to have any contact.

"Buck, tell me what you're afraid of," said Charlie, allowing the boy his space, but his question appeasing his need to know.

"I—I need to stay here," said Buck. "I need—I need to find Damek." He reached for his pocket and pulled out the wadded ball of parchment. The silver harmonica slid to the floor, creating a dull ping. Buck struggled to lift the note high enough for Charlie to take, but his arm felt so heavy. "Char—" Buck sank into unconsciousness, his arm falling. The parchment tumbled out of his hand and settled next to the instrument. A stark abyss awaited him on the other side of his eyelids, the darkness familiar, and he sensed its hold over him. He grimaced in pain, the throb in his head mounting an unstoppable attack. Buck screamed, shocking himself from his deepening sleep.

"Charlie, please, I can't go back there," said Buck. He squeezed his eyes tight, hoping to relieve some of the pressure concentrated between them, but it did not.

"Buck, you're not going anywhere," said Charlie. He knelt next to the kid, forgetting briefly that he was part of the reason Jimmy was no longer with him, that he was the reason for his introduction with the Devil. His paternal instinct mounted a campaign to comfort, but was unsure if the masquerading immortal knew what he was saying or if it was the liquor talking. Or perhaps Buck was finally trying to tell him the truth.

"That's not true," said Buck in a burst of energy and pulled himself into Charlie. "It's trying to take me back. The darkness is coming for me. Please, Charlie, don't let it take me, I don't want to go back. There's too much that needs to be done here. I can't— Charlie, let me stay here."

Buck tightened his grip even more on Charlie's shirt, but his last feat of strength began to crumble. He needed to hold on, he needed Damek. Fear consumed him and tears flowed from his eyes and his body trembled. He had failed, failed to make good on his word. His hands began to tremble as the alcohol shrouded him in a blanket of false security.

"Charlie, please," pleaded Buck, but he could not find the strength to say more. He wanted Charlie to know everything, but now, now it was too late.

Charlie stared at Buck, lost in his spellbinding emerald eyes. It was strange, but for some reason, he understood Buck was telling the truth—he truly thought he was going to disappear.

Buck fluttered his eyelids, his grip loosening.

Charlie pried Buck's fingers from his shirt. He lowered him back to the bench and held his hands. A twinge of guilt blindsided him and he felt the genuine terror in Buck. His mind began to wander, outlandish thoughts plaguing him with *what ifs* and teasing him with the secrets deep within the proverbial rabbit hole. Charlie sensed his convictions lessen and his own fears began to surface. If he did not leave now as he planned, as the Irish fellow warned, he would never leave. Yet, Buck's plight gnawed at him. He could not let go, not until he was asleep.

Buck's eyes drooped, his nose catching a whiff of sulfur. "Please," he said one last time. "Please, let me stay."

Still holding Buck's hands, Charlie inhaled deeply, contemplating the request. What did it matter if he let him stay? He was leaving.

"Please," Buck murmured, closing his eyes.

"Yes, Buck, you can stay," whispered Charlie, surrendering to the Breedling's request. "Stay as long as you like."

A spark of energy shot through Charlie's body, escaping through his hands, and he watched the muscles in Buck's face twitch before his rigid body uncurled. He felt Buck's hands fall limp and his breath steadied its rhythm. It was hard to tell if his words had given Buck any comfort, but he was certain the Breedling had heard them before drifting off to sleep. Charlie wrapped Buck's arms against his chest, the power of his words tethering them to each other, grounding the Breedling to Eden, although he was unaware of the spell he had woven or its profoundness. He stood from the bench prepared to take his leave, but caught sight of the wadded parchment. He reached for it and read the message, the ink now visible to him.

The mortal will lead you to the mortal Damek who alone has the power to amend you to your charge. Take heed, Master Breedling, the mortal knows not of this plan, and therefore must remain innocent.

Charlie reread the correspondence several more times, his anger mounting with each pass. His thoughts began to plant seeds of mistrust in his head, twisting his emotions. Buck was just like everyone else, using him as a means to an end, and in this case, to get to Damek. He felt more betrayed now than he had over their argument about Hades and a spark of hate panged in his chest. His thoughts turned dark again, blaming Buck for Jimmy's death, his duel with the Devil, opening his mind to the possibilities of supernatural wonders lurking in plain sight and shadow. Charlie crushed the parchment with his hand, stemming the surge of hatred. He had the impulse to shake Buck from his drunken slumber, force him to face his wrath, but when he looked at the Breedling all he saw was a boy, a runaway, an orphan.

Charlie took a step out of the pew. "It will be better this way," he said.

"Better for who?"

Charlie peered over his shoulder and saw the tall shadow of Father Van Lewen standing next to the statue of the Virgin Mary.

The priest moved towards the center aisle and he had the sudden desire to embrace his friend, but refrained, knowing it would only make his parting harder.

"Charlie, I know about Jimmy," said Father Van Lewen. "I am truly sorry to learn of his passing."

"Thank you," said Charlie, remaining closed off. "It was quite the ordeal, but now it leaves me free to go where I choose."

"Charlie."

"Please, Father, I have done all I need to do here," said Charlie, not wanting to belittle his cousin's death, but he needed to make his case quickly. The longer he lingered, the easier it would be for the priest to convince him to stay, for if anyone had the power to do that, it would be him. "Kalvis and Wiktor have their truce, Grocer Pawlak and I are through, and we are square as far as I'm concerned. Without Jimmy, there is nothing left. It's time I moved on."

"What about the boy?" challenged the priest. His long face grew solemn.

"Do with him as you like," said Charlie, trying to be indifferent on the subject.

"Why not take him with you?" asked Father Van Lewen.

"Absolutely not," said Charlie, his anger resurfacing. "This kid has already taken enough from me. He's not even human. He's a parasite, a reaper. For all I know he works for the Devil..." Charlie stopped, a chill passing over him. He could not speak about his encounter with Hades, and yet..."Try to understand, Damek," he added, his curiosity wondering what his old friend knew about the supernatural or what Buck wanted from him. "The boy has his secrets, dark secrets, and whatever he's hiding I simply don't want any part of it."

"But, Charlie, you already are involved, there is no need to run away," said Father Van Lewen.

"You think I don't know that?" shouted Charlie, no longer able to keep his tongue civil. "But, that doesn't matter, he doesn't want me. He never wanted me." He hung his head at the grievance.

"Charlie, what are you going on about?" asked Father Van Lewen, the priest's face puzzled.

"He's here for you," said Charlie, extending the crumpled piece of parchment.

Father Van Lewen took the note and without hesitation read it.

"You can see it, can't you?" said Charlie, watching the wrinkles on the priest's brow become more prominent. "The letters, you can see them."

"That is neither here nor there," said Father Van Lewen, trying to put forth a convincing poker face; however, he never was good at bluffing.

"Fine," said Charlie. "You can keep your secrets, but me, I'm done."

"Charlie, there is still a place for you here," said Father Van Lewen as the lit candles behind him flickered.

"This is not my home," argued Charlie. "I'm through looking after the strays no one wants and being someone else's puppet. Don't I deserve a chance to have a life? Don't I?"

Father Van Lewen sighed. Charlie was not hearing him. "Of course you do, but if there is one thing life has taught me, Charles, a man who runs has no life at all. He merely survives on the fringes and finds only regret. You leave here, now, like this, I swear to you there will be nowhere far enough for you to run. You will become miserable and reckless and in the end you'll die alone, a world away, wishing you could take this moment back."

Father Van Lewen kept his words soft, but all Charlie heard was a sermon from a preacher. He felt his blood boil.

"Don't speak to me as if I'm a member of your congregation.

I have no choice but to run as far and as fast as I can. I have nothing left in this world to take, except that which I cannot part with, Father. I will not let the Devil take my soul, nor will I involve myself any further in the affairs of the unknown. Wonder be damned, Damek. I want nothing more to do with this creature, you understand. I saved his life and I shouldn't even have done that. I'm done worrying myself to death with the affairs of others. It's high time I see to my own."

"But that is just not your way," challenged Father Van Lewen.

"Don't patronize me!" shouted Charlie, balling his hands into fists, the cooled ambers in this shoulder exploding to life, the heat spreading rapidly across his torso and down his arms.

"Charlie," said the priest with a civil tongue, taking a step towards his young friend.

Charlie responded by taking one back.

Father Van Lewen sighed. There was only one thing he could say to make Charlie change his mind, and as much as he wished there was another way there was no alternative.

"Charlie, do you remember the first conversation we had when you arrived here at St. John's? Do you remember what we talked about?"

"We…" Charlie's heart rocketed to his Adam's apple, forcing the fire within him into a full retreat. He was shocked the priest would bring up the one thing that could make him change his mind. He had underestimated his friend greatly. "We talked about my mother," he said, the thought of her quenching his temper and appealing to his good-hearted nature. "What she was like, what she hoped I'd be, the man I could be."

"And what did you ask me?" challenged Father Van Lewen.

Charlie turned his head away and looked back at Buck resting soundly in the pew, his face swollen with fear and sadness. Every fiber in his being ached to comfort the Breedling, but his anger prevented him from moving.

"I asked you to make sure I keep my promise to make good on her vision," he replied.

"Then stay, Charles." Father Van Lewen closed the distance between them and placed a hand on Charlie's shoulder.

Charlie could not withstand the strain of holding back his sorrow any longer and turned to the priest, embracing him. He cried into the cloth of his frock, letting out an agonizing cry that threatened to rip his heart in two. He knew his friend was right, but he was not ready for this challenge, nor strong enough to accept the truth. He needed to mourn Jimmy, hide away from the world. And for the first time, he could not be the man Adele Reese envisioned. Charlie pushed away from the priest, hanging his head and wiping his eyes with his sleeve. He needed to find his own way.

"Father—Damek, you have been a dear friend and have always treated me and Jimmy well. I am grateful for your concern, but I've made up my mind. I can't allow myself to go willy-nilly down the rabbit hole, for I'm afraid of what I'll find." Charlie lifted his head. "I've never asked you for anything, but now I must ask this one favor. I have done what the note asked, I have delivered him to you, now please see to this boy. I relinquish him to your care. When he wakes give him this." Charlie pulled a folded piece of paper from his pocket. "Tell him he has been allowed to stay as promised."

Father Van Lewen took the piece of paper. "Where will you go?" he asked.

"I..." Charlie paused. "I will go where it suits me."

Father Van Lewen lowered his head in somber reply. He had no choice but to respect his young friend's wishes.

Charlie gave the priest a half smile, a twinge of guilt knotting his stomach, making one last desperate attempt to change his mind, but then he thought of Jimmy and his anger returned. Charlie shook the priest's hand and headed through the church, forcing himself not to look back. He opened the door feeling bittersweet and stepped out to brave the world.

"May your journey be blessed, my young friend," prayed Father Van Lewen when the door slammed. He closed his fingers around Charlie's letter and the parchment. "And may the guardians of this world watch over you, for you have given and lost more than should be asked of you."

Dreaming

*I*n his dreams, Buck ran. He ran to get ahead of the storm, the roll of thunder resounding all around him.

It was a different time and place. The night he defied his masters the Fates. The night he let her die.

The darkness brightened as a jagged blade of lightning barreled into the earth.

In the distance, a scream rose over the thunder and as it faded it began to rain.

Buck stood soaked to the marrow, his heart breaking. He collapsed into the slosh of mud and knew it was too late.

He lifted his head, unsurprised by the appearance of two pale faces with black eyes glaring.

White fangs hung over pale pink lips and the pale faces moved towards him faster than the next bolt of lightning.

Buck gasped, responding to their paralyzing touch. His body suffered their chill and they forced him to go with them.

Eden faded and the bright hue of the palace blinded him. The smell of sulfur was present in the dead air.

The questioning began.

Buck bit his tongue and remained silent.

He felt a brutal rush of pain, lashes from a Retriever's wing.

His punishment—sentence to life in a Reformatory cell with no reprieve.

The darkness surrounded him—the humidity blanketed, followed by moments of sheer agony.

He felt guilt, regret, and disobedience. Emotions he had never before felt.

Time passed and yet not at all, until at last he was hollowed out, the grace of the Fates leaving him.

And so he made his choice. Fulfill his promise—find the Trickster and save the Shepherdess.

Breadcrumbs & Tea

Buck awoke unable to see, his breath heavy, and his heart racing. He sucked in a lungful of air to keep his heart from bursting through his chest. He blinked several times, drawing out the darkness around him and bringing forth the faint glow of candlelight. At first, he could not remember where he was, but when he heard the wind bang against the windows, he knew he was still in the church. He tried to lift himself off the wooden pew, but every inch of his body was sore. He laid his head back down, thankful he was not lying on the black stone of his former prison cell. A vengeful throb streaked across his brow, crashing against both his temples. Buck saw flashes from his dream, the broken fragments of the night the Shepherdess died and the events that followed. Buck turned his head away from the sight of the dark ceiling and the glow overhead. He slowly stretched, only to find it was a horrific mistake. The inside of his skull ignited again as if the bolts of lightning from his dream were snaking through his brain. He let out a moan and curled into a ball. He felt awful. His throat warmed and he wanted to spew. Buck pressed his hands tightly over his ear, in an attempt to compress the uncontrolled chaos in his head. He shut his eyes and swallowed back the revolting rise of vomit.

Stop—just make it stop. At any moment, he was certain he

would combust. It took a while for the throbbing to subside enough for him to try sitting up again. His body was achy, but he managed to stay upright. He also felt renewed—as though his slumber had destroyed the remaining tentacles of his past life. He felt grounded, tethered. He could not explain it, for he had yet to come across the mortal Damek. Buck pressed a hand to his forehead, in order to prevent his skull from splitting open. He tried to think of something less complicated, but the only thing that came to mind was… "Charlie."

Buck looked at the statue of the flower-crowned woman, then scanned the front of the church, but found no sign of Charlie. He leaned to check the pew behind him and then in front. Charlie was not there. Instead, he found a bundle of clothes lying neatly in a pile. He took hold of the bundle and laid it on his lap. On top was a folded piece of paper, which he set aside as he shook out the clothes. First, a pair of brown corduroy pants, though in the dim light they appeared black. Then a cotton cobalt shirt and a beige corduroy jacket. Underneath was a pair of worn Oxford shoes. Buck set the clothes next to him and opened the piece of paper.

Dear Buck,

When you wake, I will be gone. I do this with a heavy heart, although to be honest, I find myself angry and hurt because of you. I lost the last thing I cared about in this world and though you did not take him from me, I can't help but think that if you had never appeared in the orphanage, Jimmy might still be alive.

At first, I accepted it, took you under my wing, but you never truly needed me. I understand now why you clung to me like you did, your letter from the eagle spelled it out plainly enough. I should apologize for leaving you

*on such terms, but I can't bring myself to forgive you for
what has happened. I was never meant to be a part of
your world, and so this is where I say good-bye, Buck.
And as these will be my last words to you, may I impart
some advice. Always keep your word. For as promised, I
have allowed you to stay.*
  ~ Charlie ~

Buck reread the letter then set it in his lap. "I should have
figured it out sooner," he said in disbelief. "If only I realized the
power he held over me, the commanding authority in his voice…"
Buck looked back at the letter. *For as promised, I have allowed
you to stay.*

Buck felt his heart break and he wondered how the Apothecary
could have gotten it so wrong. He did not need Damek. He needed
Charlie. But now it was too late. Charlie was gone, and with him,
the words that could reaffirm him to his charge and tether him to
the Eden Wanderer, Stingy Jack.

Buck turned to the pile of clothes, with no real desire to put
them on, but the smells radiating from his filthy garments changed
his mind. He set the letter on the bench and rose from the pew.
He pulled off his ragged shirt, tossing it onto the floor and put
on the cobalt shirt. Next, he retrieved the harmonica from the
floor and placed it next to the letter. He kicked his feet out of the
patchwork trousers and pulled up the brown corduroys, their fit
spot on.

Buck felt secure in his clean clothes, but knew there was
something missing. He glanced at the naked altar and noticed a
golden bowl sitting in the center. He entered the aisle and walked
through the opening in the communion rail. He leaned over and
saw his reflection staring back at him from the water within.

Buck cupped his hands and tried to avoid drowning the floating orange hibiscus flowers as he scooped up the lukewarm water. He splashed it on his face and washed away the evidence of his suffering.

"Ahem."

Buck wiped his hands down his face, caught off guard by the presence of someone else in the church. He hesitated.

"Ahem."

Buck turned around as water dripped from his chin. In the candlelight, a tall man wearing a long black frock stood right behind him. Buck recognized the attire as the mark of a priest, having seen the wardrobe many times upon his visits to Rome. He examined the man. The priest's face was long with high cheekbones, his expression earnest.

"Can I help you, my son?" asked the priest in a bass voice.

"Excuse me, er, Father, is it? My friend Charlie brought me here and…"

"Ah, you must be Buck," greeted the priest with curious delight. Buck nodded.

"Well, where are my manners?" The priest walked up to him. "I am Father Van Lewen, pastor here at St. John's." He extended his hand to Buck. "It's all right, Buck, I won't harm you."

Buck took hold of the priest's hefty hand and gave it a shake.

Father Van Lewen studied Buck's features, finding them quite accurate from the description he was given so long ago. He had half a mind to engage in the pertinent circumstances that brought them together, but wanted to know more about this supernatural creature first.

"I see the shirt fits you well enough," said Father Van Lewen. "A little fitted in the arms, but it is all I could muster. Do the shoes fit?"

"I have not tried them on yet," said Buck. He did not care to talk about the clothes. "Please sir—I mean, Father—where is Charlie?"

"I'm afraid he left sometime after you fell asleep," said Father Van Lewen, letting go of Buck's hand. "He was rather pleased you were able to get some rest, regardless if he had to trick you to do it, but here you are, safe and sound just as he promised."

Buck frowned, further upset with himself that Charlie had been driven to trickery in order to get away from him, and could not help but wonder if it was another abnormality brought on by the Tales Teller's spell.

"In the end, his parting was bittersweet," said the priest, noticing Buck's reaction. "I know he wanted to tell you himself, but I think he used up the last of his courage. After all, losing Jimmy the way he did and then taking care of you, not to mention the strain from his dealings with Kalvis and Wiktor, I believe this time Charlie bit off more than he could chew. But then that's Charlie, always giving too much." Father Van Lewen saw his reassurance was having no effect. He cleared his throat. "I know in his letter he wanted to tell you more, explain why he tricked you, but I don't think even Charlie fully understood it all."

"Why, why did he have to go?" said Buck. "I was going to tell him the truth."

"Honestly, would you have?" challenged Father Van Lewen. He folded his hands together and placed them in front of him.

"Yes, of course I would have. To be in the dark would only make things worse for him now. He needed to know who was coming after him. He..." Buck bit his lip and hung his head. He needed to hold his tongue from enlightening another innocent mortal. "What am I supposed to do now?"

"Well, Charlie did ask me to assist you any way I can," said the priest.

Buck lifted his head. "Can you help me find Charlie?"

"No, I'm afraid Charlie did not tell me where he was going."

"Oh."

"Please, let us take a seat and talk, no?" said the priest, gesturing to the pew. He placed a trustworthy expression on his face.

Buck stared at the priest. He had no interest in talking to this man. He wanted Charlie.

Father Van Lewen saw Buck's apprehension and wondered if an incentive might help. "Buck, would you fancy a cup of tea?"

Buck felt the raw burn in his throat insisting he accept. "That would be delightful," he said.

"Marvelous, then please, make yourself at home."

Buck ambled back to the pew and whipped the beige jacket around his back. He sat on the bench and untied the shoelaces. The smell of leather hit his nostrils. Buck sneezed as he placed the shoes over his dirty feet. They were a little big, but not by much, and he found them to be quite comfortable. Once tied, he sat up and reread Charlie's letter.

Buck tried to let the words penetrate his weariness, but all he felt was failure. If he had only been square with him in the beginning instead of worrying about enlightening him or breaking any laws, he would still be here. Well, at least he hoped he would be, though that was neither here nor there. Buck folded the letter and put it as well as the silver harmonica in his jacket pocket.

"Outstanding," said Father Van Lewen. "You look like a fine young gentleman," he complimented and sat in the pew next to Buck, handing him a warm cup.

Buck breathed in the steam and felt right at home.

"I hope you like—"

"Orange peels and ginseng," Buck guessed. "It happens to be one of my favorites."

"Oh, good," said Father Van Lewen. "I am partial to Earl Grey myself."

Buck sipped his tea and scorched the roof of his mouth—*best give it a minute*. "Father…"

"Yes, my son."

"Um, Buck will do," he corrected.

"Very well, Buck," said Father Van Lewen.

"May I ask what you and Charlie talked about?"

"It's not much, I'm afraid. Charlie was in quite a hurry to leave."

"I see," said Buck, despondent.

"No, I'm not sure you do." Father Van Lewen lowered the cup from his lips. "Not once has Charlie ever raised his voice to me, but when I suggested he was being unreasonable, he would not hear of it."

"You tried to convince him to stay?" Buck tilted his head to see the priest's face.

"Of course I did. I knew Charlie would regret leaving if he did, as I am sure he does. Even my tactic to use his mother's influence on him could not change his mind. Once Charlie makes up his mind, there is no changing it. He's stubborn that way."

"I noticed," said Buck with a snicker, lightening the mood. It felt good to talk about his friend.

Father Van Lewen let out a snort. "Truly an understatement."

"Was Charlie able to tell you anything else?" asked Buck, blowing on his tea.

"Enough for me to understand his side of things."

"And he told you nothing else?"

"Nothing more that was pertinent," lied Father Van Lewen,

dropping his chin to look at him. It was not yet time to reveal his secret. "Why, is there something I should know?"

"No," lied Buck and unlike Father Van Lewen, he squirmed uncomfortably on the bench. It was bad enough he had damaged the veil over Charlie's eyes. He could not risk involving the priest unnecessarily. "Father," he continued, "I realize you may have some questions for me, but I am not ready to talk about myself yet, if it is all the same to you."

"Fair enough," said Father Van Lewen. "Then what do you wish to talk about?"

"Tell me about the young woman who came here the night before last."

"Excuse me?" Father Van Lewen's eyes widened.

"The young woman," repeated Buck. "The one who worked at the orphanage."

"Hanna—how," Father Van Lewen cut himself short.

"Is that her name? Hanna?"

"Yes," replied Father Van Lewen, realizing Buck must have been in the church the night he found Charlie beneath the statue of the Virgin Mary. "Buck, that confession was not meant for you," he scolded, his tone almost cross.

"Was it meant for you? How could you forgive something that was not yours to forgive?" asked Buck curiously, taking another sip of his tea.

Father Van Lewen drank his slowly. "You're right, Buck, it was not my sin to forgive."

"Then how could you do it?"

"Because she asked me to—the poor girl." Father Van Lewen shook his head. "It was not enough for her to tell her secret. She needed someone to show pity, tell her she had a chance to make amends."

"How is she supposed to do that? Jimmy's dead."

The priest leaned forward and pressed his forearms into his thighs. "Sometimes, Buck, we can make up for what we've done in other ways. It's much harder, of course, and it never truly satisfies our travesties, but it does help."

"I do not understand," said Buck, feeling downhearted. He had hoped the priest held such power. He wanted to be forgiven for hurting Charlie. "If you put it on the sinners to make amends, then why let them confess? If you have no power to forgive such sins, why pose as a healer if you are not one?"

"Buck, I do not pose," said Father Van Lewen, his voice remaining calm. "The act of confession is admitting your fault, trusting your secret to another living soul, having them help carry your burden. That is what I do, Buck—I help carry the burdens of others and counsel them on the appropriate course to take. My absolution is not so much genuine forgiveness as it is peace of mind."

"And this young woman, Hanna, did sharing her secret with you help lift her burden?" asked Buck. He half wondered if confessing his sins might lighten his load.

Father Van Lewen hung his head, his expression grim. "I am bound to keep the secrets of those who confess, but under the circumstances you share in this secret."

"Did it help?"

"No, Buck," replied Father Van Lewen. "Nothing could combat her sense of guilt. It wasn't enough to know Charlie still lived."

"What happened?"

"She's dead," replied the priest.

Buck gasped. "Was it the charlatan?"

"I don't believe so. The police found her body on the shore of the river early this morning, and her peach dress was intact."

The girl walking up the street—Buck recalled the girl in a peach dress near the barbershop.

"It's a terrible waste," added Father Van Lewen, leaning back against the pew. "She was a gentle soul, which is why I can understand how she couldn't go on living with such guilt. The boys in the orphanage were really the only family she had and, from my conversations with Charlie, Hanna was quite fond of Jimmy."

Buck shied away from Father Van Lewen, disappointed. There were still many things he needed to learn about mortals. It was unclear to him if the priest had any real power to speak of and, if so, wondered if it would be strong enough to reaffirm his charge. With Charlie in the wind, Father Van Lewen was the only one he could ask, and it was clear the priest had a talent for directing a confessor on the path to make amends. Buck stared into his empty cup, the death of the Shepherdess reemerging in his mind.

"Buck," said Father Van Lewen, noticing the boy's distress, "would you…"

"No!" shouted Buck and he sprang from the pew. He dropped the cup onto the marble floor and it shattered. He moved away from the broken shards into the center aisle and stood near the communion rail.

"Buck," said Father Van Lewen.

"No, Father, I—"

"Buck, it's all right to let it out, it helps."

"How is talking going to help? It is not going to change anything. It will not bring her back."

"No, it won't. But if you don't tell someone, you're going to burst or shatter from the guilt, until you cannot stand the sight of your face any longer."

"Like Hanna?"

"Precisely," said Father Van Lewen. "Is that what you wish to happen? Is this how you plan to repay Charlie for his sacrifice?"

"Leave Charlie out of this, this has nothing to do with him, not anymore," said Buck, a part of him hurt by Charlie's abandonment, even though he had no right to be upset with the mortal.

Father Van Lewen rolled his shoulders. He had hoped Buck would reveal himself by now, given him the proof that the note on the parchment was authentic, but instead, the lad was holding back, stubborn just like Charlie. Maybe Buck needed to be convinced. *Perhaps a story to loosen his tongue.*

"Then what if I told you I have something to do with this?" challenged Father Van Lewen.

"Then I would tell you, you are a crazy bird," said Buck. He crossed his arms over his chest.

"Which would be different than telling Charlie you know the Devil, how?" said Father Van Lewen.

"How—you told me Charlie did not tell you anything," said Buck.

A gust of wind whooshed through the broken stained glass window, sending a few flakes of ash into the church.

"Well, I lied," replied Father Van Lewen with a shrug.

"You cannot do that!"

"What—lie?"

"Yes!" exclaimed Buck, astonished by the priest's composed demeanor.

"Why?" asked Father Van Lewen. He took the final sip of his tea and set the cup next to him.

"Because, as a man of your station you…" Buck cut himself off and stared at the priest. There was a flicker of blue dazzling in his eyes. Buck knew that look well, having seen it many times on his mentor's face. The priest was trying to teach him a lesson.

"Buck," continued Father Van Lewen, "would you not lie to keep someone else's secret, especially if you promised them?"

"No," answered Buck.

Father Van Lewen furled his brow. "I see."

"No, Father, you have mistaken me," said Buck. "It is not that I would lie, I would simply say nothing."

"So, is that why you chose to keep yourself hidden from Charlie?"

"Father please, I have the greatest dislike for open-ended questions. Please get to the point of your lesson."

Father Van Lewen beamed. "I know what it's like to live with a secret you cannot share, Buck. I have waited many years to share mine. Would you like me to share it with you?"

"Why? I do not even know you."

"True, but I know you, Buck. I've been waiting for you for a very long time," said the priest.

"That is not possible," said Buck.

"If you say so," said the priest. "But if I can convince you otherwise, will you let me help you? Will you tell me your story?"

Buck remained speechless and unmoved. He bit the walls of his cheeks, indecisive.

"Do we have an accord?"

Buck nodded and lowered himself to the floor, propping his shoulders against the communion rail.

A Man's Word

Father Van Lewen scooted to the edge of the pew. He admired the sculpted fortress behind the altar. Amongst the stalagmite towers, there was a particular statue he was fond of, an angel kneeling in prayer at the base of the stronghold. He drew strength from it, preparing to tell the story he had not uttered to another living soul.

"I was young—oh, nine or ten, I forget now. My parents were simple people, conned into leaving their homeland by a swindler who filled their heads with nonsense, and within a few days, we were on a merchant ship bound to America. By our third day at sea, several of the passengers grew ill. The captain of the vessel helped them as best he could, but as more contracted the affliction, he had no choice but to stow us all away in the lower compartments. A day later, both my father and younger sister were the first in my family to be infected."

Father Van Lewen lowered his head and folded his hands in his lap; the ghosts of his family seemed to lend their presence in the church and he wished he could see them one last time.

"Go on, Father," said Buck, with piqued interest. He bent his knees and pressed them against his chest.

Father Van Lewen presented a soft smile. He did it for appearance sake, but deep down, it was hard to speak about such unpleasant memories.

"By the time we reached Ellis Island, out of the hundred or so souls who left port, only twenty of us survived the journey, my mother and I among them. We were destitute, starving, and tired. The sheer size of New York City was overwhelming and we were lost in it, unable to find the opportunities promised to us. But then, fortune smiled on us and we stumbled upon a homeless shelter where we were given a cot and something to eat. That first night, my mother insisted I take the bed, but I refused. I could see how worn and heartbroken she was, the loss of her husband and six children, weighting her with grief. I wanted her to get as much rest as she could, but like me, she did not sleep."

Father Van Lewen rose from the pew and walked over to the shrine of the Virgin Mary. He bowed his head in reverence, remembering the paleness of his mother's face, the delirium in her speech. He had nearly lost her that night. He genuflected and prayed silently.

Buck remained where he was, but when the priest did not return he went to him. He placed a gentle hand on the priest's shoulder to convey he was still willing to listen, though in the back of his mind all he could think about was Charlie. He looked up at the flower-crowned woman and wondered if she could answer prayers.

Father Van Lewen exhaled. "It is not easy speaking of things we've lost or that which we've suffered." He turned to look at Buck, the boy's emerald eyes full of understanding. "I believe you share in such sympathy, Buck. Heaven only knows the suffering you've seen."

Buck blinked and took a step back. "Father, how could you possibly know of my suffering?"

"Intuition," shrugged the priest, "and the words spoken by an angel."

"An angel?" Buck cocked his head, knowing an angel would never consort with a mortal—the Mistress of Heaven hated mortals. "Father, I believe you are mistaken. No angel would..."

Father Van Lewen held up his hand, cutting off Buck. He regained his feet.

"Forgive my tongue, Buck, as well as the curiosity of an old man. It is not fair for me to say angel, as I don't know what the man was who visited me in the shelter all those years ago. But what I am certain of is what he did for me and what he told me."

"Is this some sort of trick?" asked Buck, his stomach churning.

"No, Buck, this is no trick," said Father Van Lewen.

"Really?" said Buck. "How am I to know you are not tricking me? You have already lied to me once."

"You can't tell the difference?" asked Father Van Lewen. "Hmm, strange, I got the impression you had an intuitiveness about you."

"I do," defended Buck, "but even I have been tricked on occasion."

"Then I'm afraid you'll just have to find it within yourself to trust me," said Father Van Lewen.

Buck skimmed the pew and moved towards the center aisle.

"Buck, I'm no threat to you," said Father Van Lewen, taking a step towards him. "Nor am I some imposter. I am, as you see, just a man. There is nothing otherworldly about me, save for the knowledge I possess. And even then it is only a sliver to a truth I cannot even begin to understand."

"Then tell me, what is it you think you know?"

"I know you're not mortal—that much is clear to me, for the outward appearance of mortal flesh is but a shell to you, a way for you to exist, for you have traveled a great distance to be here, from a world different from my own. But the most important thing, Buck, is I know you need help."

Buck smacked his hand on the edge of the pew. "Not good enough," he replied.

"Then if you will permit me, I will finish my story," said Father Van Lewen.

Buck lowered himself onto the wooden bench, keeping his feet in the aisle. "Certainly," he agreed, unable to fight against the sincerity in the priest's request. "But be hasty, Father. Bring your story to the point."

"My mother fell ill after our first night at the shelter. I sat next to her bedside all the next day and into the night. I dabbed a cool washrag across her forehead when the fever set in, and, with each passing minute, her eyes grew more distant. One of the shelter women, who fortunately spoke some Bohemian, asked if I would like to have a priest administer last rites. Now at first you can imagine my horror, a small boy of ten having to accept his mother was about to die. I could not bear the idea and shouted at the woman to leave us. The woman stood steadfast and let me finish until I broke into tears. The woman placed a gentle hand on my back and pulled me into a safe embrace. She consoled me as best she could and without asking me again, told me she would send for the priest straight away."

Father Van Lewen paused to gain his strength.

"The priest was a frail man, with the cloudiest grey eyes. His long, silvery blond hair covered him like a cloak and his deeply bronzed skin was an image to behold. He placed a hand on my shoulder as I stood next to him and it was then I knew everything would be well. I could feel he was more than just a man, maybe even my own guardian angel."

Buck's eyes widened. He knew of whom Father Van Lewen spoke, but how? Surely the Apothecary would not seek to help a mortal?

"You speak lies," he protested.

"Buck…"

Buck was unwilling to hear any more nonsense and without a word marched up the center aisle.

"Buck, wait!"

Buck ignored the priest's calls, but as he drew closer to the low choir loft, the mind-splitting pain in his head returned. It dug into his temples, forcing him to kneel. He wanted to keep going, the front doors only a few feet away, but a force would not let him leave. Buck turned his head and saw Father Van Lewen hovering over him, his face grave with concern. Buck forced himself off the floor and crawled back into the pew, pressing the heel of his palm to his forehead. He steadied his breath, concentrating on the pain in his skull, and it took a moment for it to diminish. He rested his hand in his lap and stared at Father Van Lewen, sitting patiently in the pew across from him. Buck could not help but rethink his previous notion. If the Apothecary had visited the priest, he would have left Buck a clue to solidify the mortal's story. He had no choice but to hear him out.

"Tell me, Father," Buck said. "Tell me what this priest did for you."

"The priest knelt down in front of me and looked me square in the eye. He stared at me as if to search for something. To this day, I'm not sure what he was looking for, but whatever it was, he must have found it, then he took my hand." Father Van Lewen paused to look at his right hand. "He spoke to me. His voice was deep, full of power, and yet there was tenderness."

"What did he say?" asked Buck.

"He asked me if I would let him save my mother." Father Van Lewen lifted his eyes. "I remember thinking, what could this simple priest do for my mother? 'Let me save your mother', he said, 'and in return all I ask is a favor.' I asked him what he would have of me and the priest just smiled. I tried to refuse the tempting offer, but my mother was all I had left and with little hesitation I agreed, not caring if I had just made a pact with the Devil."

"What did he ask of you?" asked Buck, beginning to find there were many things he did not know about his mentor. What could a creature of his near-divine station possibly ask of an Eden mortal?

"I was told that one day, a young lad, who was not yet a man, would cross my path and that on that day I would assist him any way I could. When I asked him more about this lad, he told me I would know him by his ivory skin and the intensity of his emerald eyes. His face would show the pains of his trials. He told me that if I agreed to help, he would save my mother's life. How was I to say no to that?"

Father Van Lewen drifted, his mind conjuring thoughts of what might have been had he denied the offer.

"Then what happened?" asked Buck.

"The priest closed his eyes and spoke over my mother. I don't know what he said, the language at the time unfamiliar to me. But, whatever he said, when he finished my mother's eyes shot open. I knelt down on the floor and placed my hand on her brow just as the priest pulled his away. I spoke her name and she looked at me. At first, I could see the confusion in her eyes; she did not quite know where she was, but she recognized my face, and spoke my name with such fragile breath. I smiled at her with tears streaming down my face. She raised a shaky hand and I took it, pressing it against my cheek. It was cold, but I did not care. I nuzzled it, not willing to let it go. It was only when I heard the squeak of her bedsprings that I brought myself to look at the priest watching over us. I gave my mother's hand a gentle kiss and laid it safely on the bed. I rose to my feet and walked over to the priest. I extended my hand to him, which at first he was not sure whether to take. Eventually he did and we shook hands."

Father Van Lewen shied away from Buck to look at the front of the church, candlelight illuminating the altar stage.

"'Your mother will need her rest,' he instructed, 'but come night of the full moon hence, she shall be well enough to leave her bed.' I gave the priest a solemn nod and watched as he walked among the rows of beds and disappeared from sight."

Father Van Lewen turned to Buck. "As I said, I have been waiting for you for a very long time. And to be honest, I nearly gave up hope you were ever going to come. But when Charlie started talking about you I knew."

"Knew what?"

"That my wait was over," said Father Van Lewen, standing up from the pew. "It is no accident Charlie brought you here, and as unfortunate as it may be, no accident he left. In his absence, I am your link to him and he in turn is my link to you." Father Van Lewen pulled out the crumpled piece of parchment.

Buck sprang to his feet and took the message. "You are Damek!"

The Soulcatcher's Charge

Buck frowned, wrestling with his thoughts, revisiting every moment that had led him to this one. To think the Apothecary possessed the sort of power needed to scheme, to bend the will of fate all so that he would be standing in front of the one mortal who could assist him was unfathomable, but now, what did it matter? Whatever magic the Apothecary had endowed the priest with when he was a boy was no good to him now. Charlie was the one who held power over him, was able to command him, was powerful enough to tether him to Eden. And yet…Buck did not want to give up hope Damek could still fulfill his promise. All he needed was some sign. Anything that would prove the priest's magic.

"There you are, Buck," said Father Van Lewen, returning to the bench. "I've shared with you, now there is the matter of your confession."

"My confession?" said Buck, stealing away from his thoughts.

Father Van Lewen held up a hand. "I won't accept an excuse, Buck. I confessed my secret to you, now you must do the same. It will give me the insight I need in order to help you."

"But Father, I know my friend charged you with this task, but I am afraid…" said Buck.

"Buck, I have said my piece," said Father Van Lewen. He pressed his right elbow into his knee, resting his chin on his hand. "We had an accord."

Buck huffed and sat down. He did not have time for this, but it seemed there would be no talking his way out of it. "As you wish, Father, but you must bear with me in what I am to confess, for it may not make sense to you; and for reasons I cannot even begin to explain, for your safety and sanity, I cannot tell you everything."

"I am a reasonable man, Buck. Tell me what you need to," said Father Van Lewen.

"As you know, I am not of this world. I come from a race known as Breedlings, but here in Eden, we are known as soulcatchers. Breedlings are like you see me now, youth mortals, but only in appearance, for unlike mortals, we were created with no free will or souls of our own and are bound to the service of our masters with blind obedience and incontestable loyalty."

"You were a slave," said Father Van Lewen.

"In a manner of speaking I suppose, but I never quite saw it that way. It is hard for me to see it in such a way even now."

"So, what changed?"

"I think over time I grew apart from my kin, became different," said Buck, his thoughts and feet pacing. "In my world there is only neutrality and subjugation. Even the eldest creatures who have some autonomy cannot resist the impulse to obey. So, it is hard to say how or when the seed was planted to think for myself; identify right and wrong."

"And what finally brought you to this revelation?"

"My charge." Buck stood as stone, depicting his seriousness. "Along with my regular duties as a soulcatcher, I was often given special assignments by my masters. On one in particular, they asked me to seek information and discover, if I could, the hiding places of the most ancient of all creatures, who for all intents and purposes I will call the Creators."

"What happened to them?" asked Father Van Lewen curiously. "Why are they missing?"

Buck began to pace again, his nerves bubbling in his stomach. He did not want to say too much. "It is far too long a tale for me to say, Father, and under the circumstances I believe it would be in your best interest to know as little about this as possible."

"Well, it is much too late for that," insisted the priest.

Buck paused mid-stride. "Be that as it may, Father. I could not protect Charlie from seeing through the mortal veil and though you know things, your sight is not fully developed. Do me this one courtesy and let me protect you."

"All right," said Father Van Lewen, disappointed. "Go on then."

"As I was saying, long ago there was a great war that tore my world apart and forced two of the four Creators into hiding."

"Why search for them at all if they wished to remain hidden?"

"Power," replied Buck.

"I don't understand," said Father Van Lewen, puzzled.

"And you will not," said Buck. "Father, there are too many lies I would have to unravel for you just to scratch the surface of the power struggle that continually wages unseen by mortal eyes. I simply cannot."

"Then tell me what it is your masters hoped to achieve by finding them, and why they sent a mere servant on such a prestigious mission."

"Because I was their beloved, my masters' most trusted."

"And you feel your betrayal is the sin you've committed?" asked the priest.

"No, Father, on the contrary. I feel no remorse for betraying my masters or keeping secrets from them."

"What then?"

"I let someone die."

Father Van Lewen dropped his hand from his chin, awestruck. "Certainly not—I know we have just met, but I cannot believe you capable of such a travesty."

"But you thought the same of Hanna, did you not?" challenged Buck.

Father Van Lewen opened his mouth, but closed it, at a loss for words. In the absence of his voice, the wind whispered through the church as though to add its own thoughts on the matter.

"If it is any consolation," resumed Buck, "I have spent nearly two centuries trying to convince myself there was no possible way I was responsible for her death and that it was all a matter of circumstance, but as time progressed I felt a horrific sense of guilt. If only I could have broken free from my masters' hold sooner, she would still be alive."

Buck stiffened his arms to his sides. "I was simply too late, Father. And her scream rang throughout the thunderous night sky, louder than anything I have ever heard. To this very moment it still haunts me." Buck leaned his back against the pew and folded his arms in front of him, his old shame mounting within him. He suddenly felt naked and vulnerable, as if speaking his truth was stripping all mystery from him. His eyes stung and he knew he was on the verge of tears. He stared at the floor.

"What was her name?" asked Father Van Lewen.

"Iona," said Buck. "Her name was Iona Covington." His back slid down the bookend of the pew to the floor as he thought of the tragic Shepherdess. He pulled his legs into his chest and began to cry.

Father Van Lewen sat still. He had observed this type of sorrow many times before and it never got any easier to see the suffering soul. He tried to find the words to console Buck, this otherworldly creature before him, but for whatever reason he was speechless. Father Van Lewen rose, wondering how he might help Buck. The girl was dead, and by the sound of it had been for nearly two centuries. How was Buck to make amends? Father Van Lewen walked over to the creature and came down on one knee. He lifted his hand, but hesitated.

Buck brought his head out of his lap, sensing the priest's presence in front of him.

"What would you have of me, Buck?" asked Father Van Lewen.

Buck sniffled and dried his eyes. "It is too late, Father. My friend's plan has gone all wrong."

"When it comes to this, Buck, it is never too late," said Father Van Lewen.

"But Charlie…"

Father Van Lewen held up his hand to silence Buck. "I am not blind, Buck. I understand you and Charlie have created a bond that supersedes the promise I made, but there is still a chance, magic or no, I can help you. So, what is it you would've asked of Charlie?"

"I," Buck hesitated. "I would have asked him to reaffirm me to my original charge, to command me to make amends."

"I am sorry, Buck," said Father Van Lewen. He leaned away straightening himself and without another word walked away. Promise or not, he could not bind someone else's will. It went against his principles.

"Damek!" shouted Buck, forcing the priest to stop. "You promised you would help. On your mother's life you promised."

"Buck, what you ask of me cannot be done," said the priest.

"Of course it can, Damek. You said it yourself. It is not by accident Charlie brought me to you, only to leave me here with you. Look…" Buck pulled the parchment from his pocket. "The man who saved your mother all those years ago sent me this letter. Providence led me to Charlie, so Charlie could lead me to you, but even so, this moment, Charlie or no, was always meant to happen. "

"I still don't understand, Buck. By your own words, you say you have free will, so why not bind yourself to your own mission?"

"If only," Buck sighed and closed the distance between them. "Father, Damek, I may be free from the oppression and insanity of my masters, but I can never truly escape who I am or what it is I was created to do. I am a creature of servitude, a catcher of souls, and as such I must have a master. Plus, it is more than simply charging me to my course. The binding of my will also tethers me to that which I seek, allowing me to find it. Without command, the magic I possess lies dormant."

"But I am no master, Buck. I release you," said Father Van Lewen with a wave of his hand.

"If only it were that simple."

"But you said I…"

"You mistake me, Father. It is not you who is my master."

"Charlie…" Father Van Lewen lifted his eyes to the main entrance of the church where he had last seen his young friend and realized now why Charlie was running. It was more than the threat of the Devil, it was the destiny he had been handed. He lowered his gaze back to Buck to meet his acknowledgment.

"It was not intentional, I assure you," said Buck. "I would not wish this responsibility on any creature. Especially not a fragile being like you, but the deed has been done. Charlie's suffering secured my passage and in saving my life, he created the strongest of all bonds. Had he not, the orphanage fire would have surely been my end. Whatever magic indirectly bound me to you was trumped by Charlie's heroism, but he did leave me in your care, so it is possible he giving you his proxy may be enough for the magic to perform."

"Still," said Father Van Lewen, his stance uncomfortable and his hands trembling. "I cannot take your free will."

Buck smiled. "Of course you cannot," he said matter-of-factly and used his hands to illustrate his point. "Father, you are a good man. I can see now what my friend saw in you as a child. I know you would never willingly compromise yourself, but to be fair, you are not taking anything away from me that I am not willing to part with. You alone hold Charlie's voice, you are the only one I can ask this of."

Buck knelt. "Father, I know I can make amends for what I have done. Do not ask me how, but I cannot hope to do it alone. So, I humbly beg of you, please help me."

Father Van Lewen turned once more towards the altar and found the kneeling angel, realizing for the first time it was not praying, but rather awaiting orders. He looked back at Buck, the soulcatcher's head bowed before him.

"What should I do?" Father Van Lewen asked in surrender.

"There is a man I seek," said Buck. "One who can help me amend my shame. This man is not like any other. He is a forsaken man, bound to walk this earth for all eternity as a soul of flesh. I seek the Eden Wanderer, the Trickster, who in mortal life was known by the name Stingy Jack."

"And what service can this Stingy Jack provide?"

"He can help me save Iona from what you would deem a terrible fate and assist in the discovery of the Lost Creators. Please, Father, please help me, and make us both men of our words."

Father Van Lewen remained quiet. He took Buck's chin and lifted his head. He searched his emerald eyes one last time. He wanted to know more, but he held back the floodgates of his curiosity and released Buck's face, placing his hand on his head.

Buck closed his eyes.

"Through the fires of this world, Buck, you were reborn, saved by a mortal who now holds power over you. But with such power comes great danger and Charlie was not ready to accept this responsibility. In his absence, I speak as his voice, only to take that which is freely given, to bind your will in hopes of making amends, and to deliver Iona from the clutches of a horrible fate. For my part, I, Damek Van Lewen, hereby fulfill that which has bound me to you. I charge you, Buck, Breedling of the Nether, to the one you call Stingy Jack, for it is only through him you can right your wrong." Father Van Lewen paused. "Before you go, as his acting voice, I charge you with one parting task."

Buck's body tensed at the unexpected words.

"No matter where you are, whether here or among the lands from whence you came, if Charlie is to ever call on you by name, the name which he gave you, you are to appear by his side. I bind you to this, Buck, to ensure that you meet again and to give your master a chance to do with you as he wishes. For only through his words can you be forgiven for the pain you have caused him."

Father Van Lewen removed his hand and nearly collapsed from exhaustion.

Buck felt the priest's words seep deeply into his ears and spread throughout his whole body, binding his every move to the will of his new charge. He was full of purpose and his mind immediately reached out for Stingy Jack. Through the blasting winds of the Black Blizzard, he saw the lanky figure of a man walking through the blackened snow and sensed he was close. Buck tried to visualize the street sign above him, but could not. He heard the shrill call of a horn, voices of people passing, their speech deeply accented, a little airy. They came in and out of earshot and as Stingy Jack looked up, he saw a sign that read *McGregor's Tavern*.

Buck opened his eyes to find Father Van Lewen shaking, his long face pale. "Father, do you know where I may find McGregor's Tavern?"

"It is down Halstad Street in Canaryville," replied the priest, with a weak breath.

Buck gathered his feet and held out his hand. "I thank you, Damek," he said. "My friends chose well entrusting me to you."

The priest took Buck's hand and gave it a firm shake. "No, Buck, thank you," he said.

Buck puffed his chest with a newfound confidence and gave a grand bow, honoring the mortal for his sacrifice—for it was no easy feat to bind another being's will, even if freely given.

Father Van Lewen bowed his head and watched Buck pass underneath the shadow of the low balcony.

At the door Buck turned. "I almost forgot—Father!" he shouted into the church.

"Yes, Buck?" The priest's voice was frail in response.

"One day you will know," Buck shouted.

"Know what?" replied the priest.

Buck smiled. "If you kept your word." He presented a smaller bow before opening the door. He drew a deep breath ready for the charge before him and exited the church into the grim winds of the Black Blizzard in search of the Eden Wanderer known to his love, Iona Covington, as Stingy Jack.

Epilogue: Fulfillment

Father Van Lewen stood in silence, staring at the church entrance. The howl of the wind let in by Buck's departure evaporated in the stillness. Father Van Lewen's legs began to shake, the words he spoke to Buck stealing away his energy.

"What magic," he whispered, fascinated by the power of binding another's will, though thankful he would never have to perform such a feat again.

Father Van Lewen lowered himself into the nearest pew and sat up straight. He focused aimlessly on the golden bowl of floating hibiscus flowers resting on the altar. He listened carefully to the crashing wind as it rattled the stained glass windows. The eerie sound made the hair on the back of his neck prickle and he shivered.

"Settle your nerves, Damek," Father Van Lewen said under his breath. He closed his eyes and exhaled, but instantly felt the presence of a hand on his shoulder. He sat frozen, his breath stuck in his throat.

"You do your soul a great service, Damek," whispered a deep familiar voice. "And to one so willing to fulfill his promise, I leave you with this blessing. May the earth rise up to meet you; may the wind be at your back; may the waters calm your spirit; may fire vanish from your sight."

The weighted hand lifted from the priest's shoulder, removing the weakness within him. He felt renewed; strong. His life's mission, his promise was complete. Father Van Lewen genuflected and folded his hands. He lowered his head and pressed it against his fingers. A great rush of emotion ripped through him, crashing against his lightened heart and he began to sob. He truly was a man of his word.

Acknowledgments

My family has been my greatest ally in life and I couldn't have survived the crushing blows without their love and support. Thanks Mom and Budz for being my "outward voices" as I deciphered the endless mythology and chatter in my head. And to Dad for putting up with my moody crazies when I was trying to focus.

To my magnanimous team at Wise Ink and Creative Publishing: Amy Quale, Laura Zats, my editor Amanda Rutter, my designer Steven Meyer-Rassow a.k.a. Magician Steve, and my proofreader Erik Hane. Thank you all for your creative direction. The elevation you have encouraged has brought this story to its full potential and the realization of this is beyond the scope language will allow. I am eternally grateful especially to Amy and Laura for giving me the chance to fulfill this vision.

To Lord Paul and Lady Jan, thank you humbly for your patronage. It took almost a decade, but I finally got there!

To my fellow authors Andrea Savar, and Vivian Hwang; your success both delights and pushes me to catch up. It's not a competition of course, but I certainly have a lot of ground to cover to catch you. Best wishes on your continual writing endeavors.

To Mary Kaye Perrin, for without her I'd still be aimlessly stuck on draft 3.

To the best reference desk ladies ever—Robin and Susan! I would be lost without you. Thank you for getting me every book I asked for and then some. You always went above and beyond, ever since that first trip to the library when I asked you for books on the Union Stockyards and 1930s fashion.

To all my cheerleaders, and you know who you are! Thank you always for your words of encouragement.

And finally, thank you to the following businesses, authors, creators, and works who gave me inspiration and knowledge and kept the writer's block at bay:

Winona Public Library; Illinois Historical Society; Chicago Historical Society Research Center; Intercontinental Hotel & Resorts—Chicago Magnificent Mile; Yahoo Maps; Wikipedia. com; "Ethic History of Bridgeport" by University of Illinois at Chicago, April 1996; "The Gang: A Study of 1,313 Gangs in Chicago" by Fredric M. Thrasher, Ph.D, 1927; "No Promises in the Wind" by Linda Hunt, 1970; "Carnivàle" created by Daniel Knauf (HBO), 2003-2005; "The Cat From Outer Space" written by Ted Key (Walt Disney) 1978

Kimberlee Ann Bastian has a love affair with American nostalgia, mythology, and endless possibilities. When she is not in her writer's room or consuming other literary worlds, she enjoys hiking and cycling around the bluffs of her Southeastern MN home and catching up on her favorite pop culture. *The Breedling and the City in the Garden* is her debut novel.